# THE HEMLOCK FALLS MYSTERIES

**1 pretty little town in upstate New York**
**1 picturesque Inn overlooking Hemlock Gorge**
**2 talented sisters better at solving crimes than they are at their day jobs**
**1 (or more) murders**

## A WINNING RECIPE FOR MYSTERY LOVERS

*Don't miss these Hemlock Falls Mysteries . . .*

### MARINADE FOR MURDER . . .

The Quilliams's plans for the future of the Inn may end up on the cutting room floor when a group of TV cartoon writers checks in—and their producer checks out . . .

### A STEAK IN MURDER . . .

While trying to sell the locals on the idea of raising their own herds, a visiting Texas cattleman gets sent to that big trail drive in the sky. The Quilliams set out to catch the culprit and reclaim their precious Inn . . . without getting stampeded themselves!

### A TOUCH OF THE GRAPE . . .

Five women jewelry makers are a welcome change from the tourist slump the Inn is having. All that changes when two of the ladies end up dead, and the Quilliams are on the hunt for a crafty killer . . .

### DEATH DINES OUT . . .

While working for a charity in Palm Beach, the Quilliam sisters uncover a vengeful plot that has a wealthy socialite out to humiliate her husband. Now the sleuths must convince the couple to bury the hatchet—before they bury each other!

### DEATH DINES AT 8:30 . . .

This anthology of short stories by some of your favorite mystery writers is co-edited by Nick DiChario.

*continued . . .*

D1051517

## MURDER WELL-DONE . . .

When the Inn hosts the wedding rehearsal dinner for an ex-senator, someone begins cutting down the guest list in a most deadly way. And Quill and Meg have to catch a killer before the rehearsal dinner ends up being someone's last meal!

## A PINCH OF POISON . . .

Hendrick Conway is a nosy newsman who thinks something funny is going on at a local development project. But when two of his relatives are killed, the Quilliam sisters race against a deadline of their own . . .

## A DASH OF DEATH . . .

Quill and Meg are on the trail of the murderer of two local women who won a design contest. Helena Houndswood, a noted expert of stylish living, was furious when she lost. But mad enough to murder?

## A TASTE FOR MURDER . . .

The annual History Days festival takes a deadly turn when a reenactment of a seventeenth-century witch trial leads to twentieth-century murder. Since the victim is a paying guest, the least Quill and Meg could do is investigate . . .

# JUST DESSERTS

## CLAUDIA BISHOP

**BERKLEY PRIME CRIME, NEW YORK**

This is a work of fiction. Names, characters, places, and incidents either are the product of the author's imagination or are used fictitiously, and any resemblance to actual persons, living or dead, business establishments, events, or locales is entirely coincidental.

JUST DESSERTS

A Berkley Prime Crime Book / published by arrangement with the author

PRINTING HISTORY
Berkley Prime Crime mass-market edition / April 2002

All rights reserved.
Copyright © 2002 by Mary Stanton.
Cover art by Mary Anne Lasher.

This book, or parts thereof, may not be reproduced in any form without permission.
For information address: The Berkley Publishing Group,
a division of Penguin Putnam Inc.,
375 Hudson Street, New York, New York 10014.

Visit our website at
www.penguinputnam.com

ISBN: 0-425-18431-5

Berkley Prime Crime books are published
by The Berkley Publishing Group,
a division of Penguin Putnam Inc.,
375 Hudson Street, New York, New York 10014.
The name BERKLEY PRIME CRIME and the BERKLEY PRIME CRIME
design are trademarks belonging to Penguin Putnam Inc.

PRINTED IN THE UNITED STATES OF AMERICA

10  9  8  7  6  5  4  3  2  1

*For Natalee*
*With heartfelt thanks*

# Acknowledgment

I owe many thanks to Craig T. Hornsby of Red-Suspenders, who knows more about computers than Joss Roberts (thank goodness) and who helped convince me that yes, Quill could track the murderer on-line.

# CAST OF CHARACTERS

## THE INN AT HEMLOCK FALLS

| | |
|---|---|
| Sarah "Quill" Quilliam | owner/manager |
| Margaret "Meg" Quilliam | owner/master chef |
| Doreen Muxworthy-Stoker | head housekeeper |
| John Raintree | business manager |
| Kathleen Kiddermeister | head of wait staff |
| Dina Muir | receptionist |
| Bjarne Bjarnson | head sous-chef |
| Nate | bartender |
| Somerfield "Boomer" Dougherty | a guest, TV meteorologist |
| Sylvia Prince | a guest, Boomer's producer |
| Kate | a guest, actress |
| Michael | a guest, actor |
| Max | a dog |
| And others | |

## THE HEMLOCK FALLS CHAMBER OF COMMERCE

| | |
|---|---|
| Elmer Henry | mayor |
| Adela Henry | mayor's wife |
| Marge Schmidt | owner, the Croh Bar |
| Betty Hall | Marge's partner |
| Howie Murchison | a lawyer |
| Miriam Doncaster | librarian |
| Harvey Bozzel | president, Bozzel Advertising |
| Freddie Bellini | owner, Bellini's Fine Funerals |
| Esther West | owner, West's Best Dress Shoppe |
| Joss Roberts | owner, Blue Cow Computing |
| Carol Ann Spinoza | tax assessor |
| Pete Peterson | owner, Peterson's Floors & Septic |
| Harland Peterson | President, Agway Co-op |
| And others | |

## CITIZENS OF HEMLOCK FALLS

| | |
|---|---|
| Myles McHale | a private investigator |
| Andy Bishop | an internist |
| Louis Bloomfield | a cardiologist |
| Kimmie Bloomfield | Louis's wife |
| Davey Kiddermeister | sheriff |
| And others | |

# PROLOGUE

"*Good* weather for deer huntin'." Harland Peterson, his weather-beaten face ruddy with the satisfaction of being outdoors on a fine November afternoon, surveyed the sweep of rolling hills from his vantage point on the lip of Hemlock Gorge. The last of autumn's crimson tinged the maples. The sky was a blue a fellow could get lost in. The citizens of Hemlock Falls had been blessed with a slow, warm fall, and leaves still clung to the oaks and maples that grew thickly over the land near Hemlock Falls. "Good cover for deer."

Harland's cousin Petey bristled. "I've forgot more about deer than you ever knew. Them leaves ain't gonna make a damn bit of difference. And even if they do—the weather ain't gonna hold much longer. We're due for a big one."

"Says you."

"Says me? Huh. It was right on the TV this morning. Weather's not gonna hold till tomorrow, much less till Thanksgiving." Like Harland, Petey had the bulbous Peterson nose and squared-off stubborn chin. He and Harland had opened hunting season together for thirty years. Every year, Harland seemed to forget that he, Petey, bagged his buck days before anyone else did, least of all Harland, who sometimes went the whole two weeks of the season without sighting a deer at all. Petey couldn't resist a jab back at Harland, " 'Course, you know all about the weather, too, don't you, cousin? Deer and weather."

" 'Course the weather'll hold till Thanksgiving," Harland said. He tugged the bill of his John Deere hat more firmly over his eyebrows and stuck his lower lip out in a stubborn way. "Lotta deer out there, too. Mor'n usual."

"No, there ain't," Petey said. "All that new construction down by the river drove 'em off."

Their position on the north lip of the Gorge gave them a panoramic view of Hemlock Falls and its environs. The village was at their backs. The copper roof and stone walls of the Inn at Hemlock Falls sprawled across the Gorge in front of them. And to the west, a mile or so down the Hemlock River, bull-dozers and backhoes maneuvered over the construction site of the soon-to-be-completed Hemlock Falls Resort. A good quarter mile of woodland had been cleared from the dense trees at the edge of the river to make room for the new river marina and camping grounds.

"Too many new people coming into town," Petey added glumly. "Cutting down the trees, dumping their garbage, and I don't know what all. It's bound to affect the deer population. Fact."

"More people, more deer," Harland said, with the air of one who knew. "*That's* a fact. I was readin' about it just the other day. Deer do better when the land's under cultivation. And what garbage are you talking about, anyways?" Harland, who along with other members of the Hemlock Falls Chamber of Commerce had invested a not inconsiderable sum in the new resort, was sensitive to any nascent resentment of the newcomers. "There's no more garbage around here than there ever was. Any more garbage around there than there's been before, I'll go pick it up myself."

Petey jerked his thumb sideways. "Down there, innit?"

"Where? I don't see a damn thing. And don't go making up stuff to blame the workers, Pete. Can't help it if you decided not to put cash into the resort. Ain't my fault you got the guts of a earthworm." This last comment, delivered with some affection, didn't appear to ruffle Petey at all. In fact, he ignored it altogether and stared past Harland into the east side of the Gorge. He rubbed his chin, a thoughtful glint in his eye.

"You know why you never get your deer, Harland? You never get your deer 'cause you can't see worth a bucket of warm spit. I tell you I'm lookin' at garbage, you better believe I'm lookin' at garbage."

Harland squinted in the direction of Petey's gaze. He had, in fact, bowed to the inevitable and picked up a pair of magnifying glasses at the Wal-Mart some days ago. He pulled them from the pocket of his Redman coveralls and fitted them over his nose with care. The slope of woods Petey was pointing to came into focus. And Petey was right. There was a bundle of garbage insulting the landscape. Somebody had shoved a pile of old clothes and goodness knew what-all right over the edge of the Gorge. "Heck," Harland said. Whatever it was was going to get ripe, you could tell that even from here. A couple of crows had settled in the trees surrounding the pile. And crows weren't picky about how long somebody's spaghetti dinner had been lying in the sun. As a matter of fact, the longer it lay there, the better the crows liked it.

Petey's grin widened. "You going to pick it up, like you said?"

"Do I look like the town garbage collector?"

"Your exact words, cousin. Any garbage lyin' around here I'll pick it up myself. That's what you said."

"I said any garbage from the new people movin' into town. How do you know that ain't Hemlock Falls garbage?"

"How do you know it is, lessen you pick it up?" Petey's grin disappeared, to be replaced by an innocent stare. "Care to make a little bet, cousin?"

Harland grunted.

"Last one to bag a buck does the right-minded thing and clears that garbage up."

"Season won't open for two weeks yet. By then, that pile's gonna be good and ripe."

"Ahuh."

Harland ruminated, his eye on the pair of crows poised above the rags. The larger bird flew up and out of sight. "Huh."

"Of course, if you're sure that *this* year, for the first time ever, you're gonna not only get your deer but get it before me, no problem. But I ain't the one that said there was never no garbage around here. I ain't the one that was teaching my grandmother to suck eggs by telling me about how many deer we got and how good they can hide behind some ol' leaves. I ain't . . ."

"Shut up, Petey," Harland said good-naturedly. Even a stupid bet like this one added some zip to his deer hunting plans. He slipped his new spectacles back into his coverall pocket. "You got yourself a deal. I'm gonna bag that first deer, by gosh. And you're gonna pick up that mess. And won't I laugh."

• • •

Below the Petersons, the smaller crow hunched on its branch, just over the interesting scent rising from the man-sized bundle on the ground. The carrion below was too fresh a kill at the moment. But the sun was warm.

The crow could wait.

"Aw, heck," Harland said once he and Petey were in his pickup truck. He eyed the crow dubiously. "We better take a look-see now."

# CHAPTER 1

Sarah Quilliam sneezed hard, twice, and drew the drapes across her office window. It was a gorgeous day out there. The sun was bright, the air was cool and crisp, the muted colors of November were soothing. The temptation to leave her duties as manager of the Inn at Hemlock Falls and go scuff in the autumn leaves drifting across the grounds of the Inn was almost irresistible. A walk, a good long one, and then a couple of hours at her easel would blow the fuzziness from her brain and help her get back on track with the business of running the Inn.

She'd been neglecting it lately. A lot.

There were good reasons, she thought defensively. She'd been working on a painting for the last month. A good one, she hoped. And then there was the reason she was painting again.

There was Ben Harker.

Harker.

After the end of her very real relationship with Myles McHale, and the almost-relationship with John Raintree, there was Harker. Tall. Wiry. Intense. An artist—as she had been an artist, once, and was trying to be again.

They'd met when she had run up to a gallery show in New York six weeks ago—and she'd fallen, hard, in a way she thought she'd left behind when she was twenty-two. She even wore the perfume he'd bought for her—a new scent, musky, that made his presence real even when he was three hundred miles away.

Was she in love? Or not?

Quill had wasted a lot of time, staring out at the November sky, thinking about Harker and about her new painting. And then Harland Peterson and his cousin Petey had tramped along the other side of the Gorge, reminding Quill that she was here, in Hemlock Falls, and not in a studio in New York, or in Harker's arms, but here, with an inn to run.

And then she'd closed the drapes. With the drapes closed, maybe she could get to work.

Quill sat back at her desk and willed herself to go through the management notes she'd dashed off to herself in the past weeks. She would make up her personal schedule for the week. She would pay attention to business.

She sat back down at her desk and looked sternly at her desk calendar. Okay. Now. She was going to work.

She sneezed a third time and rummaged through her top desk drawer for a tissue. This cold—or whatever it was that had plagued her for the past month—was driving her nuts. Maybe she'd empty her dinky little savings account and buy Kleenex stock. Maybe the stock would triple and split and she'd make enough money to retire and just paint and not have to worry about accomplishing six impossible things before breakfast, much less three possible things before dinner.

There was a bang at her office door. She scowled, her nose buried in tissue.

The door whacked open. Doreen Muxworthy-Stoker, the Inn's head of housekeeping, rolled in like Sherman dropping in on Atlanta. Quill sighed. She didn't mind Doreen's lack of ceremony at all—except that Doreen, a dedicated republican in the best ancient Roman style—tended to burst in on registered guests in the very same way. More than a few honeymoon couples had truncated their stay at the Inn because of Doreen. "Hi, Doreen."

"Huh," Doreen said.

When Quill and her sister, Meg, had opened the Inn almost ten years ago—well, the first time they'd opened the Inn, since they had sold it once in the interim and then bought it back—Quill had plans. Big plans. Quill would set aside her stumbling career as an artist. Her sister was the best gourmet chef in the Northeast. Possibly the entire country. And Quill intended to be the best inn manager. So she'd taken a number of courses at the nearby Cornell School for Hotel Management to learn how to train her staff to be courteous, polite, well-spoken and passed them all with flying colors.

The problem, Quill thought, not for the first time, was in the application of all that stuff she'd learned. If the Hotel School ever offered a course in Transformational Management (Suppress Your Own Wimpy Personality! Learn Hitler's Best Management Style! Give Mussolini's Tactics a Try!) she'd take it.

"Huh yourself," Quill said spiritedly.

She looked at Doreen with exasperated affection. Her housekeeper's gray hair frizzed out like a dandelion gone to seed. She scowled at Quill, looking more like a cranky rooster than usual. "What?" Quill demanded, guiltily. Then, appearances clearly to the contrary, "I'm busy."

"Yeah? What with?"

Quill flinched. She couldn't fool herself, much less Doreen. Everyone had noticed her distraction in the past weeks. Between working on her new painting and the occasional (very occasional, surely) train trips to New York to visit Ben Harker, she'd been definitely derelict in her duties. "I am very, very busy with that meteorologists' conference that's scheduled for the week after next. I think I'm supposed to meet somebody about it . . ." She thumbed futilely through her desk calendar, which was filled with cryptic notes to herself. "Tomorrow? Well, at some point, although it doesn't seem to be listed here. And isn't there a contest of some kind we're supposed to set up for it? And . . ." Quill gasped suddenly and sneezed.

"You finally goin' to the doctor's about that sneezing and coughing? You got that on your calendar?"

"That's scheduled for tomorrow, too," Quill said triumphantly. That appointment, with Andy Bishop, was written down, at least. "And Meg and I are having breakfast with Kimmie Bloomfield—you know, Andy's recruited this new cardiologist for the clinic, and Meg and I are making friends with Kimmie, who just moved here . . ." she sneezed again.

"I know all that," Doreen said flatly.

"And today," Quill said sunnily, "I'm, um . . . going over accounts."

"You got your notes for the Chamber meeting?" Doreen interrupted flatly.

"The Chamber of Commerce meeting? There isn't a Chamber of Commerce meeting today."

"Yes, there is, a special session. With just the mayor and a few others. You shoulda known about this a week ago. Mor'n that, probably."

"No way." Quill tossed away yet another tissue and made a face. "We don't have a Chamber meeting scheduled until the first week in December. We just *had* a Chamber meeting last week. And a pretty dull one it was, too. I mean, there's nothing going on at all right now because everyone in town is all wrapped up in the resort construction, and I refuse to sit and listen to Harvey Bozzel drone on about how the new resort is going to mean bigger and better things for Hemlock Falls. Nothing's going to happen for the next two years until it's completed, and the Wine Festival's over, and I *won't* do the programs for the Christmas pageant because it's way too early . . . what?"

"Special session," Doreen said, with the air of one repeating obvious information to an idiot child. "You're supposed to make a presentation. About the contest."

"Contest," Quill said, doing her best to appear knowledgeable.

"The contest that the meteorologists are running," Doreen said. "It's open to the public. Boomer said so, last time he was here."

"Boomer," Quill said intelligently.

"Boomer Dougherty," Doreen said. "The weather guy. On TV. You know. Everyone knows the Boom."

Quill, who had no idea who the Boom was, at least knew that the television meteorologists were supposed to show up for a four-day convention in a few days. Apparently, Boomer was in charge of it. Quill, relieved to have assimilated that much without getting caught out by Doreen, nodded wisely.

"And the contest is open to the public," Doreen said in a you've-heard-this-before tone of voice, "and because of the prize, you know, the big 'un . . ."

Prize? Quill thought wildly. A big one?

"The Chamber figured they'd better organize the village so we don't go all hunky-ass."

"Hunky-ass?"

"You know, all gollywompers."

"You mean the Chamber wants to set up some guidelines for the local entries, so there isn't mass confusion."

"Right." Doreen smiled approvingly at her.

"And that's what this extra Chamber meeting's about."

"Right." Doreen held the office door open. She gestured commandingly. "I already talked to the mayor. And he wanted me—" she cleared her throat in a modest way "—he wanted me to make a presentation, too. So I'm going to talk after you."

"What kind of presentation?" Quill asked suspiciously, the thought of her own content-less presentation momentarily forgotten. "What are you selling now, Doreen? It's not stationery again."

This reminder of Doreen's past entrepreneurial efforts diverted her from a straightforward response. "No, ma'am. Not enough profit margin in that."

"And it's not that pyramid thingie—what is it. Nu Skin." Nu Skin had skinned more than a few guests at the Inn, before Quill had put her foot down. "Or Amway, or Tupperware, or . . ."

"I'm just goin' to give them a progress report on Cityof-Love.com."

Quill gaped at her.

Doreen shook her head. "If you hadn't been so busy goin' up and down, up and down to New York City you'd know all about it. But since nobody can count on you for weekends anymore, much less for things like this here extra session of the Chamber meeting, I'll tell you what it is. This is the web site the Chamber's sponsoring."

"Web site," Quill said. "Oh! Of course."

Doreen's glare was unflatteringly suspicious. "You sure you remember what that there's all about?"

Quill waved her hand negligently. "Of course."

"And it's different from the contest."

"Yes, yes."

"You don't know a thing about neither of 'em," Doreen said. "So look here. You let me do the talking, okay?"

"I don't even think I should *go* to the meeting, Doreen," Quill said earnestly.

"Yeah. Well, Meg's workin' on menus for the weather guys, and John's in Syracuse meeting with the resort people, which leaves you. But I," Doreen added, "am gonna back you up."

"Thank you," Quill said meekly.

"Which reminds me—are you gonna be here this weekend or not?"

Quill, who knew better than to point out their current conversation couldn't possibly have reminded Doreen of any such thing, gave a guilty sigh, which turned into a series of sneezes. "I'm not going up this weekend." She hesitated. "Ben Harker's coming here. I think. That's the plan, anyway."

Doreen's expression became instantly unreadable. "Oh, yeah?" she said.

Quill eyed her suspiciously. "Yeah."

"Sheriff's back this weekend."

Quill's heart constricted. "Myles is back?"

"Heard it down to Marge and Betty's."

Marge Schmidt and Betty Hall had the best diner food in New York State—maybe the whole country. The Croh Bar was the locus for all the gossips in Tompkins County.

And Myles was back. And Ben was coming in.

Quill rubbed her forehead.

"The Chamber's waiting on us, Quill."

"Where's the meeting?"

"I put 'em in the Lounge," Doreen said. "On account of the last of the winegrowers are all over the conference room. Come on, Quill. I'll give 'em the scoop on the contest, but they'll probably have questions for you, too, because you're supposed to be the boss."

"Boss," said Quill. "I haven't been much of a boss lately."

Doreen's beaky features softened. "So, you got a lot on your mind. And anyways, Meg's in charge of the cooking, John's in charge of the financials. Just pretend that you and me are in charge of the rest."

Quill thrust her fingers into her hair and tugged at it. "My life needs to be simplified. I should be able to go upstairs and paint when I want to, or go run out in the leaves if I want to, or go see Ben Harker in New . . ."

Doreen glared at her. "They're gonna have questions about that, too. You ask me . . ."

"I didn't hear myself asking you a thing," Quill said.

". . . and anyone *else* in this town, why you want to throw away a perfectly good man like Myles McHale . . ."

"Doreen!"

"And ignore another perfectly good man like John Raintree . . ."

"Do—"

"And go gallivanting off to New York when you have a perfectly good life here, well, you got to expect folks are going be curious. Come on. Get up.''

Quill got up. She followed Doreen down the hall to the Tavern Lounge, muttering, "My life's an open book. The Inn's an open book. Everybody in this town knows everything about everybody else even before it happens to somebody."

Before entering the Lounge, she smoothed her hair, drew a deep breath, then went in.

Some days, the Lounge was Quill's favorite part of the Inn. The plushy, low chairs were comfortable. The round tables were made of narrow-plank mahogany flooring reclaimed from a torn-down school gym. The long, polished mahogany bar that curved around the north wall dated from the days of General C. C. Hemlock, the (justly) unknown Civil War veteran who had expanded the Inn to its current size in the late nineteenth century. The Lounge was the only place in the Inn where Quill had agreed to hang her own work. Three of her paintings were on the deep-teal walls now: a huge rose, sharp, edgy, ironic; a hard-edged calla lily; and a soft, impressionist watercolor of Meg and Quill in their teens.

Harker wanted to see them. Quill smiled, thinking of how he would stand, hands clasped behind his back, and absorb the work.

Most of the core members of the Hemlock Falls Chamber of Commerce were clustered in the south corner. Leaded French doors that led to the flagstone terrace outside let in the light.

Mayor Elmer Henry and his wife, Adela, stood shoulder to shoulder. Marge Schmidt, short and formidable in a red ski sweater and heavy jeans, poked an emphatic finger into Howie Murchison's chest. Howie, the town attorney, had edged himself next to Miriam Doncaster, the town librarian. Quill wondered briefly why Hemlock Falls didn't gossip as much about Miriam and Howie's off-again, on-again romance as they did her own. The other Chamber members chattered away in a low rumble: Freddie Bellini, Harvey Bozzel, Esther West—all except the truly horrible town tax assessor, Carol Ann Spinoza, who was all by herself in the corner. Nobody talked to Carol Ann if they could help it. So she sat, blonde hair set in a perky bob and face scrubbed shiny pink, contemplating tax hikes all by herself.

Somebody, probably Nate the bartender, had seen to the coffee urns and brought out bowls of pretzels. Somebody else (probably Marge Schmidt, who should have been a general) had shoved four small tables together to make a big one.

Quill noticed three new faces in the impromptu meeting. A dark-haired, rather somber-looking man slumped next to Esther West; he wore a name tag with the cheery preprinted tagline "Hi! My Name Is" and "Joss Roberts" neatly lettered beneath it. He looked familiar, although Quill was certain she hadn't met him before. Esther made occasional flirtatious comments to him, which he received with a faint smile. The other two newcomers Quill knew: Louis Bloomfield, the new cardiologist at Andy's clinic, and of course, his wife, Kimmie. The same Kimmie Quill and Meg were going to breakfast with tomorrow morning.

Kimmie smiled and waved. Quill smiled and waved back.

"Here she is!" The mayor greeted Quill with bouncing good will and a hearty clap on the shoulder. "You ready to talk to us about the contest, Quill? We got a lot of enthusiasm going for it. That's a pretty big prize the Boomer's offering."

"It surely is," said Quill heartily, who thought she would go crazy right now, in front of everybody, unless somebody explained the context to her.

The mayor beamed. "That's okay, then. Now, if everyone's got their coffee, we'll start the meeting. Reverend?"

Quill and Doreen took the two empty chairs on either side of Carol Ann Spinoza. Carol Ann, who had been watching Esther flirt with Joss Roberts in her fixed, reptilian way, bowed her head as the Reverend Dookie Shuttleworth rose and invoked the blessing of the Almighty on the folk of Hemlock Falls. Quill caught a whiff of soap. Carol Ann was the cleanest person she had ever met.

"This plenary session of the Hemlock Falls Chamber of Commerce will come to order." Mayor Henry slapped his chubby hand on the table.

"You don't mean plenary, Elmer," Miriam Doncaster said. "Plenary means something else. You're just saying plenary because it sounds important." She appealed prettily to Howie Murchison. "It's not a plenary session, is it, Howie?" She turned back to Kimmie Bloomfield with a deprecating smile. "The mayor means that this is an *ex parte* session."

Howie, a silver-haired, comfortable sort of man in his fifties, made a "hey, whatever" face. Quill sighed. Special session of the Chamber or not, this meeting was going to amble on like all the others. The mayor cleared his throat. "Never mind that, Miriam."

"Well, just for accuracy's sake, Mayor. And for literacy's sake, too. If we all read more, if we all had respect for the written *and* the spoken word . . ."

The meeting digressed, as it almost always did, into pointless, albeit enthusiastic argument. Quill settled into the comfortable reverie usual to her at Chamber meetings.

Harker would tell her she was wasting time. Harker would tell her to get up, leave, walk away, and go back to the canvas waiting for her upstairs.

Quill sat up and thought about this.

She sneezed. Esther clicked her tongue sympathetically and pushed some Kleenex across the table. She was wearing pumpkin earrings in honor of the upcoming Thanksgiving holidays.

Harker would laugh at the pumpkin earrings.

Suddenly, she didn't want him to come here. She'd call him. Put him off. She wasn't ready for the two parts of her life to meet. She didn't want Harker, with his sardonic take on small-town customs, to laugh at Esther's pumpkin earrings.

She sneezed again. Carol Ann, whose concern for germs was pathological, shoved her chair out of the way with a pointed glare.

Quill gave her a haughty stare back. On the other hand, Carol Ann was a highly annoying part of life in Hemlock Falls. She wouldn't mind at all if Harker took a few verbal swipes at Carol Ann.

Maybe she could get cloned. Then she could be two people: one, the New York Quill, painting her heart out, spending time with Harker on the vigorous city streets; the other, the Hemlock Falls Quill, with enough time not to let her friends down.

Here's what she'd do. She'd bleach her hair blonde and gain thirty pounds, change her name and move to a distant city. She'd live under the name of Saunders, like Eeyore in *Winnie the Pooh*. She'd start a new life, where nobody knew who she was, and all the decisions she'd have to make would be new ones.

She pulled her sketch pad from her skirt pocket, and scribbled a winged donkey, flying free and labeled "For I have burst the airy bounds of earth." Then she drew a Quill with round ears and a tail and labeled it "Quill the Rat." She liked Miriam. She liked Esther. She liked them all. Even though they drove her crazy. Harker wouldn't be able to see why.

"You draw fast," Carol Ann said in her ear.

Well, she didn't like Carol Ann, but then, nobody else did, either. Carol Ann scared everybody to death.

"I was thinking," Carol Ann continued, keeping well out of the way of any contaminated air Quill might be exhaling, "of maybe taking up painting as a hobby."

"You were?"

"Yes." Carol Ann's voice was high-pitched, precise, and so sweet it made Quill's teeth ache. "You know, Carl has decided that he isn't happy in Hemlock Falls."

"Carl," Quill said, with every sign of comprehension. Then, recalling a slender, self-effacing man who usually trailed Carol Ann and her two neat children, "Oh. Carl. Your husband."

"Ex-husband," Carol Ann said in her precise little voice. She blinked once, like a cat at a mouse hole. "I understand that you're quite famous in your field?"

"Carol Ann, I don't teach," Quill said firmly, anticipating the next question. "Never."

Carol Ann cocked her head in the other direction. Carol Ann was unused to people saying no. "I see," she said in a dangerous way. She wrinkled her nose delicately. "Is that a new perfume you're wearing? Somebody should tell you. It stinks."

Quill squared her shoulders and counted to ten.

". . . The minutes, Quill?"

Quill looked up into a sea of expectant faces.

"I said you takin' the minutes?" The mayor beamed at her.

"Certainly," Quill said primly. She flipped to a clean page.

"We'll talk later," Carol Ann said.

"Okay," the mayor said, "so here's the thing. I called this meeting . . ."

His wife, Adela, drummed her fingers on the table.

"Sorry, dear. We called this meeting on account of two things. Doreen here has a report on the web site, and we got an opportunity for a great new contest that Doreen's also gonna to tell us about."

"Web site?" Quill said. She recalled, too late, Doreen's mention of the project earlier. "Oh, *that* web site."

"You missed the last meeting, Quill." Esther West's fall shipment of clothes and accessories were heavy on a harvest theme.

In addition to the plastic pumpkins dangling at her ears, a scarf printed with autumn leaves was wound around her neck. She shoved her glasses up with one long finger. Her nail polish was pumpkin-colored, too. "You were in New York with that new boyfriend of yours. Doreen's started a new business, and the Chamber's investing in it." Her eyes danced with excitement.

"It's not a dot com, is it?" Quill said. She groaned. "Of course. It's a dot com." She looked at Doreen, who grinned in satisfaction. "Tell me it's just a nice little web site. For the tourists."

"Lot more potential than that, Quill." Harvey Bozzel, Hemlock Falls's best (and only) advertising executive, smoothed his blond hair with both palms. "It's one of the hottest areas in tech biz. The hottest of the hot."

"CityofLove.com," Esther said, making it one word. She bared her teeth at Joss Roberts. "Joss here wrote the whole thing."

"Uh, not really," Joss said.

"He doesn't like her," Carol Ann said into Quill's ear. "Not really. I mean—that pumpkin nail polish." She laughed like somebody chipping ice.

"I like the nail polish," Quill said. "And Mr. Roberts seems to like Esther just fine."

Carol Ann's face didn't exactly move—like a snake's, it really never changed expression—but Quill was distinctly unsettled. "Philadelphia's the city of love," Quill said, in a game attempt to rejoin the main conversation. "At least, it's the city of brotherly love. When did we vote to call ourselves the City of Love?"

"We aren't the City of Love," the mayor said. "The web site is. It's a dating service."

"It's a what?"

"A dating service." Elmer waved his hands. "You know, if you'd used it, Quill, you wouldn't have to be runnin' off to New York City for a boyfriend. Probably could have found a good one in Syracuse."

"Not that you didn't have plenty of boyfriends here," Esther said, who had been single for a very long time. "You already have the sheriff, you have John Raintree . . ."

"Now, just a minute, guys," Quill said, feebly.

"She's going to see Dr. Bishop tomorrow morning," Carol

Ann offered. "And I'll bet I know what *that* is all about. One of the advantages of finding a man a little closer to home, Quill, is that you have a better chance of knowing his background."

Doreen, quicker on the uptake than most, decked Carol Ann with an uppercut to the chin. The tax assessor flew sideways into Quill, and then to the floor.

Esther squeaked. Marge, Howie, and the darkly morose Joss Roberts burst into laughter. Adela screamed. Dr. Bloomfield rose, gently moved Quill out of the way, and knelt by the squalling Carol Ann.

Nobody knew what would have happened next, because Harland Peterson and his cousin, Petey, burst in the French doors and startled everyone into immobility.

"Mayor," Harland said. "We got ourselves a body downstream."

# CHAPTER 2

"Another body," Quill said. "Ugh. We've had enough bodies in Hemlock Falls in the past, Meg. I'm not even sure what number this one is."

The body in the Gorge had taken up everybody's time yesterday, and Quill had retreated thankfully to her painting. When she'd come down for breakfast this morning, the wait staff had been full of speculation. It hadn't been anyone from Hemlock Falls, at least no one immediately identifiable.

Meg, absorbed in that morning's edition of the *Syracuse American*, murmured acknowledgment. The two sisters had been involved in more than one murder investigation in the past. Quill wasn't anxious to get involved in another.

"But Davey Kiddermeister thinks the body was dumped here. Whoever the poor guy is, he was killed somewhere else. A hit and run, Davey thought. Or rather, that's what the forensic guys from Ithaca thought. The mayor's worried that the news will keep the meteorologists from having their convention here, although why a convention at the Inn should worry Elmer is beyond me. Adela said something about wrecking the contest, so maybe that's what the mayor's worried about. Meg. Just what *is* this contest?" Quill poured a third cup of coffee for herself. Maybe her brain would stop being so fuzzy if she poured enough caffeine into her system. She sneezed twice. Maybe she'd be able to make a decision about which Quill she wanted to be if she could just stop sneezing. And her head ached like the dickens this morning.

"Mm-hm," Meg said.

Quill drummed her fingers on the tabletop. The table was set for three. A low arrangement of bronze chrysanthemums glowed against a deep bronze cloth, and the pottery dishes were a warm and earthy green.

Meg flipped the newspaper over.

Quill looked out the window at the waterfall just outside their Inn. In mid-November, the water ran thin and and it looked cold. The air was still clear, the sun bright. They were waiting for Kimmie Bloomfield. She was late.

Quill suppressed another sneeze. She'd been up at the crack of dawn, working on the painting, so she had to admit to being really, really tired. If she didn't leave within the hour, she was going to be late for her appointment with Andy Bishop.

She looked around the dining room with a slight sigh of satisfaction. At least the worst of the breakfast rush was over. They were understaffed, and Quill had helped wait tables.

She didn't really want to have breakfast with Kimmie Bloomfield. Kimmie was full of a nervous vitality that could be very depressing. And men and marriage were bound to be the chief topic of conversation at breakfast. Kimmie, with marriage problems, and Meg, with about-to-be-married problems, were temporarily the best of friends. And she especially didn't want to talk about her love life or anyone else's. Particularly now. Quill, who never wanted to be married again in this life or the next, had a number of things she should be doing this morning; and breakfast with Kimmie wasn't one of them.

Except for Meg. She was always there for her sister, breakfast, lunch, or dinner, and there was no getting around that, even if she wanted to.

"Oh, my gosh." Margaret Quilliam, her face pale, folded the *Syracuse American* into careful quarters and laid it on the breakfast table. "Oh, Quill." The distress in Meg's voice made Quill turn her head; at the look on her sister's face she reached out and grasped her forearm. "Meg?"

"Remember this?" Meg pointed at the paper.

The picture didn't look horrific. Just a badly angled photograph shot through the rear window of a car. The driver's neck and ears were visible. The passenger beside him turned to face the camera, mouth open, shouting.

There was a third person in the car. Quill remembered that all too well. But no picture existed of her. If there had been a picture, the police may have found her.

"You remember the carjacking we saw? The one where the kids who stole the car cracked it up? And the baby was killed?"

"Carjacking," Quill said, trying to keep the shock out of her voice. She remembered all too well.

"The Ross baby."

Quill put her coffee down. She sat up, her vagueness gone. "That baby in the car seat. George Nash, they caught him. But not the other two, the ones who got away. Overmeyer, that was the guy's name. And the girl, MaryAnn something. It was horrible. Oh, Meg. Oh, no. Are they dragging that story up again?"

"The guy's out. The one they caught and sent to jail. George Nash. They let him out."

Quill picked up the article and glanced at it. She put it down, as if physical contact with the newspaper were a contagion. She shook her head. "Overmeyer was the real murderer. They would have put him in jail for life, if they'd caught him." Those ears. Those ears and the back of his neck. George Nash had crumbled, giving the police his name but not the last name of the girl, MaryAnn, whom he had loved.

Both MaryAnn and Overmeyer had disappeared.

"I can still see it," Meg said soberly. "As if it happened this morning. George Nash looked right at me."

Quill watched her sister's face. The nightmares had plagued Meg for years. Quill herself had been fifteen, Meg had just turned eleven. They had walked to the 7-Eleven in their small Connecticut town on an errand Quill had long forgotten. But she hadn't forgotten what happened. They had walked right into a store robbery that had turned into a carjacking: *one hand pushed the heavy glass door, the other grasped Meg's fragile shoulder. The door wrenched forward. George Nash raced by her, shoving them both into the concrete wall with a frantic force, made scarier by Quill's terror of the physical invasion. Then the man stumbling after George Nash, his face distorted, shouting, "Evan! Evan!" The car roared away from the curb. She could still see the back of the driver's head, with those strange, protuberant ears.*

The kids had wrecked the car, after a twenty-mile-long police chase. Only the child had been killed.

She had done her first pen-and-ink portrait a few months after that: Meg curled in the window seat of their Connecticut house, an abandoned doll on the rug at Meg's feet. The sketch had gotten her the first scholarship.

"Are you okay?" Meg asked.

"Yes. But did this article bring it all back for you, too?"

"No. I didn't really see anything you know. You squashed me flat against your stomach." Meg shook her head decisively. "It's the shouts I remember. That poor guy, the father, shouting at the kids to stop. But I'll be fine. It was a long time ago."

"Yes," Quill said. "A long time ago." She frowned a little. "Why bring it up now though, Meg? That was twenty years ago."

"Nash broke parole," Meg said, "he's disappeared. And you know the papers—it was sensational news then and it's sensational now."

"Which brings me," Quill said, "to the body by the Gorge."

"Oh." Meg frowned. "That."

"I hope that you—" they both said simultaneously.

"Okay," Quill said, "you first."

"No investigation. No sisters in detection, no nosing in where the police should only tread, none of that."

"That's just what I was about to say," Quill said admiringly. "I mean, it's none of our business, is it?"

"Nope. As far as I'm concerned, I'm a retired detective. Come to think of it, I never wanted to be a detective in the first place."

Quill, who recalled very well how enthusiastic Meg had been about their previous forays into solving murders, raised a skeptical eyebrow but said nothing.

"I mean, I'm engaged to be married. I have a kitchen to run. The Inn's a howling success these days . . . who has time?"

"Not to mention the fact," Quill said dryly, "that the mystery surrounding this poor soul started somewhere else."

"Agreed, then, that we leave this one alone."

Quill, recalling a half-forgotten ritual they'd called the Sister Pact, pretended to spit into her palm. Meg did the same, and they shook hands over the flowers.

Then Quill sneezed. Meg, her face lightening with the diversion said, "When *are* you going to see Andy about that cold?"

"I'll get to it," Quill said evasively. "And it's not a cold."

"Of course it's a cold," Meg said in a practical way. "Unless it's allergies. What else could it be?"

Quill didn't answer her. She'd bought a used copy of the

*Merck Manual* on her last trip to New York City, which may
have been a big mistake. There were a lot of things this might
be. Most of them fatal.

"Not the dread disease, again," Meg said, with annoying pre-
science. "Come *on,* Quill."

"Go ahead. Mock. See if I care. See if I leave you anything
in my will this time."

Meg rolled her eyes. "Quill, you never get sick. And like most
totally healthy people, the few times that you do get sick, you're
impossible. The last time you got sick was the flu six years ago,
right in the middle of the convention of the Swamp Reclamation
Engineers. Did you, like most people with the flu, whine and
snivel and gulp aspirin and then go to bed for a week? Did you
make an appointment with my then-not-affianced husband, the
best—if only—internist in Hemlock Falls? You did not. You
had Howie Murchison update your will. You staggered around
here like Camille in the last act of *Traviata.*"

"Violetta," Quill corrected her. "Not that it matters. Because
I didn't."

"And you infected half the guests, besides. Honestly, Quill."

Quill glared at her. "You will be really sorry one of these
days."

"When you're dead?"

"When I'm dead."

Meg sat back in her chair, her arms folded. "Okay. So you
know what I think?"

"I know what you think. And I don't want to know any more
of what you think."

"I think this illness is psychosomatic."

"You do."

"I do.

"And what's more, I think you're, umm . . . there's a word
for it. Deflecting? No, that isn't it. Projecting? No, that isn't it,
either. Displacing! That's it. You're displacing your anxieties
about Myles and this jerk, what's his name, Harker, and your
new work onto your body!"

"Thank you so much," Quill said coldly.

"You see, I've been talking with Kimmie . . ."

"*Have* you, indeed?" Quill wondered briefly how Meg would
look with chrysanthemums up her nose.

". . . she's been in quite a lot of therapy, Quillie. You really ought to think about trying it. And *she* thinks . . ."

Quill was spared the dubious pleasure of hearing what Kimmie thought by the arrival of the woman in question.

"Sorry I'm late!" Kimmie Bloomfield breezed up to the table in a rush. A gray beret was tilted over her curly hair, and she wore a deep-pink cashmere sweater set and perfectly cut gray pants. She was smaller than Meg—who herself was shorter than Quill by a good four inches—and had a rounded, pleasantly plump figure.

Kimmie sat down in a rush of cold air and Chanel No. 14. "But Louis made such a fuss about his shirts this morning that I just couldn't get away. Honestly. Doctors. They're the worst possible husbands, Meg. It's the little tin god syndrome," she said to Quill in a condescending way. "Thank your lucky stars, Quill, that you're not involved with a doctor. It's bad enough that Meggie here is going to join the club."

Quill wiggled her eyebrows at Meg, who refused to look back.

"You're not all that late," Meg said. "And I don't have to be back in the kitchen until eleven. Well, except for right this minute. I've got a new dish I'm trying, Kimmie. I think you'll like it, but I'm not sure. Anyhow, you two have a nice time together. Be back in ten minutes."

"No food!" Kimmie cried, startling the few diners left in the room. "I've put on another ten pounds just breathing the air in here. Besides, I'm on a new diet."

"Just a taste," Meg said.

Meg disappeared through the swinging doors.

There was a long pause, which Quill finally broke by asking politely. "New diet?"

"It's wonderful," Kimmie said promptly. "No sugar. No bread. No fruits. Very few vegetables. Just meat and fish."

Quill couldn't help it. "What does Louis think?"

Kimmie snorted. "Louis. What does he know? And anyway, since the . . ." she stumbled slightly, "the accident, he's been understanding. For him, anyway."

Quill took a sip of coffee to delay any response. It was cold, and the milk had formed an unpleasant skin on the top. Kimmie had a miscarriage a few weeks before she and Louis had made their move to Hemlock Falls. From what Quill could gather, it had been very early on in the pregnancy. Quill firmly suppressed the very unkind thought that Kimmie was using the tragedy as a weapon in the war that was her marriage. "Has it helped? The diet, I mean?"

Kimmie's restless blue eyes settled briefly on Quill, then darted around the room. "Some. I wish you'd tell me your secret. How do you stay so skinny?"

Quill, who never knew how to answer these kinds of comments, made a demurring noise. Kimmie launched into a monologue with three topics: Louis's faults as a husband, diets, and the challenges presented by decorating the historic farmhouse she and Louis had moved into the week before. This last truly interested Quill. By the time Meg bounced back to the table with breakfast, she and Kimmie were having a reasonable conversation, which mitigated Quill's impatience at how late it was getting. The appointment with Andy Bishop was for ten, and she was going to be very late.

"Shirred eggs in sherry and cream." Meg slipped the warm plates onto the table and settled herself with a smile of satisfaction. "Eat it all, Quill. You're getting too thin. And I only made you one, Kimmie, since I know you're trying to cut back."

"Eggs and cream," Kimmie said, "are on my diet."

"A diet that lets you have heavy cream?" Meg said. "You're kidding."

Since Kimmie's diet seemed destined to induce heart attacks in even the very thin, Quill tuned out and tackled her eggs. When she had eaten enough, she waited vainly for a break in the conversation and finally just stood up.

"What do you think?" Meg simply ignored the flow of Kimmie's conversation and looked at her sister.

"The eggs? Terrific."

"Just terrific?" Meg scowled at Quill's plate. "You didn't finish."

"I finished as much as I could. I already had a muffin this morning, Meg."

"Are you leaving?"

"I'm leaving," Quill said firmly.

"Why?" Meg demanded. "I thought you were going to have breakfast with us. I thought you said you wanted to get to know Kimmie better." She rolled her eyes at Kimmie, "My sister. Honestly."

Quill, who had had every intention of assuring Meg that she

was going to see Andy, decided not to. "No reason," she said airily. "Thought I'd check out the construction site, see how things are going down there." Checking out the construction site of the new resort was a favorite occupation of most Hemlockians.

"Then be sure and take Max," Meg said. "He's been stuck in the kitchen with Bjarne all week because of that last set of raids on the dumpsters, and he'd love a ride." Meg giggled at Kimmie's expression. "Max is Quill's dog," she said. "Which makes me wonder, Kimmie, what are the psychological implications of pet ownership and a person's relationship with men? Or rather, a person's inability to maintain a sustained relationship?" She darted a hasty glance at Quill. "Just theoretically, you understand. Not for anyone in particular. Have you ever discussed stuff like that with your therapist?"

"Good-bye," Quill said loudly. "I'll be back. Maybe."

"Don't forget we have a meeting at eleven."

Quill, who had no recollection at all of a meeting at eleven, nodded intelligently. Then she sneezed. She had a purseful of questions for Andy, based on her thorough reading of the relevant portions of the *Merck Manual*. And she was going to be late if she didn't leave right this minute. This wasn't a cold. Or psychosomatic. Or displacement. She was sure of it.

She sneezed her way through the kitchen, noticing that Bjarne, the sous-chef, was careful to give her a wide berth. There was proof that some people, at least, had more consideration for a serious illness than others she could name. On the other hand, Max, greeting her with joyful leaps, was pitifully eager to join her.

"Come on, boy," Quill said, rumpling his ears. "I've neglected you, too. And since you appear to be the most likely candidate for my old age—we really have to start spending more time together."

# CHAPTER 3

"I don't know what else to tell you, exactly," Quill said a short time later in Andy's office. She had only been a few minutes past the time for her appointment with Andy, but she felt apologetic anyway.

"No other symptoms?"

"Nope."

Andy bit his lip and made a strangled sort of sound, like a snort. "You think it could be one of three things. A brain tumor—more specifically an astrocytoma, grade four. Amyotrophic lateral sclerosis. Or lupus."

"Lupus erythematosus," Quill said helpfully.

"Quill, you didn't unearth a copy of a *Merck Manual* from somewhere, did you?"

Better to look at the Vermeer-blue autumn sky outside the windows of Andy Bishop's hospital clinic than wonder if Andy—who had never before exhibited much of a sense of humor as far as Quill could see—was chuckling underneath his sober physician's manner. The *clank-thud* of heavy construction equipment made a distant undercurrent of sound, and she welcomed the chance for a diversion. "The new addition to your clinic is still on schedule? There's a lot of equipment still out there."

Andy blinked in a distracted way. "Uh, yeah."

"Meg said you two have been getting along well with Louis Bloomfield and his wife."

"Louis is a good guy. And a heck of a cardiologist. I was lucky to get him."

"Kimmie came to breakfast this morning. She and Meg get along really well."

"Um."

Quill did her best to dissect that "um." Did Andy find Kimmie as nosy and annoying as she did? Or did he, like her crazy sister, find Kimmie's whirligig conversational style charming and feminine?

Quill shifted at an uncomfortable thought. She and Meg had been close for years. They hadn't needed any other close women friends. When they had bought the Inn at Hemlock Falls and moved to the village, they had tried to keep up with the friends from the past, but when old friends moved out of each other's orbit, relationships were never quite the same.

Was she jealous of Meg's affection for Kimmie?

Maybe she didn't have a dread disease at all. Maybe she was jealous. Maybe she was (a) unable to manage a close relationship with anyone but her dog and (b) jealous of her own sister. And maybe all this *was* whatever Meg called it. Displacement.

"Meg seems to like Kimmie quite a bit," she ventured.

"Let's concentrate on you for the moment, Quill." Andy leaned forward, took her hand in his and turned it over and frowned at her nails. His own hand was cool and firm, like Andy himself.

Quill looked critically at her thumb; she hadn't gotten off all the burnt umber and ultramarine she'd been using while working on her new painting that morning.

"When did the symptoms start?"

Quill drew back, shifted restlessly on the gurney Andy used as an examining table, and then tucked the paper gown under her thighs. "Symptoms," she said reflectively.

Meg was flat wrong. She did have a dread disease. "I can't think. I sneeze all the time. And I ache all over. And I can't sleep."

Andy sat back. "The Inn's been incredibly busy. It's been a rigorous couple of months just in terms of the running around you've been doing. And you've been traveling quite a bit . . . and that's tiring, Quill. And you've been painting again. Meg and I are both really happy about that, by the way."

Quill pulled her lower lip. She didn't like to talk about it. Talking about being able to paint again might jinx it. She sneezed twice and her head throbbed. She was sick, dammit.

"You won't tell Meg if there's something really wrong with me, will you, Andy? You'll let me tell her first. I don't want her to worry about me."

"Meg's so busy now, she wouldn't notice if a meteor landed in the middle of Main Street," Andy said cheerfully. "And of course I wouldn't break patient confidentiality. But I don't think you need to worry too much, Quill. Basically, I think you need to slow down, get some rest, and just take it easy."

"I'm an idiot," she said aloud, suddenly embarrassed.

"We're all idiots when it comes to maintaining regular habits," Andy said comfortably. "Life tends to intervene."

"I swear," Quill muttered, "to walk two miles a day. I swear off Meg's crème brûlée. I swear to get enough sleep. I'll give up coffee. Forever."

"Lack of sleep and exercise and too much coffee may not explain this. We just won't know until the tests come back. Can you extend both arms for me? Just one more time."

Quill held her arms out. "Fine tremors," she said, her confidence in the severity of her problem coming back. "In *both* hands."

"Hm." Andy went to the small built-in desk in the far corner of the examining room and made a note on her chart. "Get dressed, kiddo. I'll be back." He left, carrying the chart.

Quill waited a few moments after the door closed, until the tremors stopped. That was the annoying thing: the shaking came and went. She'd go for hours, even a day or two with no problem at all.

It didn't make any sense. She *had* a dread disease. Meg would be sorry when she died. And so would the rest of them.

She'd folded her clothes carefully when she'd taken them off. She put them on just as carefully, concentrating on each item: the long denim skirt, made out of that lovely Tencil, that draped so well; warm tights; midcalf boots; a beautiful sweater in a rosy cream, a gift from Meg. She frowned at the sleeve. More paint, dammit. Rose madder, from the look of it. She'd had a devil of a time with the upper corner of the background this morning. She'd dropped the brush on her sleeve while trying to fix the canvas.

She peered at herself in the mirror over Andy's desk. There was paint in her hair, too. She'd wound it into a long braid, to keep the ends from the paint, and much good it had done her, because she'd tripped on her carpeting and fallen right into her palate.

She imagined Andy's chart:

Thirty-six-year-old unmarried female, five eight, one hundred and twenty-five pounds, reports weight loss, sleeplessness, and periodic weakness in extremities, especially right arm, nausea, light-headedness. Rule out . . . what?

Hysteria, Quill thought gloomily, neurasthenia, if that fine old Victorian diagnosis still applied. Creative frenzy—that's what was wrong with her. But good it was to have it back. That beneficent, ferocious monkey on her shoulder, whispering in her ear, filling her conscious mind with great, looping washes of color and shape, shoving everything else aside.

"Tests," Andy said as he came back in. "We're going to order some tests." He carried a syringe and a small box of cylinders.

Quill winced. "Blood samples. Do I have to pee in a cup, too?"

"You'll have to pee in a cup."

Quill shoved up her sleeve and whooshed at the prick of the needle as Andy drew blood. He filled three cylinders in his precise way, set them on top of her chart and looked directly at her.

"Now listen to me, Quill. I want you to get some sleep, cut back on the coffee, and get out and walk as much as you can. And there's no excuse for the weight loss, not with a sister who's the greatest gourmet chef in upstate New York." He patted his own flat stomach. "I've got to watch it all the time."

"You only have to watch it part of the time," Quill pointed out. "Meg cooks in New York at La Strazza two days a week."

He grinned. "But she's all mine the other five."

"Andy? You won't . . . that is . . ."

"No. I won't talk about your visit today, if you'd rather I didn't." He gave her a small glass jar with her name printed on the label: "Sarah Quilliam," and underneath that, a heading "Patient ID."

Except she wasn't patient. She wanted to get back to the canvas.

"Quill?"

"Sorry, yes, the cup."

"Fill it and leave it on the shelf in the bathroom."

"I know, I know." Quill waved the jar at him. "Go. Get out.

Go hassle some other sorry patient. Oh, Andy?"

He turned, his hand on the door, his attention obviously on the day's work ahead.

"You don't think . . . I mean. It's just stress, right? A little overwork?"

He nodded. "Maybe. Chances are ninety percent or better that it's stress. But we'll find out."

And the other 10 percent?

Andy had left the door slightly ajar. And he'd dropped the chart in the metal holder fixed to the face of the door. Shirley Peterson would pick it up and file it.

Quill filched the chart and ducked back into the examining room. Andy's handwriting was as neat and precise as Andy himself. *". . . Ten pound weight loss w/in last 30d . . . 3 recent, intermittent episodes of marked tremors all extremities, esp. right side."* Blah, blah, blah.

And there it was, at the end, scrawled quickly, in pencil, as if recording in an erasable medium meant it was of transitory concern: *rule out stress-related allergies, psychosomatic illness, caffeine poisoning . . .*

"Allergies!" Quill exploded indignantly. "I've never been allergic to a thing in my life. And too much coffee?" Balzac, she suddenly recalled, had died from drinking too much coffee. Something like forty cups in one day.

"Thanks, Quill! Were you going to bring that to me?" Sheila Peterson shoved the door open, grabbed the chart from Quill's hand and backed out, obviously in a hurry. Shirley was usually in a hurry. She had five kids, three in high school, and one in college who commuted to Syracuse. The oldest lived at home, too, and worked for her husband Petey's business (Peterson's Floor Covering and Septic Systems, Inc.) Quill couldn't imagine how Shirley managed to hold down a full-time job. She was Quill's age, but her hair was graying. When she didn't smile, the lines around her mouth and eyes added fifteen years to her face. Talk about stress. But Shirley wasn't sneezing and her legs and arms seemed to work perfectly well.

Quill followed her out the door, intent on getting the chart. Shirley came to a brief halt and waved the chart in the air. "Did you want to see it? That new Patient's Rights bill, you're allowed to, you know. Or is there something else I can do for

you? No? Okay, then." She resumed her half trot down the hall.
"And don't forget the urine sample!"

"I didn't forget the sample," Quill said to Max some minutes
later. "And I didn't come out any smarter than I went in. Allergies! Too much coffee! Phooey!"

Max, curled into the passenger seat of her new Honda, made
a noncommittal sound somewhere between a yelp and whine.

"So. No dread disease. At least," she added hopefully, "not a
dread disease that's immediately apparent." She stared out into
the parking lot. At least three new physicians were joining
Andy's practice, including Louis Bloomfield. The addition to
the clinic was as long as the original building.

She shook her head. This was stupid. She was wasting Andy's
time, wasting Shirley's time. Wasting her own. She felt fine.
There wasn't anything wrong that couldn't be put down to er-
ratic hours of sleep, or too much caffeine, or standing in one
place for hours in front of the easel. She sneezed. And a bad
cold.

The easel. The vision of her painting engulfed her again—
the painting that would be, if she could just get the time to finish
it. "Time, Max. I don't have any time." And she'd been wrong
about the rose madder. It needed another color. She sat at the
wheel, engrossed. Blue. Some sort of blue.

Max whined and stuck his wet nose in her palm. Guiltily,
Quill rumpled his ears. She should have walked to the clinic.
Max would have enjoyed it, and she needed the exercise. But
there wasn't time. As it was, she had to steal the hours to work
on the painting from her duties as manager of the Inn; no way
could she afford the time the two-mile hike from the Inn to the
clinic would take. She just needed to relax, that's all. She could
hold the elusive shade of blue in her mind in the few minutes
it would take to get back to the Inn, back to the easel.

She put the Honda in gear and drove through Hemlock Falls
at an (unusually) decorous pace. Which meant she missed the
light at Main and Hemlock Drive. She braked and waited with
rising impatience while an endless line of construction vehicles
lumbered through the intersection. Most were on their way to
the new resort being built on the lip of Hemlock Gorge. Some
turned off to Andy's clinic.

The light turned green. Quill put her foot on the accelerator.

A cheerful construction worker with a red flag jumped from the back of a pickup and signaled her to stop. Quill put her foot on the brake again. A huge crane grumbled slowly through the intersection against the green. The light turned red just as the crane cleared the road. Quill bit her lip, hard, fighting annoyance.

It was good, the growth in Hemlock Falls. Everybody said so, and everybody was right. When the new resort was finished, hundreds, maybe thousands of tourists would stroll the sidewalks and admire the cobblestone buildings. They'd get hungry and come up to the Inn and order huge gourmet meals and watch the waterfall right outside their dining room windows. She could put up with the mess made by the crews and with the blocked roads. Everyone else did.

Quill glanced at her watch, and then tapped the wheel impatiently. She stared at the intersection, willing it clear. Several gravel trucks jounced through on their way to the resort. The builders had located it three miles south of the Inn, at a spot over the Gorge where the Hemlock River ran slow and deep. Meg and Quill swam there in the summertime.

She'd been up to the site a lot, at first. So had the rest of the village. The huge complex was supposed to open just before Christmas next year, but most residents of Hemlock Falls were skeptical about the pace of the work.

Quill wondered why construction guys never seemed to actually *do* anything, like dig or shovel. There were the guys that drove trucks back and forth. And the guy that walked up and down the site with a clipboard. And another two guys that stood in earnest conversation. Quill wondered about the project job descriptions: Road Walker. Clip Board Reader. Discussers.

A car horn blared at her.

Quill's attention jerked back to the traffic light. Green. She looked in the rearview mirror. A long line of cars was backed up behind her. The light in front of her turned yellow, then red. The Flag Waver stared at her accusingly. There was absolutely no through traffic as the light stayed red. This time, a lot of horns blared at her.

Quill sank down behind the wheel. She'd traded in her aging Oldsmobile just last week for her new Honda. Maybe no one would recognize the new car. She hummed carelessly, "La, la. Oh, la."

Then Max, for reasons known only to him and his dog gods, stuck his head out the window and started to bark. Quill put her head on the wheel and sighed. Everyone in town knew Max. And almost no one really appreciated him except Quill herself. In fact, there was what Quill considered to be an active and unfair prejudice against Max in Hemlock Falls. Which meant that nobody would be giving Max a ride except her, or the dogcatcher, and the dogcatcher drove a beat-up Chevy pickup. So everybody would know that the whole traffic jam was her fault, even though she was temporarily disguised in a new car.

"It's the garbage can thing, Max," she said. "If you'd just stay away from the garbage cans, you would be universally approved and loved. Honest."

Max, who even Quill had to admit was perhaps the ugliest dog in the world, looked pleased.

"Lady!" the Red Flag Waver yelled. He began to jump up and down. "Lady! Will you *please* get a move on?!"

"So it's green," Quill muttered. "Fine. Just fine." She gunned the motor and made it through just before the light turned again.

She looked back a little guiltily. The car immediately behind her hadn't made it through, which meant the rest of them would have to wait through another cycle. "Well, at least we made it through, Max," she said cheerfully. "So the cork's out of the bottle. Traffic will be running smoothly in no time."

Quill was at the top of the drive to the Inn before her cheeks cooled off. She barely registered the view of the Inn—the copper roof, the sprawling green velvet grounds, and the surrounding trees displaying the last gold/red burst of autumn. She'd park in the guest lot, sneak up to her room and get the blue mixed on her palate before anyone dragged her into the day. Cheerfully, she wound her way through the crowded parking lot to her parking space.

A bright-blue Jeep stood smugly in her parking spot.

"Dammit, Max."

She backed up, narrowly missed a Toyota, and bumped over the curb to turn around into the main drive. The driveway angled along the side of the Inn then curved around the front entrance, which faced Hemlock Gorge and the waterfall. She could park in front of the big oak doors there and let guests maneuver around the Honda, which would be rude, inconsiderate, and quick. Or she could take the back drive to the sheds that housed

Mike the groundskeeper's trucks and mowers, and let Mike maneuver around her car, which would put him into a fine old temper and cost her five minutes in the walk back to the Inn.

Or she could park in the herb gardens off Meg's kitchen. That'd be the quickest of all. The gravel path was wide enough for guests to stroll three abreast, and the only crop there in mid-November was Brussels sprouts, which Meg hated anyway. And the Honda was technically a sport-utility vehicle. It should handle Brussels sprouts with ease.

She parked the Honda and banged into the kitchen, Max at her heels, to find her sister and her housekeeper staring at her from their stools at the stainless-steel prep counter in the middle of the room.

"Are you crazy?" Meg demanded. She was small, almost four inches shorter than Quill, with gray eyes and dark brown hair. When she was indignant (a frequent occurrence) she seemed bigger.

Quill looked at her, puzzled. She'd done something weird to her hair in the hour or so Quill had been gone. Meg's hair was short. It was also thick and glossy, and usually fell into place without a lot of effort on her part, a fact that always annoyed Quill a lot. Her own hair was recalcitrant: there was too much of it, it was too curly, and the color was somewhere between carrots and tomatoes. "What did you do to your hair?"

"Never mind my hair." Meg poked at it uncertainly. "Kimmie hared off when you did, and Dina said she wanted to try styling it. Does it look stupid?"

"You curled it and moussed it. What will Andy think? I think it looks, umm . . . maybe better the other way. Are you experimenting for the wedding?"

"Never mind my hair, Quill. Why did you park your new car in the Brussels sprouts?"

Quill looked over her shoulder. The Honda's steel gray made a nice contrast with the green spikes of the vegetable. "I have to get upstairs. I'm in a hurry."

"Well, you can't get upstairs, not yet," Doreen said truculently. Doreen had been experimenting with her hair, too. She was going to be a bridesmaid, if Meg's wedding to Andy ever came off. The housekeeper's frizzy gray was now a sort of silvery blue.

"That I like," Quill said. "Your hair, I mean. Did Dina do it?"

"Yuh. Don't know why that girl wants to mess around with that Ph.D. when she could make a good livin' as a hairdresser with none of the fuss."

Meg rolled her eyes. Doreen scowled ferociously at her.

Quill sighed: everyone was in a mood. The exact shade of blue she needed for her painting was already beginning to fade from her mind.

Doreen switched her beady gaze to Quill. "Anyways. That guy from the weathermen's convention is here about the banquet for Saturday. You remember? You two had an appointment with him at eleven. It's eleven-thirty now. Where you been?"

"They're meteorologists, Doreen," Meg said crossly. "Don't call them weathermen."

"Okay, guys." Quill sat down on a stool at the prep table and put on her competent innkeeper look. "Let's all calm down. I'm here, ready to keep the meteorologists happy."

"Yeah?" Doreen asked skeptically. "You sure you haven't got more important things to do?"

Meg ran her hands through her hair, flattening the curls and making her look more like herself. "Where *have* you been, Quill? We stuck him in the Lounge and gave him some brioche, a lot of brioche. Come to think of it, I'm now out of brioche." She tugged at her hair. "I could have talked to him myself *and* made another batch of brioche in the time you were gone."

"No," Quill and Doreen said simultaneously. Meg's temper was mercurial at best, especially when the topic was food. Quill, Doreen, and their business manager, John Raintree, had a long-standing rule never to let Meg be alone with any guest who wanted to discuss menus.

"John could have handled it," Quill said a little guiltily. "I'm sorry. I just went for a walk."

"You din't go anywhere for a walk, you took the car," Doreen said remorselessly. "Joyriding, most like. And you know that John's not here—he's got that three-day meeting with the investment bankers in Syracuse. You two talked about it yesterday. You were supposed to take over for him, here. Not to mention what you're supposed to be doin' as your regular job. Look at this. Dina brought these—" Doreen waved a handful of pink telephone messages in Quill's face. "—which shoulda been answered this morning. Travel agencies and a couple more bookings for Christmas. Plus, we got no busboys for lunch on

account of we worked the ones we do got to death and we need
more, so Kath and Peter are settin' up for lunch. You gonna get
around to hirin' more staff or are we just going to let 'em all
die like the mules on the railroad?"

Quill shook her head. "What mules on the railroad? As a
matter of fact, what railroad? And don't pick on me, Doreen."

"I wouldn't pick on you if I wasn't worried about the way
you're actin'."

Quill had no response to this. Except that she wished Doreen's affection, which was genuine, showed itself in less bel-
ligerent ways.

"So," Doreen continued remorselessly, "Dina also said to tell
you that Harker called three times this morning, and do you
want her to tell him that you're dead, or what?" Doreen sniffed,
which made her look a bit like a rooster with a runny nose.
"Drivin' all over when we got this work to do. Is that Harker
here in Hemlock Falls? Is that who you were seein'? I thought
he was still in New York."

Harker. On top of all this, there was Harker.

The perfect shade of blue for the canvas slid sideways and
was gone. Quill slapped down the feeling of panic that she'd
never get that blue back again. "Doreen—nobody's going to die
of overwork. And yes, I'll get to hiring more staff. We had a
lot of response to the ad we ran in the *Gazette*. I've got five
interviews set up for tomorrow morning."

"Huh," Doreen grunted.

"And yes, I'll answer these messages, and yes, I'll be in my
office in two seconds flat to meet this weatherman." She grabbed
the messages on her way through the swinging doors to the
dining room.

She waved at Kathleen Kiddermeister and Peter Hairston,
both busy with setting the covers for lunch, each with that ag-
grieved, virtuous air people get when they know they're doing
you a favor by condescending to do a job beneath them.
"Thanks, guys," Quill called fervently. "I'll be back to give you
a hand in a minute."

"We don't need a hand," Kathleen said coolly, "we need
about a dozen more bodies." She nodded crisply at Quill, and
then smiled warmly at Peter Hairston.

Quill got the point. Kathleen wasn't in a bad temper gener-
ally; she was specifically annoyed with Quill. Quill refused to

feel guilty. Kathleen's little brother, Davey Kiddermeister, was currently the sheriff of Hemlock Falls. Both Kathleen and her brother admired Myles McHale, formerly sheriff and Davey's boss, and formerly Quill's own Myles McHale. Both of these formerlies annoyed Kathleen. It wasn't fair. Davey wasn't an especially good sheriff, because he was dumb, but he wasn't terrible, either. Kath's worry that Davey was going to get himself killed was not realistic. "And you haven't even *met* Harker," Quill said aloud.

Quill decided to act on advice she'd gotten from a recent course in employee relations she'd taken at the Cornell School for Hotel Management. Confront and defuse, the professor had said. Don't let employee issues build up. Act immediately! Excellent managers are calm, decisive, and fair.

Quill wandered over to table seven, where Kathleen primly folded napkins into swan shapes. The table had a full view of the Gorge. Quill looked at the glorious cascade of water without her usual pleasure. "Um, Kathleen."

"What?" Kathleen snapped a swan flat and refolded the napkin. She'd been the Inn's head waitress for the nine years they'd been in (and out) of business. Kath herself was calm, decisive, and fair, and a lot smarter than her younger brother, Davey. Davey's appointment to the sheriff's position was fairly recent—his sole qualification that he had been Myles' deputy.

"Kath," Quill tried again. "About Harker . . ."

"I don't give a hoot about your love life," Kathleen said virtuously.

"You do too give a hoot about my love life. Now, Kath, I'm going to be calm, decisive, and fair about this." She drew breath. "You're upset with me because I've met someone who's interested in me, Kath. Me. Not in chasing criminals all over the world like Myles, or . . . um." She wasn't going to get into the really tangled issue of her other relationship with John Raintree, who Kath liked almost as much as she liked Myles. ". . . Whatever," she added lamely.

"Fine," Kathleen said. She pinched the swan's head into a shapeless mass and refolded the napkin.

"So, I don't think that these—these opinions you have about, well, you know. My love life. They just shouldn't make a difference."

"I have no idea what you're talking about."

Quill straightened up and stuck her chin out a little.

"Kath, I've been calm, decisive, and fair about this. So don't take it out on me, okay?"

"And clear?" Kathleen said. "What about clear?"

"It should be perfectly clear."

"Well, it's not. You're never clear. That course you took said managers should be calm, decisive, firm, and *clear*. You made Peter and me take it, too. You always forget the clear part, Quill. And the calm part and all the rest of it, as a matter of fact. Those management courses," Kathleen said, working herself into an even greater huff, "are *hooey!*"

"I'm very calm," Quill said. "But it's not going to last."

Kathleen shook her head.

Quill stalked out of the dining room and into the reception area, where she was pretty sure she was going to get the same kind of attitude from Dina Muir, their receptionist. Dina had been studying for her doctorate in freshwater pond ecology for almost all the time she'd worked for the Inn at Hemlock Falls. She had stronger opinions about Quill's love life than Kathleen did.

# CHAPTER 4

Dina sat behind the fine mahogany reception desk in the foyer. She was round-faced and pretty. Her hair, Quill saw, hadn't been moussed or tinted or curled and looked just fine.

"There you are," Dina said.

"Here I am," Quill agreed. "The flowers look great, Dina." Two huge Chinese vases flanked the cobblestone fireplace that was almost all that was left of the original Inn. They were filled with bronze chrysanthemums from the gardens out back, and the flowers' spicy scent filled the air.

"Thanks. I like doing them. And since you weren't here this morning . . ."

"I was busy," Quill said firmly, clearly, and decisively.

Dina made a face. "Harker called. Again."

"Thanks."

"Like, are you going to call him back? Because I can just, like, tell him you're too busy, or something. Permanently busy. Maybe even dead. And the sheriff called, too."

Quill knew whom Dina meant by the sheriff. Nobody in Hemlock Falls seemed willing to acknowledge Myles wasn't sheriff anymore. It made her want to scream. "Myles isn't the sheriff anymore, Dina. He's a chief investigator for WorldSec."

"Sheriff *Kiddermeister*," Dina said, with emphasis, "wants to know if you're going to need any traffic control this weekend for the meteorologists' convention. We're all booked, and half the convention guys are staying at the Marriott, and with all the construction in town, he'll need to take on some extra men, because there was this big traffic jam on Main Street already this morning, and nobody knows why. Davey figures if we get traffic jams for no reason, there'll be even worse traffic jams if there's more people here."

"Oh."

Dina looked prim. "And Davey shouldn't be having to worry about stuff like this anyhow, Quill. Not with this murder on his hands. He has far more important things to do."

"Murder? What murder? Oh, you mean that poor guy whose body was found in the Gorge? I thought he was killed somewhere else and dumped here. I mean, it's horrible to think about, but it isn't a problem for Hemlock Falls, is it?"

Quill couldn't quite place Dina's expression. Smug, that was it. And slightly superior. "Dina?"

"I think we should just let the professionals handle it, don't you, Quill?"

"Of course we should let the professionals handle it. Why wouldn't we let the professionals handle it? What in heaven's name do you mean?"

"Well, Davey said, no offense, Quill, that you and Meg should just butt out. I mean, we didn't intend for it to sound like that, of course, but I think you should butt out, too."

"I have no intention of butting in," Quill said tartly. "Those cases Meg and I solved before, well, there were good reasons why we had to get involved, Dina."

"And besides," Dina said, quite fiercely, "he's *my* boyfriend. So, no disrespect, Quill, but hands off. Okay?"

"What?" Quill asked.

Dina, defensive, but gallant in the course of true love, stuck her chin out. "It's that Carol Ann who pointed it out, Quill."

"Pointed what out?"

"That you're kind of, like, on the loose."

"On the loose?"

"You know, you went through the sheriff, I mean Myles, and then there's poor old John, and this creepola from New York . . ."

"Carol Ann Spinoza said this?"

"And Esther, and Miriam Doncaster, too. I mean, are any of the guys safe here is what Carol Ann wants to know? So, like I say. Stay out of this murder, okay?"

Quill decided that no, she wasn't going to have a fit of hysterics. "Okay," she said. And all of you, all of you will be really, really sorry when I'm dead of whatever this is. "I think," she said aloud, "that I'm going to rest in my office now. I'm not feeling very well."

"Hang on a minute," Dina said with a truly repellent lack of sympathy. "So, like, where were you this morning, anyhow? There's tons of messages. I mean, it's great that we're so busy and I really appreciate the raise you gave everybody last month, although I think that maybe this job is, like, just as important to the public as Nate's."

"Nate? What does Nate have to do with this? Nate's the bartender."

"I mean, bartenders get tips. I don't. I mean, really, Quill, fifteen percent? What kind of raise is that?"

"It's a good raise."

"It'd be a good raise if I'd been making twenty bucks an hour. Which I'm not. Like, what am I? Chopped liver?"

Only Dina could jump from phone messages to her salary and find it logical. "I am going crazy," Quill said. She thrust her hands into her hair and tugged at it. "This is me, going into my office. I will be here when the phone rings. I will be here for the meeting with the meteorologist about the banquet Saturday. I will call Davey about the extra traffic guys. I will not be here to give you another raise. Got it?"

"Got it. Although how you expect me to be as cheerful as this job needs me to be when I've got this huge tuition bill absolutely staring at me next quarter and Nate is making money hand over fist and spends it all on *bowling,* beats me. I make more money hairdressing. Maybe I should open a hair salon here."

Quill banged into her office and sank into her chair. She shut her eyes tight.

That wonderful blue that had haunted her was gone. If she'd gone upstairs and mixed it right away, she could have gotten it back. A soft silver with the cerulean? Azure and white? She should have written some ideas down this morning at Andy's office.

Except she wasn't sure her hand could have held the pen.

She glanced over her shoulder, although she knew she was alone. She held her hands out. The tremor was gone, wasn't it? From the left hand for certain, and the right was better. She'd skipped the coffee this morning. That must have helped.

The tremor wasn't gone. She made a fist.

Andy had said before it would take a while to get off the caffeine, and to take something for the caffeine headache. She opened the top drawer of her desk and scrabbled through the pencils and paper clips for the ibuprofen. Two left. And she'd bought the large bottle not a week ago.

"Hey!" Quill jumped as Meg banged cheerfully through the door. Her sister stopped in midstride. "You okay?"

"I'm fine." Quill dry-swallowed the ibuprofen. "Caffeine headache. I skimped on coffee this morning. So. What's this banquet about? Who's it for?"

Meg opened her mouth, and then closed it. She sank into the couch facing Quill's desk. It had been re-covered since they'd bought the Inn back from Marge Schmidt that spring, and Quill wasn't sure if she liked the new pattern: orange-red poppies on a pale bronze field.

"Quill?"

Quill jerked her attention back to Meg. Her sister's clear gray eyes were narrowed. "You've been so—not with it. Are you okay?"

"You know what it's like when I'm working, Meg."

"I'd almost forgotten." Relieved, Meg smiled with enormous affection. "It's been a while since you've been able to paint. How's the canvas coming?"

"Don't ask. Now, about this banquet."

"I don't know anything about the banquet, or the guys that will be eating the banquet, or even exactly how many. You're supposed to know all that stuff."

"I've got some notes somewhere. John booked them. He always writes everything down." Quill shut the top drawer to her desk, then opened it again. She was sure she'd put the notes in the drawer yesterday. Or was it the day before?

The intercom buzzer rang and she punched the button, grateful for the mild distraction.

"He's here." Dina's voice was tinny, but the sulkiness came through loud and clear.

"Who's here?"

"Somerfield Dougherty."

The penny dropped, suddenly, of course. "Boomer Dougherty? The weatherman? I mean the meteorologist? The Channel Fourteen guy?" Quill remembered the first time she'd seen

Boomer Dougherty on TV. He was the sort of guy you felt you'd known for years.

"Yes, Quill. He's chairman of this convention." There was a mumble from the background. "Of course she knows who you are," Dina's voice said to the mumble. "She's, like, in total control of this event, Mr. Dougherty. She always is."

At least Dina kept the squabbles in the family. Quill belatedly recalled that Somerfield was indeed the Channel 14 guy who had booked the meteorologists' convention at the Inn. "Boomer," as he was called, was notorious for two reasons: he was never right about the weather, and he scared the knickers off his disproportionately large share of the viewing audience with his inaccurate, doom-filled prophecies. Quill made a face at Meg, who promptly made one back.

"Remember the blizzard of '97?" Meg whispered.

"Do I. Two people were killed in the traffic jam that resulted from his prediction it was going to be the storm of the century. The families won a pile of money from the lawsuits."

"I've already met him," Meg said reassuringly. "He's okay."

"Send him in, please, Dina," Quill said in her most Competent Innkeeper voice. She tugged her sweater into place and folded her hands onto her desk blotter.

# CHAPTER 5

Somerfield Dougherty didn't so much enter as roll into Quill's office like a tank advancing on Beirut. He was enormously fat. Everyone who watched Channel 14 knew that—and probably most of the people who didn't: Somerfield's bulk was notorious. Quill, who had a vague notion that television added pounds to those in front of the cameras, was surprised to see that the meteorologist was even larger in person than he was on camera. Flesh rolled from his ears to his collar and disappeared into his crisp white shirt. He was a solid, gigantic column all the way down. He wore a beautifully cut dark blue suit, a rep tie, all of it custom-made. And he carried himself with a benign authority that made no apology for his bulk.

Somerfield's shrewd blue eyes were almost buried above his mounded cheeks. They returned Quill's look with a decided challenge: I'm fat. So what? So bloody what?

"It's very nice to meet you, Mr. Dougherty."

He extended a hand the size of a six-pound ham. Quill rose and took it; the palm was warm, slightly sweaty, the flesh firm. "Call me Boomer," he said. His eyes probed hers. "I've wanted to meet you for a long time, Ms. Quilliam. But every time I'm here, you're running off to New York."

"Well. Yes. Um—Boomer. And you know my sister, Margaret Quilliam."

"The chef!" Boomer swiveled his great neck and beamed at Meg. "We've met many times before." Then, to Quill, he said, "I guess you can tell how highly I regard her profession, little lady." He looked down at his bulk with satisfaction and grinned.

"Thank you." Meg blinked and tugged her hair flatter.

"Would you care to sit down?" Quill looked a little desperately around the office, which suddenly seemed claustrophobic. "Umm. Perhaps on the couch?" It was a long couch—and Meg was small.

Boomer sank into it with a cheerful groan. "Great place here, just great. You've heard me mention it on the show."

Meg, squashed into the farthest corner of the couch, nodded politely, "Yes, thanks, I have. And speaking of the show, will you miss it, the night of the banquet? Is someone covering the show for you?"

"Oh, no. I'm going to broadcast from here. It's going to be a killer show." His blue eyes narrowed in a sudden, vicious spasm. "See, there's always someone ready to step into the spotlight in this business. So you don't give 'em an edge. Not the slightest edge. When I travel away from the studio, I take my camera guy with me. Even though it's impossible to replace the Boomer. Although there's plenty what've tried. Plenty."

"It's pretty competitive, I take it. The weather business?" Quill moved the cloisonné bowl on her desk to the left, then to the right again. Normally, she didn't mind these polite business preliminaries. Today they made her impatient. She picked up a pencil and doodled restlessly on her yellow pad. "Now, about your banquet, Mr. Dougherty."

"Greed," Boomer said flatly. "S'all about greed."

"Fine food is not about greed, Mr. Dougherty," Meg said indignantly.

Quill craned her head slightly to get a look at Meg's socks; the choice was usually a barometer of her mood. Black, with red and green squiggles. Sunny, with possible thundershowers? She bit her lip. She didn't think she could take one of Meg's squalls today. And what was it with the weather similes? Better than references to Boomer's bulk, at any rate.

"I know all about food," Boomer said with a generous wave of his hand. "No, I'm talking about the greed for fame. Yes, sir, the greed for fame. 'Specially this little broadie that works as my producer, Sylvia Prince. Tough little—ah—witch soon as stab you in the back as look at you."

Quill pasted a smile on her face.

"Oh," Boomer added hastily, insincerely, "Sylvia's nice as can be to your face. Lot of that in TV. But ready to stomp you flat the minute you screw up, and dance on the corpse after that. Lot of that in Sylvia Prince."

"Sylvia Prince," Quill said.

"You bet. She'll be here to oversee the arrangements."

Quill did a rapid sketch of a flattened Boomer with a cheerful lady dancing on his back. She scribbled squishy bits of Boomer around the edges, trying to get the effect of a dropped pie. "It's a tough business, television," she murmured sympathetically. "Now, we're going to need a precise head count for the banquet, Mr.—um—Boomer."

"Tough? You got any idea how tough?"

"Well, actually, yes." Quill added Helena Houndswood's face to the doodle. The TV star had vacationed at the Inn some years ago and ended up a suspect in a series of gruesome murders.

"I came up from nothing. Nothing." Boomer folded his hands over his gargantuan belly. "What's more, when did you ever see a guy my size make it big? I remember the early days. Started in radio, you know, and . . ."

Quill tuned out; Boomer's reminiscences sounded suspiciously like Ted Knight's infamous "it all started in a five-thousand-watt radio station twenty years ago" speech on the reruns of *The Mary Tyler Moore Show.* Tuning out was an extremely useful skill, and she was proud of it. She'd cultivated it after she joined the Hemlock Falls Chamber of Commerce as secretary. And she'd gotten a lot better. The Chamber meetings tended to stupendous irrelevancies, so she'd had a lot of practice.

"Miss Quilliam!" Boomer shouted.

Quill came to attention with a start. Boomer's face was flushed, and he looked mean. "You haven't heard a word I've said, have you?"

Quill looked helplessly at Meg. Her sister sat with her chin resting on her drawn-up knees. There was no way to read the expression on her face. "Shakespeare," Meg said, after a long pause.

"Shakespeare?"

"You missed the part about Boomer's undergrad degree in English lit. Renaissance English lit, to be precise. And about the competition."

"Oh, no, I got the part about the competition. Miss Prince

and the perils of leaving the TV show to the competition. Right?"

"Not that competition. The cooking competition."

"I cook," Boomer said. "I'm a damn good cook, too. And *I'm* friggin' literate. Not like some."

Some who? Quill thought wildly. Some other English lit majors? Big, fat TV meteorologists whose scare tactics were on par with the nuttier evangelists prophesizing hell? Cooks?

"And the banquet's just like my shows." Boomer's angry flush was gone. "You know, you can't keep the folks at home glued to the tube with mingy little reports about the weather. No, sir, I pack more thrills and chills into my three minutes than a rolly-coaster ride, and I mean to do it with the banquet, too. People expect me to be *big!*"

"Yes," Quill said. "So you want competitively big food? Giant turkeys? A steamship round?"

"Nothing's bigger than the Bard," Boomer said.

Quill waited.

"I want to put these folks on their mettle. Got guys coming in from all over the country. I want to give them a little something to look forward to. First off, I'm giving a panel on 'Forecasting as Infotainment.' "

"Infotainment?" Quill couldn't stop the next question. "What's infotainment?"

"You know, how to keep the audience guessing what's next. *Info*rmation and enter*tainment*."

Meg cleared her throat. "I don't want to guess about the weather. I want to know if I should take an umbrella when I go on a picnic. Or put on my snow boots."

"Huh," Boomer scoffed. "Fat lot of success you'd have in the weather business, begging your pardon. So, we got almost all the attendees signed up for my panel. And we got a full day of guest speakers. But at night—that's when we really get down and party. To start off, I'm bringing in a troupe of actors from New York. We're going to do a couple of scenes from *Wives*."

"*The Merry Wives of Windsor*," Meg supplied.

"You remember I starred in that Equity Showcase in New York in September." Boomer paused expectantly.

"No," Quill said.

"Yes," Meg said.

"Made all the papers," Boomer said with an injured air.

"And your weather show," Meg said innocently.

"See, the thing with an Equity Showcase is that they need a big name to draw the folks in. That way they get to perform the classics and still make a bit of the old *dinero*." He rolled his forefinger and thumb together.

Boomer Dougherty performing Shakespeare? It took Quill a moment. Then she remembered the play from a course she'd taken in undergraduate school. "We're . . . you mean you? You're going to . . . oh. I see. Falstaff."

Boomer patted his belly. "None better. None bigger. I do a pretty fabulous Falstaff, if I do say so myself."

"Sounds like fun," Meg said, doubtfully.

"We can take care of the staging for you," Quill said. "We've had performers here before."

"We have?" Meg said blankly.

"Of course we have, Meg. You remember the Rudyard Kipling Condensation Society. They performed right out on the terrace." Quill stopped. The meeting had ended in a bit of a debacle, come to think of it, mostly due to the corpse. Solving that crime had been one of her more interesting cases. "Anyway, we can provide lighting, and a minimum set, and chairs for the audience. I think a few scenes from Shakespeare would be terrific."

"The competition," Meg prodded gloomily.

Boomer expanded—to the detriment of the couch springs. "Yeah, the competition. See, cooking's quite a hobby of mine, like I said, and the guys already got it in their convention packets."

"What did they get in their convention packets?"

Boomer withdrew a large envelope from his suit coat pocket and handed it over. Quill opened it, and read:

## FOOD OF SWEET AND BITTER FANCY

*The BOOMER sez: Cook on! Got a recipe the Bard himself would like? Then turn it on and turn it in. To the Boomer that is—and I'll cook the winner and serve it forth at the food fest Sat. Nite. I'll make sure it's "As You Like It!"—First Prize: One thousand dollars. Entry Fee: Twenty dollars.*

"A thousand dollars?" Quill said. "Good heavens!" So that's why the Chamber was all agog. A thousand dollars was a lot of money.

"That's to make sure I get everyone's attention. The Boomer doesn't do things in a small way," he said modestly.

"And where," Meg asked in a dangerously quiet voice, "do you intend to prepare the winning recipe? Not in *my* kitchen."

"Oh, don't worry about that, little lady. I already made a great contact in the town—you have a pretty good little chef at the Croh Bar, and I talked to them about borrowing their kitchen. Had to pay a bit for it, of course."

"That's Marge Schmidt's place," Quill said. "Marge and Betty Hall's." She kept her eye on Meg. Marge and Betty served some of the best diner food in New York State. They weren't precisely Meg's culinary rivals, but with Meg, you never knew.

"I," Meg said with a virtuous air, "would have lent you my kitchen for free."

"No need for that. The contestants turn in the recipes on Friday, the banquet's Saturday, and I have all morning to toddle on down to the Croh Bar and make up the winning entry."

Meg's eyes narrowed in challenge. "You are not, I take it, expecting me to enter this contest."

"A pro like you? No way. This is strictly for amateurs. Matter of fact, I'm putting some publicity out about it, in a modest way, of course. I met the stringer for your newspaper . . . that *Hemlock Gazette,* is it called? Nice old lady. Looks a little like a rooster, but then, so did my old ma."

"Doreen? You gave Doreen a press release about the contest?" Quill tugged her lower lip thoughtfully.

"Yup. Said her hubby published the town paper, and I gave her an interview. It's always," he added with a lavish gesture, "a good thing to keep in with the little guys."

"Little guys," Meg said meditatively. She tugged restlessly at her socks. Quill, far too experienced with the astonishing range of rudeness demonstrated by so many of the Inn's guests, said firmly, "I'm sure Stoke, that is, Doreen's husband, Axminister Stoker, will give you all the publicity you need, Boomer. Now, about the menu."

"Yeah. The menu. The way I see it is this. You have the three-star rating, Meg. And I got the bucks. You cook me and my guys up a storm, and I look good. Plenty of desserts, mind.

I don't expect too much out of this competition and I like a good dessert. We got forty folks registered. You got the list I sent that Indian, Raintree?"

"*Mr.* Raintree," Quill said pleasantly, but with a warning undertone. "One of my closest friends. And yes, we have the list."

"Good. I was thinking maybe you, Quill, could make some name tags. You're a pretty famous artist, aren't you? That's what I heard, anyway. I had my people show me some of your work."

Meg's eyes widened. Her mouth opened. She placed both feet on the floor, prepared to rise. Quill, who had no wish to hear her sister's impassioned defense of My Sister the Famous Artist—which usually included an exhaustive list of her awards—said loudly, "We'll get a copy of the suggested menu to you tomorrow, Mr. Dougherty. But no, I don't do name tags."

Boomer dragged a Palm Pilot from his capacious suitcoat. "Great. Tuesday," he muttered aloud, as his finger tapped at the tiny keys. "Menu to come. Can you e-mail that?"

"We're not really computer literate here, Boomer," Quill said apologetically. "I've got an e-mail address and so does Meg. But the Inn as such doesn't have an address."

" 'Course you do," Boomer said tolerantly.

"We've always intended to set up a fully computerized system, but we've grown so quickly in the past few months that—"

Meg cut her off. "We'd be happy to e-mail it, Boomer."

"But, Meg, we don't . . ."

"We do. There's a lot you've missed in the past months."

"You've got a nice web site," Boomer said in an approving way.

"Web site? What web site?" Memos, Quill thought, she'd have to send out a memo reminding everyone else to write memos. How was she supposed to keep up with what was going on if no one ever sent her a memo?

"We'll take care of it, Boomer," Meg said briskly.

"Excuse me," Quill said. "Hello?" She tapped the bronze nameplate on her desk: Sarah Quilliam, Manager. "Yours says 'Master Chef,' doesn't it?" She smiled at Boomer. "I'll take care of it."

"Good. Now. This is Tuesday. Banquet's Friday. I'm gonna send that little broadie I told you about . . ."

Quill pretended to consult her notes. "Miss Sylvia Prince?" she asked, a little sarcastically.

"Sylvia Prince, right. Anyhow, I'm sending her down tomorrow to do the prep work. Make sure all the invites show up. Arrange for local publicity. Get footage for background, so we have the option of turning the conference into a show we can sell to cable. And I'm going to announce that you, Meg, will judge the contest."

Meg made a face.

"Come on," Boomer said. "Who else could judge it?"

"Okay. I guess. What's this about cable TV?" Meg asked.

"Always a market for programming. Depends on how good the presentations are. And I'm one that likes to make a buck. Anyway, you got any questions about the banquet, you talk to Sylvia. I like to send Sylvia out on the road. Keeps her out of my hair and away from my job."

Boomer rose from the couch. It was like watching a sequoia re-right itself after being chopped down. "Now, the actors I hired for the scene from the Bard'll be down by train Friday afternoon, Quill. Six of 'em. I booked them into the Marriott since you're filled up here. But if you could send the house van to pick them up from the Marriott and bring 'em over here, I'd be a grateful guy. And I'll be back here myself on Friday, so we can make sure there's no slipups." His genial expression faded, to be replaced by quite a predatory look. "I don't like slipups."

"We'll do our best to see that there aren't any." Quill hoped Meg noticed her super-businesslike expression. "We'll take care of all of it."

Meg gave Boomer her sweetest smile. "Just one more thing. Did you want to put a cap on the budget for the banquet, Mr. Dougherty?"

"Cap? Nah. Do what you have to do."

The door slammed, and he was gone.

"Wow," Meg said. "No budget! A free hand with the food." She raised one fist in the air: "Yes!"

"I hope he pays his bills."

"The station pays his bills. He's a fabulous customer." Meg frowned. "On the other hand, I do *not* want some cockeyed amateur dessert competition messing up my menu. We'll put it on a separate table. Better than that, we'll set up a special place away from the banquet altogether. In the Lounge, perhaps."

"Meg. What's this about a web site?"

Meg either didn't hear this, or didn't care to answer. She jumped to her feet and hopped around the floor, waving her arms. "Dance of joy," she warbled. "La-la-*la*! No end to the funds!"

The intercom buzzer rang, and Quill said, "What is it, Dina?"

"It's that guy, Harker, Do you want me to tell him . . ."

"No. Don't tell him I'm dead. Put him on hold for just a second."

"Harker," Meg said. She stopped her exuberant jumping around. "From the Dance of the Unlimited Budget to Harker. I'm going to take off my shoes and get back to the kitchen."

"What?"

"Just kidding, Quill. Let me know what's going on, okay?"

"Me let *you* know what's going on!" Quill said. "What's this about a web site?"

Meg tilted her head to one side. "If you'd been at the staff meetings on Monday mornings for the past weeks, you would have learned something about the web site. About both web sites."

"Both web sites? We have two web sites?"

"We have one. Hemlock Falls has another one." Meg wasn't finished with her tirade. "But have you taken any interest at all in these technological marvels? No, you were in New York, or headed to New York, or coming back from New York. What you were *not* doing was painting, managing, letting your nearest and dearest meet this paragon of perfection who is messing up *your whole life!*"

"You could have sent me a memo."

"To Quill. From Meg. Get a grip."

Quill threw her sketch pad at her. It fluttered weakly to the floor. Meg mouthed, "Missed me," pulled a rude face and left.

Quill didn't wait for the door to close before she picked up the phone. "Harker," she said, loudly enough for both Dina and Meg to hear. "Boy, have I missed you!"

# CHAPTER 6

She'd fallen in love with Harker a month ago. It felt like love, anyway, because she had no decisions to make, no questions to ask, and it was so right that she didn't want to talk about it, even with Meg. He was an artist—working for her old gallery—the one that had carried her work all those years ago in New York. Francis, the owner, an old friend had called:

"I've got someone you have to meet."

Francis had always called Quill often, just to check. Just to see if the terrible drought that had stilled her hands and blinded her eyes was over. To see if he would get more than the few sketches and small canvases she'd sent in pitiful trickles over the past nine years.

"And he's got to meet you, sweetie. Come down. Just for a couple of days."

She'd gone to New York. She'd walked into the gallery, already exhilarated by the pull of the city, walked in to the well-loved scents of paint and the varnish on the frames, to the shock and delight of new artists' works on the walls, the joy of seeing old friends' latest works, the familiar feel of Francis's smooth cheeks against her own. Walked in to see Harker himself, dark, focused, intent, not handsome, but strong, with the most beautiful hands she had ever seen.

"You're not working, Quilliam," he'd said, without preliminary. "You haven't worked for nine years. That's wrong. And it's a waste."

• • •

"Are you working?" he asked now. Quill could hear the background noise of the city through the phone: the wail of a police siren, horns blaring, and the rush of traffic. "How's the cold?"

"I worked last night," Quill said. She sneezed. "Until about three. And this morning . . . no. Too much stuff to get out of the way."

"So are you all set to see me this weekend? I'll hop the train from Penn Station."

Quill hesitated. She wasn't sure. She just wasn't sure. Maybe she wanted them separate, her life here, her life in New York. Every week Harker called and asked to come visit. Every week Quill said no. Except last week. Last week she had said yes. She bit her lip. She was pulled in two.

"Quill, it's time for them to meet me." Harker took life as he found it: a battle, a war to be won, a fight. He was mercurial, committed, and meticulous. And rigorously logical, when it suited him. "I love you. We love each other. You have a life up there that's an important part of you. Please."

Quill didn't stop to think this time. If she stopped to think, she'd never make up her mind. "Yes. I'd like that. But . . ."

"But?"

"I don't want you to look at the painting. Not just yet. And the place will be a zoo, so I may not be able to spend a lot of time with you. During the day."

"And at night?"

Her whole body responded to the smile in his voice. "The nights are ours," she said lightly.

"Oh, bad movie line, Quill! That's great." The relief in his voice was almost palpable. "I was beginning to think I'd never see the famous Hemlock Falls."

She'd have to talk to John, to Meg. And they'd want to know, immediately, right then: what was she going to do?

"I want to meet Meg, and Doreen, and the entire Chamber of Commerce, if I can. God! Spending time among the simple country folk. Sounds fabulous."

"Yes," Quill said, "I guess it is time. But they're not simple, Harker. They're my friends."

"Uh-huh. Saturday morning, then. The train's in at ten." His voice dropped and took on his Serious Artist tone. "Where are you right now?"

The first time he'd asked this, she'd been here, at the Inn, after a long, breathless weekend with him in the city. And she'd said, "The office," and then realized he'd meant her art, not her actual physical location. And how could she explain that deep, instinctive knowledge of another human being even to her sister?

"Background, still," Quill said into the phone. "I thought I'd figured out the colors this morning, but it slipped away."

"That rose is wrong for it?"

"Very. It's muddy. But I don't want you to see it, not yet."

"Whenever you're ready," he said calmly. "Anything I can bring?"

Quill thought. She ordered her paints through the mail, but she liked to think of Harker at Pearl Paint among the brushes and tubes. "I'm low on charcoal."

"Charcoal it is. Now, what's new in Hemlock Falls?"

She was in the middle of a vivid description of Boomer Dougherty's contest when Doreen barreled into her office and stood, arms folded under her meager bosom. Quill reluctantly said good-bye and hung up. "What now?" she demanded.

"Chamber meetin'."

"We just had a Chamber meeting. Yesterday. I've had it up to here with Chamber meetings. I absolutely do not want to go to another Chamber meeting."

"We didn't get through the best part yesterday," Doreen said. "We didn't talk about the contest. On account of the murder . . ."

"And on account of you socking Carol Ann Spinoza in the jaw."

"Yeah, well, there's that." Doreen grinned. "Anyways, it's almost one o'clock. I ordered coffee and cheesecake for the Lounge. We gotta git."

Quill sighed. "You didn't do any permanent damage, I hope. To Carol Ann?"

"Nah. But I give her something to think about, that one. It'll be a while before she shows up at a Chamber meeting again, I'll tell ya that."

It was exactly three minutes after one before Carol Ann Spinoza showed up at the second *ex parte* session of the Hemlock Falls Chamber of Commerce. Her nose was bluish, and there was a faint dark shadow on her jaw, but other than that, she seemed perfectly fine. True, Quill caught Carol Ann's curiously flat glance on Doreen now and then, and once she felt a faint chill on the back of her own neck when Carol Ann thought that she, Quill, wasn't aware of her, but by and large Carol was her usual self: perky, sticky sweet, and ominous.

Almost all the core Chamber members were there, tucked into the same corner of the Tavern Lounge where they had been the day before. Neither of the Bloomfields nor Josh Roberts had turned up. (Which Quill thought was just as well: time enough for the new members to experience the furor of Hemlockians chasing after a thousand-dollar prize.) But except for Harland and Petey, the Hemlock Falls regulars were there in force: Marge Schmidt, Betty Hall, Miriam Doncaster, Howie Murchison (who usually could be counted on to maintain reasonable decorum), Esther West, and the others. Quill was not at all sanguine: she still recalled the debacle resulting from the infamous Jell-O Architecture Contest some years ago; Hemlockians took their competitions seriously.

Mayor Henry rapped the table with the gavel, called the meeting to order, and said, "Ladies and gentlemen of the Hemlock Falls Chamber of Commerce. It is with a great deal of pride in our town that I announce to you all that I have persuaded Mr. Somerfield Dougherty—Boomer to his friends, of which I am proud to count myself one—anyhow, Boomer is the famous TV weatherman, who graciously has allowed us to enter this great contest for a mere twenty-dollar entry fee."

"What d'ya mean, 'persuaded'?" Marge Schmidt interrupted truculently. "Far's I know, he came up with this idea to let us go after that thousand bucks all on his own. And for a 'mere' twenty-buck entry fee. Phooey."

The mayor's lower lip protruded. Marge, who maintained her sturdy shape by lifting weights, ignored this sign of mayoral displeasure. "What I want to know is, how come?"

"How come? What do you mean, how come?" Adela Henry said, with equal belligerence. "The mayor just told you that he, and may I say, I myself, were instrumental in convincing Boomer to open the contest to the town. He did it, Marge Schmidt, because he likes us. And he likes this town."

Marge shook her head decisively, with an air of Alaric refusing a request not to sack Rome. "I don't get it. And I don't like what I don't get. What I think is this, I think he's trying to get out of paying that thousand bucks at all. Just like," she added somewhat mysteriously, "raffling the mule."

"Raffling the mule?" Miriam Doncaster said.

"It's an old scam," Howie said easily. "You sell raffle tickets for a dollar to win a mule. The winner of the raffle doesn't get the mule—he gets his dollar back. But that's illegal, Marge, in New York State."

"How I figure it is, this bozo stands to make a buck off of us. Somehow. And I'm not sure I like that. Not by a long shot."

This was met with respectful silence. Marge was the richest resident of Tompkins County. She'd started out dirt-poor and with a high school education. If anyone knew about money, Marge Schmidt did.

"What's more," Marge shifted herself forward in her chair, "what's he going to do with the recipe that does win? Who has the rights to it? I figure that Howie, here, should draw up a contract that lays out fair and square . . ."

"It's because he's fat," Carol Ann said suddenly. "I think Boomer Dougherty is the fattest person I've ever seen in my life, and the reason he wants more people to enter the contest is because he just wants to eat. It's disgusting."

"Morbid obesity isn't disgusting," Miriam Doncaster said. "There's been a lot of research on it lately, and it's both cruel and wrong to castigate a person because of weight."

"Now hold on," Elmer Henry said in alarm. "What are you talking about, castigating this poor guy!"

"Castigate doesn't mean that, Mayor," Miriam said. "Castigate means . . ."

Quill tuned out and doodled on her notepad until Doreen passed around copies of the contest handout and the discussion of whether or not Boomer should be asked to lower the contest fee was voted on. (Fifteen to one in favor of keeping the entry fee as offered. The "no" vote was Marge's.)

She sat patiently through the discussion of who would make the handbills announcing the competition (Harvey Bozzel) and who would distribute them around town (the Ladies Fireman's Auxiliary), and even took notes. At the end of the meeting, for once, everyone seemed in agreement that the contest was a good thing for the village, and as long as "no big deal" was made of the body found on the slopes of Hemlock Gorge, nothing at all could be anticipated to wreck the successful inclusion of Bard-related recipes to Boomer's Food of Sweet and Bitter Fancy.

"The thing is," Mayor Henry explained at the close of the

meeting (with an apologetic look at Quill), "we seem to get these murders that draw the wrong kind of attention to this town. And right now, with this very nice, big prize that Boomer's so generously made available to all of us—well, we just don't want anything to get in the way of a fine and fair competition."

Quill nodded with the rest of the Chamber members. Someone from the kitchen had seen to it that coffee was served, and she sipped gratefully at her (sixth? seventh?) cup of the day.

The mayor continued, "Now as near as we can tell, this ol' boy that Harland and Petey found down by the Gorge had an unfortunate accident somewheres else and got dumped here. Looks like maybe a hit and run . . ."

Quill, before she could stop herself, asked: "Does anyone know who he is?"

Elmer's ears got red. "Now, Quill . . ."

"This is just what we were talking about before." Carol Ann's prissy little voice cut through the mayor's speech like a hot knife through cold butter. She exchanged a significant glance with Esther West, and murmured, "David *is* the last single man in Hemlock Falls! And she would be working very closely with him. Long nights, together." Then, at room-temperature volume, she continued, "This is none of your business, Miss Sarah Quilliam. And you and your detecting—" Here Carol Ann laughed ha-ha, a bit like ice cubes dropping in a porcelain sink. "—are just not welcome." She paused and added primly, "At this time."

"That's just it, Quill, y'see," Elmer said. "This isn't Hemlock Falls business, so we just want you to . . . to, ah . . ."

"Butt out." Carol Ann again.

Quill rose to her feet with as much dignity as she could muster. She was glad to notice that the coffee cup she held in her left hand didn't shake at all. "Of course. I was just . . . it's just that the poor man. We don't know his name, and if we keep referring to him as it, or you . . ." She turned and did the best she could to loom over Carol. "It doesn't seem humane, somehow."

Carol smiled tightly. "Oh, we know his name. At least, Davey does. His name was Nash. George Nash."

# CHAPTER 7

"Pow, right in the kisser?" Meg asked. "Again?" She added some crushed ice to a stainless-steel bowl, and then shoved it in front of Doreen. "Here. Soak your knuckles in that."

Quill, apologetic, tried to explain one more time. "I was so surprised that they'd identified the guy, the cup just flew to the left. And Carol Ann's face was in the way."

"And then Carol Ann swung at you and Doreen swung at her and wham." Meg shook her head. "We're going to get sued yet, you know."

Quill and Doreen had fled into the kitchen to find Meg, leaving Carol Ann behind shrieking for revenge. The lunch staff worked busily around them, seemingly indifferent to Doreen's loud recitation of the events in the Lounge. But an occasional snort of laughter from the dishwashers ruffled Quill as she sat, elbows propped on the prep table, chin in her hands. She didn't have time for this. She just didn't have time for this. George Nash? George *Nash*? She'd have to talk to Davey. And Myles was back. She could see him and ask him to run a discreet check. Most important was not to tell Meg. Not now, not until she thought about what it meant. And why, of all places, George Nash had ended up dead in Hemlock Falls.

"Quill?" Meg poked at her with a wooden spoon. "Earth to Quill."

Doreen examined her knuckles critically. "Been a long time since I landed a good one. They look pretty swole. Should keep 'em toughened up more."

"But not on Carol Ann!" Quill said, setting the troubling thoughts of George Nash aside. "Just wait, Doreen. We're going to find our tax assessment going up a billion percent. How could you?"

"Do you know what she was intimatin'?"

Quill sneezed twice. She had a headache. Her stomach hurt. She wanted to know why, after all these years, George Nash's body had shown up practically at their back door. "Yes, I know what she was intimating."

"Well, I don't know what she was intimating," Meg said. "Tell me."

"It was about how Quill's got her eye set on every man in this here town," Doreen said.

Meg shrieked joyfully. "My sister, the vamp!"

"Who cares what Carol Ann thinks?" Quill said crossly. "But she's going to be out for my blood now, Doreen." She groaned. "And to think she wanted me to teach her to paint. Ugh. Maybe I should offer to teach her to paint. For free."

"You don't teach," Meg said. "You've never taught in your life."

"I told her that. But she thought I was just being nasty. And she made a crack about the perfume Harker gave me," she added indignantly.

Neither Doreen nor Meg said anything for a second, and then Meg drew breath, "Well, since you asked . . ."

"I didn't. And then yesterday, she made a crack about poor Esther's pumpkin earrings . . ."

"No," Meg said, agreeably interested. "Pumpkin? Ugh."

"It doesn't matter," Doreen said. "That was yesterday. Today was today."

"Well, so what," Quill said crossly. "Esther can dress up in a Ronald McDonald suit for all I care. She's a very nice woman, and how she dresses is her own business. I defended her, and that just made Carol Ann madder. I mean, she was mad *before* Doreen socked her in the jaw. And now she's socked her twice."

"Esther *would* dress up in a Ronald McDonald suit, if that Joss Roberts would pay some attention to her," Doreen said. "Matter of fact, so would Carol Ann Spinoza."

"Joss Roberts is the guy who wrote the web site, isn't he?" Meg said.

"He's hot," Doreen said, with a helpful air.

"I guess he is," Meg said cheerfully. "So what else happened at the Chamber meeting today? I mean, what was the name of the guy in the Gorge?"

"It doesn't matter," Quill said, a little too quickly.

"I forgot," Doreen said honestly. "What with the brouhaha and all."

"And what about this blasted dessert contest, then," Meg said. "I suppose I'm going to be tasting five billion variations of tapioca. Or lime-pistachio."

"Probably. But Boomer's supposed to help, and he'll like it. He seems to like any kind of food at all." Quill put her head down on the prep table and gently thumped her forehead against the cool stainless steel. It felt good. "Everyone wants to contribute a dessert. Even though the entry fee *is* twenty dollars."

"Practically the whole Chamber wants a shot at that thousand bucks," Doreen agreed. She ticked off the names with one bony finger. "Esther, Marge, Adela, Miriam, that there doctor's wife . . ."

"She wasn't there," Quill said.

"She told me this morning," Doreen said.

"Kimmie?" Meg said. She nodded in what Quill thought was a proprietary way. "Good, she needs the diversion. She's got a lot of negative stuff going on in her life right now."

"Such as what?" Quill said testily. "She seems to be married to a perfectly nice man and she's got a wonderful new farm-house to decorate. Everybody has tough times, Meg." Her sneezes were defiantly headed into a cough.

"Ooh, la, la," Meg said. "What put you in a mood?"

"She don't know what she wants," Doreen diagnosed succinctly. "Haven't you noticed? She gets like this when she has to make a big decision. She grabs on to you, Meg, cause you two can count on each other, and she's a little jealous of your new best friend, is all."

"Thank you, Dr. Freud," Quill said coldly.

Meg reached over and hugged Quill with deep affection. "I will always love you, sweetie."

"I need an aspirin," Quill said. "Or an ibuprofen. My head is killing me."

"The desserts!" Doreen said loudly, dragging the conversation back to the point. "There's more of 'em want to join the contest."

"Such as whom?" Meg asked, highly interested. "What about Marge and Betty Hall?"

"No professionals," Doreen said. "Din't you read the rules?"

"Of course," Quill said. "I wondered why Marge was so snarky about that entry fee."

"And the padre is goin' to send something. And Freddie Bellini. He and the missus both like to bake."

"The last time I went to a party at Freddie Bellini's house, he had a cake shaped like a casket for dessert," Quill said.

"So? Funeral directors gotta eat. They like desserts, too. What's wrong with that? Even Joss Roberts, that new guy with the computer store is gonna send in a recipe. He," she said with a significant look at Quill, "can make a cake shaped like a laptop, for all of me. And you stop bein' snippy."

Quill scowled. "I am not being snippy. But Marge does have a point, now that I think about it. Why Hemlock Falls? What did we ever do for Boomer? And he invested in the web site? The City of Love dot com thing? Does he have relatives here or something?"

"Maybe it's the resort that's going up," Meg said, with a noticeable lack of interest in the whole topic. "Didn't Harvey Bozzel write that the resort's going to make Hemlock Falls a rich and wealthy tourist area, and Boomer wants in on the ground floor? Nobody gives a hoot why, Quill."

Doreen fixed Quill with a merciless gaze. "He likes this town, Boomer does. And he likes the people in it. Why else would he invest in the web site? He got Joss up here to build the thing. Invested some of his own money in it. He's a Hemlock Falls booster."

Quill fixed Doreen with the sternest glance she could muster right back. "We've got a dead man in the Gorge. What about that?"

Meg and Doreen looked at each other, then at Quill. "What," Meg asked carefully, "does that have to do with the price of bananas in Brazil? And I thought we agreed. No detecting."

"I don't know," Quill said. "But it's an anomaly. And Boomer's sudden interest in Hemlock Falls is another anomaly. Two anomalies in one week . . ."

"Boomer's been around longer than that dead guy," Doreen said.

"Whatever." Quill paused for a moment. She didn't want Meg

to know about George Nash. Too many memories, and neither of them had time to investigate a case. Until she knew if it was a case or not. But she did want to know all she could about Boomer, and it wouldn't matter if Meg heard that. Boomer hadn't murdered anyone. "Begin at the beginning about Boomer. And stop when you've come to the end."

Doreen gave a gusty, oh-how-I-suffer sigh. "Boomer Dougherty came to Hemlock Falls in September for a three-day vacation. He liked it. This was when you were in New York City gallivanting. Boomer went down to the Croh Bar a coupla times and started talkin' to Esther and Carol Ann and them. He's a lonely guy, too, you know. Never married on account of his career. And his fat, of course. That has to account for some of it. He came to a Chamber meeting that Monday."

"Which Monday?" Quill asked, bewildered.

"The Monday he was here," Doreen said patiently. "He said he had a young friend he was tryin' to he'p out. This Joss Roberts, who needed a job on accounta he just come out of a rehab place, only nobody's supposed to know that part. Drinks a bit, I guess. We cooked up the datin' service idear. Boomer got the Chamber of Commerce to help out, and there you are. Got it?"

"Joss Roberts, Boomer, web site," Quill said. "Okay. Do I know Joss Roberts already? I think I know him. I mean, I saw him at the Chamber meeting yesterday, but I didn't speak to him. He's familiar, though, for some reason."

"He stayed here a few weeks ago while he was getting his office set up," Meg said. "You probably saw him around the Inn."

"Computer programmer," Doreen said importantly. "Not only is he the key to City of Love, but he did our web site, too."

"Okay. I've obviously missed a whole lot of stuff these past few weeks. Tell me about this new business."

Doreen's wrinkles folded into a huge smile. "One of my better idears, if I do say so myself."

" 'Better,' " Quill repeated. "Better implies that there was a best before this one, Doreen. And try as I might, I haven't seen one of your businesses result in anything but doom, death, and disaster for the guests. Remember the ex-wrestler minister and the Church of the Rolling Punches, or whatever it was? And the nudists? I mean, dot-com companies are the snake oil salesmen of the millennium. Instead of a dog-and-pony show, you've got

PowerPoint presentations, but the principle's the same. They count on suckers. How many people have gone bust putting their life savings into a sure thing that turned out to be smoke and mirrors? It all started," she added loudly, "with that dumb tulip scandal in Holland, three hundred years ago. And people never learn, Doreen! And they don't make one red cent."

"Hold on." Doreen held up one hand, like a traffic cop. "We're already makin' money on it."

"Making money how? What in the heck is it?"

"They said in the meeting. Din't you hear? A datin' service."

"A dating service?"

"Really, Quill." Meg, in the middle of preparing a *demiglace*, took a delicate sip of the mixture with a pious air. "If you hadn't been so caught up in *things* recently, you might have invested in it, too."

"He's comin' up here this weekend," Doreen said in a low voice to Meg. "That Harker."

"Oh yeah?"

The two of them looked speculative.

Quill ruminated. If she took exception to her sister's tone of voice when she'd said "things," the discussion would degenerate into an argument over art, Harker, and goodness knows what other "things" could be laid at her door. If she pounced on Meg's revelation that she, too, had been drawn into investing into one of Doreen's nutty schemes, well . . . She leaned over and looked under the prep table at Meg's socks. She hadn't changed them since the interview with Boomer that morning, so the risk of an explosion was high. "Okay," she said finally, "tell me about it."

"Do better than that, I'll show ya. Come on into my office."

Quill looked an inquiry at her sister, who shook her head. "I've seen it. And this glaze keeps crystallizing, so I need to fiddle with it. The web site is actually pretty neat, Quill. Ours is okay—the standard stuff, because we couldn't afford to get fancy—but CityofLove.com is very cool."

Doreen had a small office—really more of a large closet—just off the storage rooms. This was where she kept the house-keeping staff's personnel files, records of the inventory of cleaning supplies, and the linen counts. She switched on the overhead light and sat down at her desk. She tapped away on a slim, top-of-the-line laptop computer. Another piece of evidence of change in the past month. Quill pulled a chair across the highly polished linoleum and sat down as close as she could to the screen.

"I'll show you ours first."

Meg was right. TheInn@HemlockFalls.com was nice, but strictly standard stuff. The photos of the grounds, the waterfall, and the twenty-seven rooms and suites the Inn had to offer were taken straight from the advertising brochure Harvey Bozzel put together for them every year.

"I done most of the work on that myself," Doreen said. "Hadda learn HTML."

Quill decided not to ask. But she made an admiring noise. Doreen shrugged carelessly, then said, "You were asking about Joss? Joss Roberts? Now *he* knows a thing or two about computers. Take a look."

Doreen tapped away, brow furrowed in concentration. "He helped us with the software and the architecture. He set up shop in that empty store right next to Nickerson's. That's where he's got the server. Calls it Blue Cow Computing."

"There's several new businesses in town," Quill said, "but I don't quite remember seeing it."

"That's 'cause you been gallivanting," Doreen said sternly. She turned to face Quill while the laptop squalled the modem connection to the Internet and repeated, "You've been gallivanting."

The computer made a musical noise: the first dozen notes of "You Can't Hurry Love." The screen glowed and a plummy voice intoned: "Welcome . . . to the City of Love!"

"That's Boomer Dougherty!" Quill sat up too quickly, and a charley horse shot through her right hip. She stifled a yelp and Doreen gave her a penetrating look.

"So," Doreen said flatly. "That's what happens when you haul off wearin' yourself out." She turned back to the screen. "Yep, that's Boomer. We're making a lot of money on account of him agreein' to invest. Mentioned the web site a coupla times on his TV show. And he got us a good break on the commercials."

"How in the world did you get Boomer to help, again?" His interest in Hemlock Falls was beginning to bother her. And she hadn't heard a legitimate reason yet. "And why would he?"

"Oh, he and Joss Roberts go back a ways, I guess. Costs a bundle to set this kinda thing up, I can tell you. But Joss is willin' to wait for his cash . . . They call it sweat equity, y'know."

"I know."

"And since Boomer's given us a leg up with the TV exposure, we started makin' money right off the bat."

By now, Doreen's tapping fingers had called up the "City of Love" features page. A coy little questionnaire appeared first, headed "Tell Us About Your True Love!"

"See, you put in 'woman' lookin' for a 'man.' Then you put in your age . . ." She tapped in 36. Quill frowned. "And then, like, if you don't want the man to smoke or drink and like that . . . and then where you want to meet your true love, because it won't do no good if the guy's in L.A. or whatever."

The scroll bar showed New York, then the Rochester/Syracuse area.

"And then you sign up and go." Doreen clicked and said, "Gimme your credit card number."

"No."

"Now look, missy. It's a mere twenty-four ninety-five a month to get the chance to meet the man of your dreams."

"I've already met . . ." Quill shut up.

"Look, here. See them? Testimonials."

Quill squinted over Doreen's shoulder. *I met the man of my dreams!* gushed someone called Bootsie. *Chuck and I met online and he moved in the very next day. We're getting married next week!*

"Next week?" Quill said. "Doreen! These people are crazy!"

"Joss fixed it so we don't get nobody from the state prisons and that." She looked thoughtful. "I don't know about the loony bins, though. We'll have to see about that."

"What! The prisons?"

"Accessed the New York State prisoner's list." Doreen made a squinchy sort of face. "Come to think of it, he said not to tell anybody; anyhow, we don't want any trouble. So, this here Bootsie found the man of her dreams and they're gettin' married, just like that." Doreen snapped her fingers. "Amazing, innit? Now, give me your credit card."

"No!"

"All right. I'll sign up you myself. It'll be a birthday present."

"It's not my birthday, and I don't want to sign up."

Doreen pulled open a file drawer, found an Amex bill,

(stamped PAID, for once) and tapped in the credit card number. "Now, we gotta wait till tomorrow, till that clears, but in the meantime, we let you get a look at the goodies."

Clickety-click went Doreen's fingers. And then, to the computerized strains of "Some Enchanted Evening," the screen came alive with men.

"These here are your City of Love Perfect Mates." Doreen's voice was loud over the tinny music. "See, I ast the Love Guide for a guy from thirty to fifty, who likes women like you."

"What do you mean, 'women like me'?"

"Oh, you know, 'skinny beauty likes art and dogs.' "

"I am not skinny," Quill said with some indignation. Then, drawn to the screen with a sort of helpless fascination, she began reading. "My goodness, Doreen, what a lot of lawyers."

"There's a lot of lawyers everywhere," Doreen pointed out.

Each of the text paragraphs describing Quill's perfect mates had a small color photo next to it. Quill frowned a little. "But there's no names. I mean, there's names, but names are like High, Wide, and Handsome? And Counselor of Love?"

"Huh-uh. You get to choose yourself a handle. One I picked for you is Art."

"Art?"

"On account of that's what you do when you're supposed to be runnin' this Inn."

"But I sound like a guy, Do—" Quill interrupted herself. "Art. Fine. As if I *cared*."

"See, with a handle, you don't have to let anyone know who you really are on account of Joss and I don't want stalkers and rapists, and that. And you got to pick a password. Go on, pick on."

"What about STOPIT."

"Hm. 'Kay, then." Doreen tapped S-T-O-P-I-T as if squashing ants. "Now. You're ready. You pick one of these guys, e-mail him, callin' him by his handle. And he e-mails you back and you kinda go from there."

"An awful lot of men seem to like walks on the beach," Quill said, scanning the personal ads. "Last time I walked on the beach I didn't see any of them. And everybody seems to like movies. And long walks in the park."

"The Love King can he'p you with that. Gets kinda boring after a while." Doreen clicked away, and the screen read: "Let us help! We will write your personal ad so that you are irresistible to the one you love! For only $24.95, send us your personal description and a photo!"

"www.bozzelads.com?" Quill shook her head, as if to clear it. "That's Harvey."

"Good old Harve. Wanna see some more of your true loves?"

"No," Quill said.

Doreen clicked once and the men were back.

"My gosh, that's Howie Murchison!" Quill squinted at the tiny photo. It was indeed Howie, leaning against a tree, dressed in jeans and a denim shirt, and wearing a red bandanna around his neck. He grinned into the camera. " 'Here comes the judge,' " Quill read aloud. " 'Fifty-six-year-old white male professional looking for smart, independent female who likes long walks on the beach, quiet evenings at home, movies . . .' " Quill sat back. "I don't believe it. My gosh. And what about Miriam Doncaster? I thought they were dating? Or is that off?"

"Somebody smart as Mr. Murchison knows the more you got to pick from, the better chance you got." Doreen, who had been married four times to Quill's sure and certain knowledge, added, "Weren't for me bein' happy with Stoke, you can bet your behind I'd be advertisin' on this, too."

"Somebody as smart as Howie ought to know better altogether," Quill said vigorously. "Phooey, Doreen. I'm glad you and the Chamber are making money. I'm glad we're fully computerized and on-line with our own web site. But this City of Love stuff is just—weird. And maybe even dangerous. How do you know these guys are telling the truth about themselves?" She reached over Doreen's shoulder and tapped the keyboard herself. "Look at that one: 'Hot Lover Looking For Hot Lips.' Ugh!"

Doreen read the rest of the ad, eyebrows raised. "We might oughta get the Reverend Shuttleworth in on this. Sort take a look at the ads before they go on-line."

"Sure. Forget about the First Amendment." Quill got up. "Phooey again. If you want me, leave me a message."

"You going to be paintin'?"

"Painting," Quill said vaguely. And she would, too, if she could find Davey Kiddermeister and grill him about George Nash first. The intercom buzzed imperiously. "Nuts!" Quill said. "It's for you, Doreen. I'm not here."

Doreen pushed the audio button with a firm thumb and barked "Yuh?"

"Somebody named Sylvia Prince is here to check in." The transmission made Dina's voice tinny. "Is Quill there?"

Quill shook her head and mouthed, "No."

"Yuh."

"She says she's supposed to meet with you, Quill. She's Boomer's assistant." An indignant squawk interrupted her. She returned to the intercom after a brief interval. "Sorry. She says the only thing she'd assist Boomer with is a haircut with a lawn-mower. She's an assistant producer."

"She's not due until tomorrow," Quill said. "She's early."

"She says she knows she's early and she's sorry but she wasn't sure about the weather so she drove up today. We've got room," Dina added. "Some of the winegrowers checked out this morning."

"This here's a big account," Doreen said. "And it's lunchtime. You get her settled and Quill will meet her in the dining room in twenty minutes."

"Hey," Quill said. "I have to work this afternoon."

"Over and out," Dina said.

"Ten-four," Doreen said.

"Ten-four? What do you mean ten-four? Ten-four what?"

Quill reached past Doreen and pushed the End button on the keyboard. "My life," she said crossly, "is not my own."

She sneezed twice and went to see about lunch with Boomer's broadie, Sylvia Prince.

# CHAPTER 8

"Man, oh man. What they sat about your sister's true. This is fabulous stuff." Sylvia Prince took a huge bite of the wild-mushroom chicken breasts in heavy cream.

Quill looked at her watch. Past two o'clock. Davey got off patrol at three-thirty. She sighed and settled back to deal with Sylvia Prince.

Sylvia had the buffed and polished look that characterized so many of the TV people Quill had met over the years. She was blonde, athletically thin, and dressed like a Wall Street broker. Her face was exceptionally narrow, like a hawk's, and her eyes were set widely apart. They appeared to be a sort of violet-blue, but with contact lenses, one never knew. She may have been in her late thirties, but Quill had the impression she was older.

Quill found her almost alarmingly decisive and opinionated. "We've kept Chicken Quilliam on the menu for years. It's one of Meg's signature pieces."

"I hope it's on for many more." Sylvia finished the last bite and leaned back with a sigh. "I don't suppose she does as well with desserts?"

"Sure! We've a nice raspberry coulis."

"Something chocolate," Sylvia said wistfully.

"Seven-layer torte," Quill said briskly. "Three varieties of chocolate, crushed English walnuts, crème fraiche, and whatever fruit Meg's working with at the moment. And an espresso?" She wiggled her fingers at Kathleen, who came and took the order. She returned with two pieces, and the muttered comment to Quill: "The kitchen says you're getting too skinny."

Sylvia took her time with the torte, clearly savoring every bit.

"Thank you so much for this, Quill. You're a genius."

"You're welcome. But Meg's the genius here."

"I don't mean the dessert. The dessert is a gift from the gods. I mean for not saying, 'How do you keep so skinny?' Or, 'I wish I could eat like a horse.' "

"How about that tactful old classic, 'Do you throw up after you eat?' "

Sylvia shouted, "No! I'm telling you, sweetie, anyone tries that one on me, they get a slap up the side of the head." She leaned across the chrysanthemums and said in an undertone, "You know how crazy this makes Boomer?"

"Pretty crazy, I should think."

"Yeah. I make it a point to stuff myself with pasta whenever I have to eat with the big, fat son of a gun. And every so often I come up with an idea for our medical feature on the short life spans of people with morbid obesity."

"You know, to be fair," Quill said with some reserve, "it is a disease. And heavy people have a lot more nasty comments to deal with than very thin people."

"Of course it's a disease. For some," Sylvia said. "But Boomer just plain likes to eat. There's no metabolic problem there. He's just damn greedy. Take it from me. I've known the bastard for years. When he started in the business, he was just your average burly guy on the make. In my highly informed and objective opinion, he stuffed his gut to make himself stand out. He doesn't have any other marketable talent, that's for sure." She grinned at Quill's expression. "We've disliked each other for years."

"Why? And if it's difficult, why work together?"

"You think jobs in television grow on trees? Hey. Channel Fourteen's an affiliate station. One of the big four. I've got a toehold in the big time, and I'd rather have a toehold in the big time than a whole foot smack in the middle of cable." She shuddered. "Some of those channels broadcast to an audience of three little old men in Boca Raton with a letch for mud wrestling. My job's not much, and neither is Boomer's, but it's something. As for why I loathe Boomer . . ." She put her elbows on the table and regarded Quill with a frank and engaging smile. "He's an egoist. You know the old Zen question: if a tree falls in the forest, ya da da ya da da?"

"Actually, it's an old slipsologist question," Quill said dryly, "but, yes, I'm familiar with it."

"Well, if Boomer isn't there to hear it, it hasn't fallen at all. That man genuinely doesn't understand there are other points of view. That other people exist in reference to someone or something other than Boomer."

"Was he ever married?" Quill asked curiously. "Does he have children? Parents usually can empathize better than other people."

"Parents." The word dropped oddly into the silence. "No. I think Boomer has what he calls a 'squeeze' somewhere, but as far as. I know, no kids. Me, either, for that matter. How about you?"

"I was married a long time ago. But no children."

"Hostages to fortune," Sylvia said briskly. "You're, what, in your early thirties?"

Quill nodded. "Well, middle, anyway," she added honestly.

"That's the worst time. For me anyway, and for most of my women friends who haven't had kids already. There's some sort of weird *thing* that happens. You're going along, happy as a clam trying to make a career and *wham,* just like that you find yourself mooning over kids in the drugstore, or offering to be an honorary aunt to your married friends' kids." She shook her head, as if to get rid of something in her hair. And then, so softly that Quill couldn't be sure that Sylvia meant her to hear, she said, "And you dream. No. You have nightmares. About what might have been. You look back on the stupid choices you made when you were just a kid yourself, about men, about kids . . . that takes a while to get through. But get through it you do."

Uncomfortable with this, Quill brought the conversation back to the present. "Speaking of getting through. Was there anything specific about the banquet you wanted to cover?"

Sylvia's blue eyes were shrewd. She looked at Quill for a long moment, and then said mildly, "Not a lot. This looks like a well-run place. Any problems that you can see?"

"Well," Quill said, who was strict about following the Innkeeper's Third Rule of Good Business (Mostly Tell the Truth), "we might have a problem with the wait staff." She gave a brief rundown of the growth problems currently plaguing Hemlock Falls, and the subsequent effect on the Inn's employment roster.

"But we're interviewing more waiters tomorrow. And we should have everybody well up to speed by Saturday."

"Good. But you let me know how that goes, Quill. There's not much that would make Boomer madder than having soup in his lap, or his food delivered cold. Take it from me. This banquet is a big deal for him. He does it every year. And he's never gone back to the same place twice. Something's always gone wrong."

"Why did he choose Hemlock Falls to begin with?" Quill asked.

Sylvia shrugged. "Someone put a bee in his bonnet. It's weird. He wasn't at all happy about putting the banquet on up here at first. Then he read about you, and heard about Meg, and he seemed a little happier with it. Not that Boomer's ever really happy," she added sarcastically. "But at least he stopped screaming about being stuck in some out of the way burg with a female chef."

"You're kidding." Try as she might to make sense of this— it didn't add up. "He seemed perfectly happy to have the Inn here. More than happy. And Sylvia, why would Boomer invest all this time and money into Hemlock Falls itself?"

"You mean CityofLove.com?" Sylvia's face twisted in a wry smile. "The dating service is a good idea. If I get any more desperate for male companionship, I was thinking about trying it myself. But if you sit back and take a look at it? The answer's simple. Money. And Boomer's as greedy for that as he is for food. Greedier, even. Your little town's a great place to try this out as a business idea. Everybody knows everyone else's business here, am I right?"

Quill pulled a face.

"I thought so. Word gets around fast in a town this size. Suddenly you've got a whole lot of users without any advertising costs at all, so the site looks good right away. This is a pretty affluent area so you've got people paying for it right away. And if it works here, Boomer can take it national. Same thing with the recipe contest. I mean, that may look like a one-off right now, but then again, maybe it isn't. Look at Emeril."

"Boomer as a celebrity chef?"

Sylvia shrugged. "Why not? There's a limit to how famous you're gonna get forecasting weather. But who knows why the hell Boomer does anything. All I know is, if you haven't got a crackerjack wait staff on hand, I'm going to hear about it, big time."

"I'll let you know every step of the way," Quill promised.

"Good. So. You all seem to know what you're doing. Boomer sent me up here because, one, he likes to jerk me around, and two, the man is a walking case study of an obsessive-compulsive. Oh, I'll meander on down to this Croh Bar, where the out-of-town contestants are supposed to make their damn desserts and introduce myself to the locals, but I'm counting on you to tell me if there's a problem." She reached across the table and Quill shook her hand. "Deal?"

"Deal." Quill got up to leave, feeling dismissed.

"You'll keep me current, though, won't you? Boomer'll call fifteen or sixteen times tomorrow wanting to know if I'm on top of things. I'll want to get a sort of progress report pretty often."

"Of course," Quill said. And then she went off to interrogate Davey Kiddermeister.

# CHAPTER 9

Quill drove to the municipal building and parked in the city lot. She sat staring at the building, overwhelmed with memories. She hadn't been there since the day Myles had left, since she had told him, finally and forever, that they couldn't make a life together.

That last talk had been in his office, Myles behind the desk, Quill sitting in the steel gray chair in the corner, weeping.

Myles McHale had joined the Tompkins County sheriff's department after twenty years in the Homicide Division of the NYPD, a few years after Meg and Quill had opened the Inn at Hemlock Falls. In the early months of their relationship, Quill had learned almost nothing about his life there; by accident, she'd discovered his career had been a brilliant one. And as Quill had discovered over time, no one working in law enforcement in metropolitan areas escaped without scars—both emotional and physical. Although an easy man to love, Myles had not been an easy man to know.

Myles hadn't left Hemlock Falls after they'd parted. He had purchased an old cobblestone house at the east end of Hemlock Gorge when he'd taken the sheriff's job; now he spent long days restoring it. But the investigation job he had taken, after he'd resigned as sheriff, kept him out of the country for months on end. And although Quill ran into him in the village when he was back, she hadn't spent any time at all in the places where they'd been together. Not his home, not the long walks along the Hemlock River, not the restaurants in nearby Ithaca, where the Tompkins County headquarters were.

And this stupid, ugly municipal building. Another place where the two of them had spent long hours.

The black-and-white cruiser was in its accustomed spot. Quill turned off the Honda's engine and sat for a moment, staring at the dull orange brick and the verdigris metal roof. She had a strange, eerie sense that there was another Quill at her side. A ghostly Quill who had made a different choice in life.

This Quill had married Myles, had a child perhaps, had moved to the cobblestone by the river with him. This Quill was going to meet Myles in his office, just before the two of them would drive to Ithaca for a glass of wine at Francine's.

Quill sneezed. Right. She was an idiot, and going loopy to boot. She got out of the car, shivering suddenly in the chill air. Sometime during the day, the air had cooled. The out-of-season warmth was gone, replaced by the usual November chill.

She ran across the asphalt to the door marked Sheriff's Office and below, in smaller letters: Jail. She knocked and pushed the door open at the same time. There was a small anteroom, covered in peeling brown linoleum, and not quite clean, now that Myles wasn't there. The door to the office itself was open, and Quill saw that Davey Kiddermeister was sitting on the desk, ear to the phone, dressed in his black-and-grays. He glimpsed Quill and turned bright pink. Quill waved cheerily. Davey was cursed with fair skin, very pale blond hair, and visible feelings. Myles would have been a hard act for any new sheriff to follow; it was particularly hard for Davey, who had grown up in Hemlock Falls, and who, although sincere in his commitment to keeping Hemlock Falls crime-free, was the kind of guy who was happiest when everybody liked him. He had been far more effective as a deputy than he was as sheriff. But hardest of all on Davey was the blush. Davey blushed at the drop of a hat.

"Hi, Dav—I mean, hello, Sheriff." Quill kept her voice low, as people do when interrupting a phone conversation. "No, don't hang up. I'll wait."

Davey hung up the phone. "It was just my mom."

"Oh." Quill searched her innkeeper's memory for Mrs. Kiddermeister. A widow. Retired from a career as a school aide. A nice lady, who wished both her children were happily married. "How is she? Is she getting along better with her diabetes?"

"Hum," Davey said. His cheeks flamed crimson. "Dina said you might be by."

"She did?" Quill blinked. She'd been pretty certain that she'd disabused Dina of any notion that she, Quill, was taking up detecting again.

"Yeah. And she said to tell you not to spread it around, but that we're unofficially engaged."

"Davey! How nice," Quill said, pleased.

"Uh-huh. Well, like I said, it's unofficial." He wriggled, as if his shirt were itchy.

"And when will it be official?" Quill settled into the steel gray chair. That hadn't changed since Myles had left. It was still miserably uncomfortable.

Davey waved his arms in the air in a bewildered way. Quill stiffened. Ho. So the gossip about her supposed vampy behavior hadn't been limited to the Chamber members or her receptionist. "I see," she said, conscious of asperity. "I have no intention of . . . of . . . having any intentions. Toward you, I mean."

Davy moved around the desk and stood in front of her. "That's okay," he said, a little huskily. "The intentions part, I mean. You must be lonely with the sheriff gone . . ."

Even Davey kept calling Myles the sheriff.

". . . and this guy you're running up to see in New York all the time. Well, there's no need to do that at all, miss, I mean . . . Quill." His roseate complexion made his eyes very blue.

"Davey, you're what . . . twenty-two?"

"Twenty-six!" he said, his tone injured.

"Fine. Try to behave like it then, will you? Listen. I need to know something about George Nash." Quill, having decided that confidence, determination, and authority were the best tactics to use with Davey, settled firmly onto the chair and made her expression as severe as possible.

"You do?"

"Yes. And quickly, if you please. I have a lot to do today."

"Well, I don't know, Quill, I mean, Miss Quilliam. The sheriff never . . ."

"Davey, *you're* the sheriff."

"I—Oh. Yeah."

"Can I see the autopsy report, please?" Quill held out her hand in a very authoritative way, she thought.

"Can't give that to members of the public, ma'am."

"I'm not exactly a member of the public," Quill said frostily.

"Am I? You have seen me here before, David. Discussing cases with the sheriff."

Davey, not bothering to work this through to any sensible conclusion, shrugged and moved to the file cabinet in the far corner. "The coroner's office just faxed it to me. Haven't had a chance to file it, yet." He picked up a sheaf of papers from the top of the cabinet and brought them over to her. "I was going to give Doc Bishop a call, to get me through some of the language."

Quill, scanning it, swallowed hard at the photos of the body, and went straight to the cause of death.

"Injuries consistent with vehicular homicide," she read aloud. "The preliminary reports on the paint found on the body—my goodness, Davey. They think it was a silver Honda. That's . . ."

"The color of your Honda."

"The color of my Honda," Quill agreed. "Oh, poor man. Death occurred at least twelve hours before the body was discovered. And the body had been moved. And—this is interesting, Davey, he'd only been wrapped in that tarp for a few hours at most."

"How do they know that, anyway?" Davey asked. "I mean, they can just flat out tell?"

"Maggots," Quill said briefly. She read on. "You want to know more? The life cycle of the maggots found in the folds of the tarp were shorter than the maggots found in the, um, eyes. Ugh." She placed the autopsy report on the desk. "Well. Did you get any information about George Nash himself?"

"They pulled his record. He had a sheet. Ex-con. Just out a few days, before he was hit."

Davey handed that over, too. Quill read carefully. There was the account of the old, terrible accident. She let out her breath. Neither she nor Meg was mentioned in the witness column.

"Rotten case, that was," Davey said cheerily. "Carjacking. A little kid died."

"Yes," Quill said. "The Ross baby."

"You know about that?"

"It says so right here." She set Nash's conviction history on top of the autopsy. "Are you conducting an investigation, Davey?"

"Me? No, ma'am. Last Nash was seen was in Syracuse, some eighteen hours before death was alleged to occur."

"It wasn't alleged," Quill said.

"Ma'am?"

"He's dead, isn't he? Never mind. It's upsetting, looking at this stuff."

"Don't I know it!" Davey's complexion bloomed rose. "And those pitchers. Jeez. Anyhow, Syracuse is handling it. I just sent in my report. Want to see that?"

"Love to," Quill said heartily.

Davey's report was painstakingly printed on a Tompkins County Incident Report sheet. Quill read it twice. "There were just the two witnesses? Harland and Petey?"

"Well, they found the poor bastard, sorry, ma'am. Seems that they had this bet going and weren't going to pick up the garbage until deer hunting season was over . . ."

"Deer hunt . . . ? Never mind."

"Anyway, they got to thinking it would have been more of a hassle to leave it there, on account of they thought it was . . ."

"Stop," Quill said. "But neither Harland nor Petey saw anything suspicious before they discovered the body? I saw them up on the ridge the day they found it, you know. They'd been there quite a while."

"I don't think so," Davey said cautiously. "But you never know."

Quill bit back exasperation. "I think I'll drop by Harland's and talk with him a bit. You don't mind, do you?"

"Mind? No, ma'am."

"And if I find out anything, I'll be sure to let you know."

"Sure thing. Thanks, Miss Quilliam."

"You're welcome, Davey."

Back in the Honda, Quill cheered herself up by thinking that if she were interested in pursuing her career as an amateur detective, you couldn't ask for a better local sheriff than David Thomas Kiddermeister. He hadn't frowned at her questions. He didn't lecture her at length—well, no, that wasn't fair—Myles had been prone to pith, and his lectures had been short. At any rate, Davey didn't warn her about the dangers of mixing in with the professionals. Or tell her not to put herself in harm's way. In fact, Davey had been nicely oblivious to her whole investigative effort.

Harland Peterson, on the other hand, was not as well-mannered.

"Dang it, Quill," he said, when she found him in the middle of milking time at his dairy farm. "I thought you were gonna stay out of this. Thought the mayor and Marge both gave you what for."

"You weren't at the Chamber meeting today," Quill said.

"Well, no, ma'am, I wasn't," Harland conceded.

Quill let the silence run on. The dairy barn was very pleasant at this time of day, if rather smelly. The milk cows presented themselves peacefully to the automated milking machine, their brown eyes sleepily content. Quill reached out and tentatively patted the nearest cow on the nose.

"That's Glory, that is," Harland said.

"She's very nice," Quill said admiringly.

"Send you some of the burger, if you want," Harland said. "Gotta send her off to the butcher's next week. She's been down a couple of gallons, past month or two. She's getting on." He thumped the cow's flank. "Aren't you, old girl."

Quill stepped back a bit. None of this seemed fair, somehow, to the cow. "So, what I wanted to ask, Harland, was how long you and Petey were up on the Gorge?"

"Awhile. Deer hunting starts in two weeks. We were deciding where to go first."

"An hour while? Fifteen minute while? What a while?"

Harland moved down the line with a slap on Glory's rump. The milking machine rumbled along behind him. "Say, an hour or two. You know how it is. You get to jawin'."

"You didn't see anyone dump the, er—"

"Body? Nope. Would have noticed that for sure."

"Any cars you didn't recognize? I mean, you know most of the cars in town by now."

"Lotta new folk, what with the resort and all."

"But most of the workers park by the site in the morning, when the shift starts. And then they're in those darn dump trucks all day long."

"Thought I saw you, didn't I?" Harland said.

"I don't know. Did you?"

"Yep. You bought that SUV, in the silver color. Was pretty sure I saw you headin' out toward Route Fifteen. Couldn't'ta been though. You were smack in the middle of the Chamber meeting when I come in to tell about the body."

"Yes," Quill said thoughtfully. "Yes, I was."

After declining Harland's offer of the best parts of poor Glory, Quill drove back to the Inn.

So, for what it was worth, she had a lead. Her own car's make and model, headed toward Syracuse. How many new-model silver SUVs had been sold in Syracuse in the time that the new model year was available? It seemed to her that the next model year was usually available to buyers in August, or maybe it was September. It'd be easy enough to check with the Honda dealer. And if she could talk Davey into turning the lead over to the Syracuse police department, they might track down the vehicle.

And then what?

Quill parked at the back of the kitchen and sat still for a long while, thinking.

Did she want to find out who killed George Nash?

Yes, she did. She wanted to know. If there hadn't been that connection. If she and Meg hadn't been involved, no matter how innocently, she could turn the lead over to the proper authorities and let the whole thing go.

She closed her eyes, hearing again that long-ago squeal of tires. The shouts of the distraught father.

Maybe she should just let it alone.

Maybe.

She'd think about it. She'd work on her painting, find the surcease of thought that intense work always gave her, and think about it.

On her way, finally, to go upstairs to her canvas, Quill stopped and said hello to Dina.

"That Sylvia Prince," Dina said. "She's kind of scary."

"Tough," Quill said. "But she's had to be. And I don't think she's scary. I think she has a perfectly awful life. I think it's sad."

"Boomer left a couple of calls for her. He wants her to call back by two o'clock, and if she doesn't reach him at the first number he left, he left about twenty million other numbers for her to call, and she'd better get back to him by five at the latest. Honestly, Quill, that guy just doesn't let go."

"I can see," Quill said. She bit her lip. "Sometimes there's a lot of virtue in just letting go. Don't you think?"

"Oh, yeah," Dina said. "Life's just too darn short."

"That, too," Quill said.

# CHAPTER 10

"Tell me honestly, Meg. How much money did you put into that dot com thing?" Quill sat on the couch in her suite, facing the French doors. Outside, the sky was dark with stars sprinkled like so many computer cursors across the horizon. She'd spent what remained of the afternoon working on the canvas. It hadn't gone well. She'd kept thinking about Sylvia Prince and a life spent working with somebody she hated. She kept thinking about the Ross baby and George Nash ending up dead in the Gorge, mistaken for a bag of garbage. Then she'd showered and washed her hair and sprayed on her new perfume and thought about Harker.

She'd startled Meg with an energetic hug when her sister came by.

But physically she felt horrible. Her arms and legs ached. Her head throbbed like the devil. She kept her hands firmly clasped on her knees, so that Meg wouldn't see the tremors and give her sixteen kinds of holy hell for working too hard and drinking too much coffee.

Meg curled next to her, an after-dinner glass of sauterne in her hand. Andy was on night shift at the clinic.

"My last paycheck, that's all I contributed. I own a tenth of a tenth of a point or something. John put some of the Inn's funds in it, so you own some, too. It really is making money, you know."

"But the costs of creating that kind of site—that's hundreds of thousands of dollars. Did everybody in Hemlock Falls invest in it?"

"Quite a few," Meg said. "I think what convinced everybody

was Boomer Dougherty's support. He's giving us fantastic exposure. You don't watch his weather report, but maybe you should. He's on the eleven o'clock news. Check it out before you go to bed." She yawned and stretched. "God, I'm pooped. I'm going to jog around the herb garden and see if I can wake myself up. Why don't you come with me?"

"Jog around the herb garden? It's ten-thirty at night."

"It'll help you sleep. And it's a nice, mild night out, Quill. Since we've gotten so busy, I've had to schedule my jogs later and later. As a matter of fact, I was going to discuss getting a treadmill. This nice weather isn't going to last very much longer, and since Sherri's gym closed, we'll have to drive all the way to Syracuse to find a place to exercise indoors in the winter."

Quill rubbed the back of her neck, keeping her right hand as steady as she could. "I'm going to turn in early. I'll go with you tomorrow."

"You said that yesterday. This *is* tomorrow."

"Well, I mean tomorrow, as in Wednesday, which it is tomorrow," Quill said calmly. "Go on, Meg. I want to make it an early night. I've set up five job interviews to hire new wait staff in the morning. I've already met with Sylvia Prince to go over Boomer's banquet plans, but even though she says she's leaving everything up to us, she's the sort of person who'll want reports every half hour, like The Weather Channel. And then there's the, umm . . ." She nodded toward the easel standing in its corner. She'd draped a sheet over it.

"How much longer until it's finished?"

Quill made a face.

"Well. All right, then." Meg shifted from one foot to the other. "Be sure to get to bed early. You've got to get some rest, too, sweetie. You look all in."

"I will."

"This weekend. You can paint this weekend. John will be back and he can handle a lot of the meteorologists' stuff for you."

"The weekend's out."

"Harker's coming up!" Meg scowled. "I'd forgotten. Well, at least I'll have a chance to meet him. But is this the best time, Quill? I won't be able to do much more than say hi. I'll be busy in the kitchen."

"You've already decided you're not going to like him." Quill was aware of how suddenly quarrelsome she sounded.

"I'll like Harker just fine, Quill. He sounds interesting, sexy. You've said he's smart, talented, crazy about your own work . . ." Meg rubbed her cheeks. "I just can't see a guy like that living in the country, that's all."

"You haven't met him yet."

"Do I have to meet him to know that he's so . . . so . . . New York? If he's what you say he is, he's going to want you to move there."

"It's okay for you to think about moving to New York, but not me?" Quill felt she was being very cool.

"So you *are* thinking of moving to New York! And what's this about me? I'm not moving to New York. Who said I was moving—"

"You did! A couple of months ago. Remember? Andy had that job offer from Columbia and you were going to run off and marry *him* without saying a word to me or anyone else."

"No."

"So there. Don't you dare tell me how to conduct my love life."

"I wouldn't dream of telling you how to conduct your love life!" Meg's cheeks flushed. "Have a glass of wine or something. Watch a little television. You're overdoing it, Quill. That's why you're looking so thin."

"I'm looking fine."

"You look like a slat off a picket fence." Meg got up, stalked out, and slammed the door behind her.

Quill got to her feet. She made it to her bed, and when she did, she dropped into sleep like a stone into a well.

"Well, folks, it's a gloomy seven o'clock in the morning and it looks like the first major storm of the year is gonna blast the city of Syracuse and suburbs sometime late this afternoon." Boomer Dougherty's huge form nearly obliterated the weather map behind him. His Mercator-map face dominated the television screen.

Quill hated early-morning TV. And she hated it even more when the weather report forecast bad weather. Right now, the sun shone directly into her living room, flooding the room with fresh yellow. She sipped at her orange juice and poked listlessly at the omelet in front of her.

Meg frowned at her from the little stove that was the focal point of Quill's small kitchen, then walked to the corner shelf to lower the volume on the television set perched there.

"That's okay." Quill swallowed a forkful of egg. "Leave it on, if you would. I want to hear what Boomer has to say. Have you heard him talk about us before?"

"Ever since he decided to have the meteorologists' convention here a month ago, he's managed to mention either the Inn or the City of Love at least once a day." Meg jigged impatiently from one foot to the other. She was wearing a sweatshirt with a recipe for roadkill on it. "Are you feeling any better this morning?"

Quill rose from the chair she'd pulled to the breakfast bar and poured herself more orange juice. "I'm fine. I overslept, though. If you hadn't bombed in here insisting on making this omelet, I'd still be asleep."

"You're the only person I know who does her best work before six o'clock in the morning. I thought you'd be up."

"Garbage collectors do."

"And newspaper delivery guys."

"And some artists. I wanted to paint this morning, but I just couldn't wake myself up."

"Ssh. Will you listen to that guy!" Meg folded her arms indignantly under her small bosom and leaned against the kitchen counter, her eyes intent on the TV screen. "He's off on the Doom, Death, and Disaster trolley again."

The weather map behind Boomer was gone. The screen was filled with video images of cars buried in drifts of snow. Thick, fat flakes whipped a lone figure wading along bundled in scarves, wool cap, and heavy boots. Quill shivered involuntarily.

"All that footage's from the blizzard of '77," Meg said in disgust. "He uses it every time he makes a winter forecast. And the footage of those tornadoes in Kansas in the summer."

"Could it be twelve inches of the dangerous white stuff? We'll have to wait and see, folks!" The camera pulled in for a closeup of Boomer's worried face. His voice dropped. "Might think about staying home today, might think about keeping the kiddies inside. We'll keep you up to the minute, so stay tuned to Channel Fourteen and the Boomer! I just hope the storm doesn't snow us in at the weathermen's conference up in Hemlock Falls this week, where I'll be broadcasting the weather each and every night, on location."

Boomer's signature tune (ominous beats on a kettledrum) sounded briefly. The camera cut to the credits, which rolled over a visual of a rambling, copper-roofed mansion perched on the lip of a waterfall.

"That's us!" Quill said.

"Yep." Meg clicked off the television and set a cup of coffee down in front of her. "Say what you like about Boomer, he's been giving us a lot of free air time. When he doesn't run a picture of the Inn, he uses a shot of the web site."

"The City of Love?" Quill rolled her eyes and sipped at the coffee. "Is this decaf?"

"I hate decaf. You hate decaf. No, it's not decaf."

Quill put the cup down.

Meg's eyes narrowed. "So what's going on?"

"Nothing's going on. I'm just cutting back, that's all. Since everyone in town seems to know that I saw Andy yesterday . . ."

"You didn't say a word to me, Quill, and Andy won't tell me!"

"Well, he shouldn't tell you," Quill said crossly. "But I'll tell you if you really need to know."

"It's stress, right? A fine thing your own sister won't tell you she's stressed and you have to hear about your sister's doctor's visit from the whole town."

"The only reason the whole town knows about it is because of that nosy Carol Ann," Quill said in exasperation. "It was just a routine office visit. And who cares, anyway?"

"The whole town cares because you stuck the entire Chamber of Commerce in a traffic jam, and the only reason everyone isn't mad at you is because they think you have a dread disease. "I told them if you had a dread disease, I'd be the first to know about it, and you don't. Traffic was backed up to the municipal building." She laughed suddenly. "You used to drive a cab like that in New York."

Quill smiled reluctantly.

Meg leaned over the counter and put her hand on Quill's hair. It was a light, loving touch. Quill felt an absurd urge to weep. "I'm going to ask one more time, and then I swear I won't mention it again. Are you all right?"

"Yes! Honestly, Meg, just cut it out, okay? I mean, I think I'm in love, really truly in love, for the first time in my life, and I want to paint for the first time in years, I mean really want to paint, the way that I used to need to paint and I'm not getting as much sleep as I usually do, and here you are harassing me and I don't need harassing, I need you to leave me alone!" She stopped, out of breath, and braced herself.

"Okay," Meg said calmly.

"Okay?"

"Yes. You're absolutely right. Everyone leans on you, Quill, and nobody wants you to fall over, so, yes, okay, we'll leave you alone." She cupped her hands around Quill's wrist. "We've been jerks," she said with sudden fierceness. "Just jerks. And you don't deserve it."

"No, you haven't."

"Oh, yes, we have. I have everything I want in this life, Quill. Andy, the best place to cook in the known universe, the best sister, that's you, Quill. And good friends. And what have you got? No work, two busted relationships with men who adore you, and you're looking awful, just awful."

"Hey!" Quill said indignantly.

"And it's all because we lean on you. Your life stinks because of me, Quill, and I'm going to make it up to you."

"My life does *not* stink, thank you very much."

"Oh, yes, it does." Meg paced up and down. Her socks this morning were an earnest blue. "You've handled everything up until now alone. All alone. Well, you aren't going to have to anymore. I called John last night, and he's going to cut the Syracuse meeting short and come back and take over all of the stuff you have to do for the Inn. And then you can be alone! To work! To go back to Myles! To have some time for yourself."

"Go back to Myles? I'd rather have all my teeth pulled out. With a backhoe."

"Don't be ridiculous."

"Don't you dare tell me not to be ridiculous. I am in the middle of the best relationship I've ever had in my life."

"Oh yeah? To a guy I've never even met? Somebody who hasn't even been up here to visit you in the place where you live and work? Phooey."

"Just shut up," Quill muttered. "I'm just trying to decide what to do with my life. I'm trying to decide if I have a life."

"Shut up, huh? Let me tell you right this minute, Sarah Quilliam, that you do have a life. Your life is what you do, right this minute. It's getting up in the morning and coming into the kitchen and having coffee with me, John, and Doreen. It's making the guests comfortable. It's designing the Inn. It's the work you do on your canvas. That's your life. What you do everyday is your life. Not what you plan to do next week."

Quill took a minute to sort this speech out, to see if (a) it made any sense and (b) if she should be insulted. She wasn't sure. "Thanks," she said dubiously.

"Not a bit of it." Meg drew herself up to her full five-feet-two-inch height and squared her shoulders.

Quill recognized this stance with some alarm: it was Meg, being noble. When Meg was noble, she sang songs of martyrdom in the kitchen and all the sous-chefs threatened to quit, mostly because Meg had a voice like a flattened eggbeater. Quill had been wrong about the earnest blue socks. They were a martyr's blue, a this-is-a-hell-of-a-way-to-spend-an-Easter blue.

Meg gave Quill a hug, patted her back, then turned and headed toward the door. "That's it, I've finished. You're free. Go to it."

"But . . ."

"No. You're going to say you have to interview people for the new wait staff, or Kathleen and Peter will die of overwork . . ."

"I didn't say that. Doreen said—"

"Well, John can't cut loose until this afternoon, so Doreen and I are going to interview the candidates for the new wait staff this morning."

"Oh." Quill thought about this, then said, "All right. I guess. We need at least two full time and three part time. And the part time's only until after the New Year's rush."

"Got it."

"And make sure that the ones that you hire get a chance to talk with Kathleen and Peter before you take them on. You remember that course I took in Managing Employee Satisfaction. Employees *need* to support the hiring of new employees. It's critical."

"Will do. And I'll send up lunch on a tray, all right? You make sure you eat it."

The door closed.

Quill was alone, feeling as if she'd survived a tiny tornado.

She stood up. She pulled at the waistband of her jeans; they were loose, but she'd finish the omelet and she'd eat all of the lunch Meg sent up, and with any luck, she wouldn't have to go out and buy new clothes.

She walked around her living room.

Unlike the rest of the Inn, which was furnished with antiques and expensive chintz, her own living quarters were sleek, almost austere. The floors were covered in cream Berber carpet, the couch facing the French doors to her balcony was a neutral leather, and the few pieces of art she had on the walls were not her own, but Ansel Adams black-and-white photographs.

Her easel stood in the south corner, to catch the best daylight. Myles had installed track lighting so that she could work deep into the night if she wanted to.

Myles.

She was suddenly aware of him, as if he were at her shoulder. If she turned quickly, would she actually see him? Tall, broad-shouldered, his dark hair turning gray, ready communication in his eyes.

Quill pressed her fingers over her own eyes. She was going to work, dammit, and it would be Harker at her side, not Myles, Harker with his intent, passionate focus on the things that meant the most to her in this life.

She went to the huge pine apothecary cabinet that stored her paints and brushes and pulled the top drawer open. There were her palate, her brushes, cleaned and neatly arranged on terry cloth. She passed her hand lightly over the brushes, then took one stride and gently pulled the canvas drop off the easel.

An explosion of color greeted her. She responded to color the way she responded to Harker's lovemaking, her skin alive to it. And her best work, the work that most approached the visions in her mind's eye, was saturated with exuberant crimsons, shouting blues, living greens.

The phone rang. She jerked away from the painting with a cry of annoyance and picked it up.

"Quill?"

She focused suddenly. "Hey, Harker." She turned her back to the painting. "You're up!"

"Are you working?"

Quill hesitated. "About to, but . . ."

"You're not letting the rubes get to you, are you?"

"They aren't rubes, Ben."

"Fine. Whatever. I keep forgetting that your liberal principles are coloring your perspective." He chuckled. "Sorry about that. Get it? I said—"

"I heard what you said." Suddenly, Quill didn't like him very much.

"Sorry." She heard him yawn heavily. "I've had a rough time of it down here without you."

Quill's heart softened.

"I'll call tonight, then. And I'll see you in four days. I love you, Quill." She heard the gentle click of the phone and cradled the receiver.

"All right, all right, all right," she whispered, but the sound of her own voice didn't work to call her concentration back. She could call him right back. Catch him before he went out somewhere. Tell him not to come. Not right now. Maybe later.

How much later?

Quill, traitorously, envisioned a very long time before Harker came up to Hemlock Falls.

She stomped to the French doors and flung them open to the chilly morning. Her rooms were on the second floor, right over the kitchen, facing the vegetable gardens. She heard Meg's voice singing (sort of) the opening bars of the Song of the Volga Boatmen, over and over again. The clashing of pot lids punctuated the pause between each "Yo-oh, heave-ho!"

There'd been a frost overnight, and the grass glistened with its thick cobwebs. The Honda still stood in the middle of the Brussels sprouts.

Quill smiled and rubbed her arms against the cold. She raised her face to the sky. If she stood here, not thinking, she could get to the place in her head where she could work. She didn't really see the canvas when she painted. She saw what the canvas should be.

"Worse than the blizzard of '77," a voice below her whispered. "That's what Boomer Dougherty said on TV. Let's bag the job interview and get home. You want to get snowed in up here?"

Quill bent over the balustrade. Below her, two women had just come out of the back door to the kitchen. Both were shrugging themselves into their coats. Quill could only see the tops of their heads: one brown, one drugstore blonde.

"We're not going to get snowed in up here. And if we do, so what? It's gorgeous." The blonde.

"Ssh! Keep your voice down." The brunette turned uneasily and peered back through the kitchen door. "I don't care how pretty this place is, or how much in tips we're going to make, the woman who runs the kitchen is nuts. And if we get bad weather this winter, like Boomer says, I'm not going to chance driving back and forth to work all the way up here, anyway."

"Ho!" Meg yelled from inside. Then a crash as the pot lid landed against a wall. She'd reached the finale.

"She threw the pot. She threw the pot at the wall." The whisperer was the blonde. "And did you hear her about my gum? I can't work if I can't chew gum."

"You can't walk and chew gum at the same time," her friend said, unkindly. "Okay. Okay. Tell you what. Marge Schmidt's hiring at the Croh Bar. Tips aren't as good, but she's not crazy. And we don't have to worry about driving up a hill like this one in bad weather. Only thing we do have to worry about is traffic jams on Main Street."

"There was a doozy of one yesterday," the blonde said glumly.

*"No cinnamon!"* Meg's voice roared suddenly. "Nutmeg, *nutmeg, nutmeg!"*

"Come *on!"* The blonde clutched at the brunette.

"It's just Bjarne," Quill said, leaning so far over the balustrade that she could feel her face turn red. "Meg's just yelling at Bjarne. He's our head chef—Meg's the master chef, and they've been having this ongoing argument about spices and neither one of them wants to give in. And we keep the drive salted."

The blonde jumped and looked around wildly.

"This is a great place to work," Quill said. "Truly."

The brunette looked up, saw Quill's face and nodded to herself with an "oh, yeah?" expression. Quill heard the kitchen door open and shut, and somebody else came out onto the flagstone path.

"Kimmie? Kimmie Bloomfield?" Quill said in surprise.

Kimmie looked around, too. Quill wondered briefly why people just didn't look up if the voice they were hearing came from up. "Up here," Quill said patiently.

Kimmie squinted against the sun. "Quill?"

"Did you come for breakfast?"

"Actually, I came for a job."

"Good luck," the brunette muttered. The blonde said, "Jeez!" and the two of them trudged off, presumably to the parking lot.

"A job?" Quill looked hard at Kimmie. There were shadows under her eyes, and her face looked drawn.

"Yes."

"But . . ." Quill stopped herself just in time. "Umm . . . come on up, why don't you?"

"I thought you were working."

"Who told you that?" Quill asked suspiciously. "Honestly, does the whole *town* have to know everything about everything?"

"Well, Meg told me, actually. I thought I'd be talking to you about the job, you see, and when I asked where you were . . ." Her voice wavered. "Anyhow, I really could use a job." Near tears, Quill thought. Oh, dear. "But I don't want to interrupt you."

"I haven't started yet. I could use some coffee before I do." Kimmie nodded uncertainly.

Quill went inside and shut the doors firmly against the chill. She threw the drop over the painting, closed the drawers on her palate, and took a cautious sip of coffee. It'd been standing too long. She dumped it, ground the beans, and just finished pouring the water into the filter as Kimmie knocked.

Kimmie settled on the edge of the couch and launched into inconsequent chatter. Quill looked at her with her painter's eye. She really was a very pretty woman, with short black hair cut into feathery curls, a beautiful porcelain complexion, and light, changeable eyes. She used very little makeup, just a dash of bright-red lipstick. She was slightly taller than Meg, but not much, and had a rounded figure, unlike Meg's slight, athletic build.

Logically, the three of them should be fast friends. Kimmie could talk knowledgeably about painting, had a passion for decorating and a real enthusiasm for the one-hundred-and-fifty-year-old farmhouse she and Louis were remodeling.

"So," Quill said, when the stream of Kimmie's nervous chatter slowed for the coffee. "You didn't mention you were looking for work last week. Has . . . um, anything happened?" She floundered for a moment. She couldn't think of a question that wasn't too nosy.

"Beautiful cups." Kimmie held up her coffee cup to the sunlight. "That's a lovely bird in the center of the design. I've seen the pattern before, but I can't place it."

"It's one of Helena Houndswood's lines. That's a rose-breasted grosbeak. Some of the designers live here in Hemlock Falls."

"Well, it's beautiful," Kimmie said passionately, and burst into tears. "Louis wants a divorce!"

Quill got up and went for the Kleenex.

# CHAPTER 11

"It's the usual story," Quill said to Meg at lunch. "I'm not indifferent, or unsympathetic, but gosh, Meg, men can be such jerks. They've been married fifteen years. She worked while he went to medical school, set aside her own master's degree—you've heard it all before. I've heard it all before."

"It's going to embarrass Louis big time if she ends up waiting tables here." Meg put her feet up on the fireplace fender and rocked her chair on its back legs. The kitchen was winding down from a frantic lunch hour: the huge dishwasher was on its fifth cycle, and the air smelled of soap, disinfectant, and old garlic. Quill sat beside Meg. They both sipped squash soup.

Meg made a face. "I was right about the cinnamon. Bjarne!"

Bjarne slouched against the wash sink and shot a hunted glance Meg's way. One of the busboys sluiced squash soup into the disposal.

"I was right about the cinnamon!"

"You were right about the cinnamon," he said gloomily. "I was not wrong about the nutmeg, precisely, but I shall consider it."

"Hah." Meg set the soup on the floor. Quill, who thought the soup was terrific, eyed her warily. But Meg appeared to be in a sunny mood. "Is Kimmie really angry? And I can't believe she actually needs the money. I mean, Louis can afford to support her. He's a doctor, for cripe's sake."

"I don't think she wants to embarrass him as much as she just wants to keep busy. And there's not a lot to keep busy with in Hemlock Falls. And don't be such a snob, Meg. Half the wait staff here are in grad school at Cornell. It's an honorable job."

"So you want to hire her."

"We can use her. Certainly through the holiday season. And she said she could work any shift. She wants to start right away. Since the meteorologist convention is over the Thanksgiving holiday, it's good timing. I know Dina wants to go home, and so does Peter, and Kath could use some time off."

"They'll reconcile just before the banquet," Meg said, gloomily. "And we'll have all these new hires, and no old hands and it'll be a mess."

"How *did* the interviews go?" Quill asked brightly. "Are we all staffed up?"

"Staffed up," Meg said, "Umm. Well, not a lot of them worked out, really. But it gave me a little time I hadn't thought I'd have this morning. I worked a little on the banquet for Boomer. Want to see my ideas?" Meg leaped to her feet and dashed to the clipboard that hung by the huge white board that held the approved menu schedule.

"So, I take it we're not all staffed up."

"We *are* going to be staffed up. Just as soon as John gets in. I called him right away on his cell phone, and I caught him just as he was leaving Syracuse."

"So now poor John's got another hassle on his hands."

"Everything," Meg said frostily, "is under control."

Meg's face was pink, and her hair stood on end. Quill made a diplomatic retreat. "I'm dying to hear about the banquet menu."

Meg's eyes narrowed, but she said, readily, "Bjarne was wrong about the soup—" A defiant crash from the prep table let both of them know Bjarne had overheard this. "—but he had a great idea," Meg added loudly. "We're going to try a squash terrine. Plus, I called the wholesalers, and we've got beautiful cranberries coming this afternoon. I'm going to do a series of cranberry chutneys, Quill, which will absolutely knock. Your. Socks. Off." She used her finger for punctuation, a habit Quill usually found so irritating that they ended up in a squabble.

But Quill, who'd been thinking about the impossibility of John recruiting anyone from Syracuse to work for minimum wage plus tips an hour away from their home in the depths of winter, decided the menu could wait. "And who," she said coldly, "is going to serve these chutneys? You didn't hire even one person, Meg?"

"Kimmie," Meg said. She dawdled her way back to the rocking chair and perched on the edge. "That's one."

"I can see it now. Doreen hollered at them and you sang to them. And you offered them jobs and *not one person* wanted to work here."

"I'll admit it, Quill. I'm not all that good at the personnel side of things." Somebody behind her went, "Hah!" Bjarne, Quill thought, getting back at Meg for the nutmeg and the crack about the soup. Meg ignored the interjection with aplomb. "I mean, you've had all those courses at the Cornell Hotel School. And you're the one experienced at these things, so yes, you should have run the interviews, I admit it."

"We should have waited for John to talk to them."

"Maybe he can call some of them back," Meg said, hopefully.

"Hemlock Falls isn't exactly swimming in the unemployed," Quill said crossly. "I guess I can give the Hotel School a call and see if they have any students available to tide us over during the Thanksgiving holiday."

"Well, most of them had listened to that idiot Boomer and his scare forecast," Meg said even more crossly. "They were worried about getting snowed in. It wasn't all my fault. You'd think this was the Yukon, for Pete's sake. And the banquet's four days off—if it does snow it'll have melted by then. We've got plenty of time."

"Temps," John Raintree said as he came in the back door. He shrugged off his raincoat and tossed it onto a free coat hook. "I stopped by a temp agency in Syracuse and got a list of part-timers in Tompkins County."

"Hey, John," Meg said in a pleased way. "Just like the cavalry coming to the rescue. How did you know we'd need more staff?"

John looked tired, but he managed a grin. There were shadows under his black eyes, and his coppery skin was dull. "Good guess," he said dryly. "When you called me to tell me you and Doreen were going to do the interviews, I just took a precaution."

"So that's settled," Meg said happily. "Good. I'm going to mess around with my chutneys now." She bounced out of the chair, and John settled in her place.

He reached out and took Quill's hand. "How are *you* doing?"

Quill forced a smile. She wanted to say, "Better, now that

you're back" or "John, it's so good to see you," but their friendship had been strained almost to the breaking point in the past few months, and she didn't dare. "I'm okay. But it's good that you're back. As usual, there was a crisis. How did the meeting with the investors go? I hope you didn't have to come back just on our account."

"I was getting tired of the Hilton, anyway." John released her hand and stared thoughtfully into the fireplace grate.

"You *look* tired," Quill said. "Haven't you been getting any sleep?"

When the construction of the new resort had become a reality, the mayor had been quick to recruit John as the town's business manager to represent their interests with the international conglomerate. John had an M.B.A. from a prestigious downstate school—and he had been born and raised in Hemlock Falls. Quill had been concerned that juggling the two positions would wear her old friend out. He smiled at her now.

"You know I like it. The project's pretty much on schedule, but we're running out of space in town for a couple of new businesses that want to open shop here." John looked at her. "And our own balance sheet is looking pretty good."

"That's wonderful," Quill said warmly. "I can't tell you how terrific that sounds."

"I wish you looked as good as that sounds." John's tone was kind. "You've lost even more weight, Quill."

She sneezed.

"And you still have that cold. How's the paint—"

Quill held up one hand. "Fine, just don't talk about it."

"The Jinx?"

"The Jinx." She took a breath. "And John, I have a friend coming to visit me this weekend. I just . . . thought you'd like to know."

He didn't move. But she could feel him shrink.

"Harker?" he asked after a moment.

"Yes. I thought it was time for him to meet everybody."

John nodded. "Quill," he said. "Oh, Quill."

Quill's voice rose. She couldn't help it. "And he'll be staying until Monday. So he'll have a chance to see the Inn at its most, most . . . whatever."

John didn't say anything. Quill grasped her hands tightly.

"You sure you're feeling all right?"

"If," Quill said evenly, "one more person asks me how I'm feeling, I'm going to scream."

"Then go on up and work the scream out on canvas."

"She can't." Doreen marched into the kitchen, her lips compressed. "We got an emergency situation and it's all hands on deck."

"What emergency situation?" Quill jumped up.

"Snow." Doreen pointed dramatically. John, Quill, and Meg followed her to the windows facing the vegetable gardens. A faint gray washed the blue sky, and the sun was misty.

"Why is the Honda parked in the Brussels sprouts?" John shook his head. "Why did I even ask? It's not snowing, Doreen."

"Not now, it ain't. We got maybe ten, twelve inches headed this way," Doreen said grimly. "The TV's full of it. Somebody better go up and give Dina a hand with the checkouts."

"The winegrowers aren't due to leave until tomorrow," John said.

"Well, some of them are leaving now. Coupla of them were in the Lounge where we got the TV on all the time over the bar. Blizzard," Doreen said, with satisfaction. "A big 'un."

The entire kitchen rocked with groans. Bjarne flung a dish-cloth into the sink. Meg yelled, "The cranberries!" and leaped for the wall phone. Doreen stood with her arms folded.

"Okay," Quill said. "We've been through this before."

John nodded. "I'll get Mike to see to the snow blade and the emergency generator. Quill, if you could give the temp agency a call, maybe we can get the van up here with the temp staff before we get any kind of significant snow."

"Sure. And I'll get Dina to find the guests and let them know. A lot of them might want to check out early." A slight grimace crossed John's face, and she couldn't help laughing. "Did you ever check on the blizzard insurance?"

"As a matter of fact, I did. And yes, we have coverage for business lost due to Acts of God."

At the end of the practiced whirl of preparations (boards on the north windows, which dated from the mid-1800s; stockpiles of water and gasoline for the generator; extra blankets and guest toiletry kits for stranded travelers), Quill got a call from Betsy Peterson at the train station: the temporary wait staff had arrived by train—would someone come to pick them up?

Quill, who'd moved the Honda out of the Brussels sprouts
and into the equipment garage, found herself the only person
without a specific task, and moved the Honda out of the garage
and onto the road.

The sky was hazy with soft gray clouds. A pale sun waned
behind the gray. A few preliminary flakes spat through the air,
which was soft, and surprisingly warm. If Quill hadn't known
better, she would have gone out in her lightest winter coat and
without boots. As it was, she wore her heaviest down parka, her
heavy gloves, and fleece-lined boots. Her feet were hot, and her
neck was sweaty.

Quill drove through the village feeling pleasantly competent
and secure. Most of the buildings in Hemlock Falls dated from
the mid-1800s, and years of experience with the homicidal
weather of upstate New York had gone into their construction.
Almost all of the cobblestone buildings were equipped with
working shutters, and the townspeople were busy securing them.
The sidewalk in front of Nickerson's Hardware was clear of the
stack of new garbage cans, snow blowers, and shovels that were
normally displayed. The snowplows were being readied at the
municipal building. Davey Kiddermeister and his two new dep-
uties (the hires were courtesy of the increased village budget,
due to the town's expansion) cruised the streets.

Quill pulled into the train station. The structure was one of
her favorite parts of the village, recalling, as it did, the architecture of the far larger train stations from the Victorian era.
Quill parked and walked into the building. The temp workers
were scattered throughout the small interior. The marble floor
was tracked with snow and mud. Quill counted five people waiting: two women and three men. Four of them were bundled to
the ears. Quill shook hands with each of them, noting the vol-
ubility of the oldest lady, the unshaven chin of a guy who looked
as if he'd be happier interviewing for a job driving the snowplow, the odd silence of one man who was so wrapped up in
hat, parka, and scarf that she couldn't begin to tell how old he
was, much less see his face. She introduced herself, thanked
them for coming up, and directed them to the Honda. She
stopped for a word with Betsy Peterson, sitting placidly behind
the ticket window.

"If we're going to get all that snow, Quill, are you going to
need the extra help?" At one time, Quill had a pretty good grip

on the network of Petersons in Hemlock Falls. She could place the older generation, like Betsy; it was the younger ones that confused her. "How's Jackson doing with the cows?" Quill asked companionably.

"You're thinking of Alma's Jackson," Betsy said. "I'm Harland's younger brother's wife. Dickie."

"How's Dickie, then?" Quill asked.

"Dickie's fine. Thought maybe I'd give him a call, though. Check some of these suckers out." She nodded in the direction of the Honda, where the temporary workers sat patiently. "You know he took one of the deputy jobs, as soon as the town posted the job. Some of those birds look pretty suspicious to me, Quill. Why can't you use people you know?"

"We need the help for the banquet," Quill said, too experienced in small-town life to feel especially offended. "And everybody seems to be working at something else, these days."

"True enough," Betsy said. "But if you find yourself murdered in your beds one morning, don't go a-blaming me."

"I certainly won't," Quill promised.

"So. You planning on putting those birds up at the Inn, or what? Thought the big doings with the dessert contest weren't until Saturday."

"They aren't. The problem is the training time. We need at least a day to orient them, and another day to run through serving. And the convention isn't until Saturday, so with any luck, the snow'll be gone. Or at least manageable."

"Doubt it." Betsy shook her head. "I truly doubt it." She squinted at Quill. "You mind what I said about those people."

"I'll do that."

"What is it about imminent disasters that makes people paranoid?" she asked Sylvia Prince an hour later. The temp workers were safely delivered into Kathleen's capable hands. Quill found Sylvia in the Tavern Lounge, a drink in front of her, and reported the successful solution to the waiter problem. "Except," she added, "for the fact that Betsy Peterson, at least, seems to think they are all murderers."

"Maybe they are," Sylvia said cheerfully. "Can I treat you to a scotch?"

"No scotch." Quill sat across from Sylvia. She'd changed out of her gray wool suit into jeans and a sweater. Somehow, this made her look tougher, not more relaxed. "But I'll have a glass of wine. This has been one of those days when I've been run off my feet."

"Can't be too hard a life," Sylvia said. Her tone was sardonic, but Quill guessed that she was pleased with the company. "This place is beautiful."

"Thank you."

"And that's your work on the wall over there?"

Quill didn't turn. "Yes," she said. She could feel her face going warm, the way it did when people commented on her work.

"Hm." Sylvia's smile broadened at Quill's evident consternation. "I don't have a clue about art. What am I supposed to say? Looks good enough to me."

Quill turned around and looked critically at her rose. Nate had stoked the fire and the warm light dimmed the vividness of the flower. "Well, you know, at the time, it looked good enough to me, too." She gasped, involuntarily. "Oh, no."

"What?" Sylvia took a last sip of her scotch, and then waved at Nate for another.

"Carol Ann Spinoza," Quill hissed. "See? That clean-looking blonde who just walked in. Quick. Look busy."

"Channel Fourteen," Sylvia began in a loud voice, "is an affiliate station of the National Broadcasting Company. Founded in . . ." She broke off and stared rudely at Carol Ann, just like Lewis Carroll's Caterpillar. "And *who*, may I ask, are *you*?"

Quill got to her feet, reluctantly. The downside of having been an innkeeper for almost ten years was that her courtesy reflexes were by now, involuntary. "Carol Ann? This is Sylvia Prince. Sylvia? This is Carol Ann Spinoza, our local tax assessor."

"How do you do?" Carol Ann said primly. "May I sit down?" Sylvia shrugged. "Suit yourself."

Carol Ann sat down. Nate deposited Sylvia's scotch in front of her and a glass of Australian Shiraz in front of Quill.

"I will have a glass of Chablis," Carol Ann said.

Nate showed his teeth in a smile. He'd recently cultured a thick, bushy beard. This, and his bearlike brown eyes, gave him a deceptively formidable expression. "The two-dollar Chablis or the six-fifty Chablis?"

Carol Ann, in addition to being the meanest person in Tompkins County, was also the most dedicated freeloader. "The better quality wine, I think," she said thoughtfully.

Quill, who knew very well that Nate's question was the preface to an immediate demand for cash (not by any means the usual practice at the Tavern Lounge), said quickly, "It's on the house, of course, Nate. I didn't expect to see you here right now, Carol Ann. I thought the village offices were closed for the blizzard."

"The obligations of my job supercede any inconvenience posed by the weather." Carol Ann's voice became exceptionally syrupy when she was up to something.

"What the hell kind of tax assessing can you do in a blizzard?" Sylvia asked.

Carol Ann didn't answer this. As a matter of fact, it was clear she was determined to ignore Sylvia altogether. She blinked snakily at Quill. "I've been looking for you," she said sweetly. "All over. That Doreen said you were out. I thought you might be up in your room." The light in the Lounge was dim, but Quill could see the purplish place on Carol Ann's chin where Doreen had landed a good one. "But you weren't. I do like what you're working on, Quill. But I'm afraid I might have smudged it a teeny bit when I put the canvas back on."

Quill set her teeth. "Oh," she said.

Carol Ann rubbed at a spot of azure blue on her thumb with intense concentration, and then clasped her hands neatly in front of her. "Sorry," she said.

There was a fairly long silence. Sylvia looked interested; rather in the way a person looks at a new species of spider. Quill was counting backward from one hundred. At fifty-six, she said brightly, "So. Can I do something for you?" Like push you bit by bit into the Disposall? she added mentally.

"Well, yes. I need to see your occupancy permit."

"The occupancy permit?"

"The one that sets the quota for the number of people allowed in the Inn. Oooh. Thank you." She smiled brightly at Nate as he slapped the Chablis in front of Carol Ann. "The six-fifty Chablis," he said.

Quill—who knew perfectly well that the only Chablis they carried was a truly repellent Gallo label that they sold, reluctantly, for a dollar seventy-five—sent Nate a fierce mental message, which he apparently picked up because he went away.

"The occupancy rate," Sylvia prompted, to Quill's annoyance.

Carol Ann sipped delicately. "Delicious," she pronounced. "Yes, well. Those persons you have occupying the servant's quarters. Just how legal are they?"

This took Quill a minute to figure out. "You mean those two rooms next to John Raintree's apartment in the carriage house. Where we've housed the temporary help from Syracuse."

"Not Mexicans, then," Sylvia said innocently.

Quill shot her a glance. Sylvia winked.

"Two women in one room. Three men in the other. And just the one bathroom. I'm not sure at all," Carol Ann said earnestly, "that the carriage house is zoned commercial. And if it isn't, Quill, I'm afraid it's my duty to bring this to the attention of the proper authorities."

"Then bring it you must," Quill said. "Is there anything else?"

"Well, you know that the tax code bases your assessment on the number of guests you have room for, so the other thing I need to know is if you are going to—you said they were temp workers? Legal workers and that."

Quill nodded. She was reasonably certain her teeth would fall out if she didn't stop grinding them, but she didn't care. Carol Ann's preferred interrogation technique was of the Chinese water torture variety. If she lost her temper now, she wouldn't find out what Carol was after until the assessment hearing.

"If you are going to pay them partly through room and board, it's probably okay. But if you going to charge them room and board, that puts them into the guest category, legally speaking, and I'm afraid that we're looking at reassessment. Tax-wise, that is."

"They're living there for free. Until the banquet. Then they go home."

"Oooh! The banquet. I'd forgotten about that. And you know? My littlest one? Amber-Lynn?"

Amber-Lynn. Oh, yes. The fat kid with the foghorn voice.

"You know, when she heard about the thousand dollars, she said to me 'Mommy?' She said, 'Mommy, what chance do we have to get that thousand dollars? We sure could use it now that Daddy's gone.' 'Sweetie,' I said. 'I just don't know.' 'Mommy,' she said, 'I just bet if you made those oatmeal-granola rolled cookies and put them in that ol' contest, *you'd* win just like that.' " Carol Ann finished the wine and set it on the tabletop with a sharp whack. "Trouble is, I haven't come up with a good Shakespeare title, like everyone else."

"Goneril's Granola Cookies," Sylvia said promptly.

Carol Ann frowned. "That sounds quite nasty."

"Oh, not that nasty." Sylvia screwed up her face in thought. "But I see what you mean. It does sound a lot like gonorrhea." (Carol Ann winced.) "What about Reagan's Rolled Cookies?"

"You mean, like the president? It has to be Shakespeare."

Quill cleared her throat. "She's a character in King Lear. One of the king's daughters."

"Then it would be Princess Reagan's Rolled Cookies," Carol Ann corrected. "Yes. I like that. Well." She rose and nodded her head in satisfaction. "I see. Thank you for the wine, Quill."

Neither Quill nor Sylvia said a word until Carol Ann was safely out the door. "Holy God," Sylvia said. "What a bitch." There was a certain degree of admiration in her tone. "And was that all about what I thought it was all about? She wants you to make sure she gets the thousand bucks? Hoo. Hoo! Station politics aren't a patch on that broad."

"Do you suppose the snow's started yet?" Quill asked a little wistfully. "Maybe she'll get stuck in a drift and they won't find her until spring."

"Blizzard?" Sylvia laughed. "You know who predicted that blizzard? My big, fat boss, that's who." She grinned widely at Quill. "Don't haul out the gas lanterns yet, sweetie."

# CHAPTER 12

"This is the Boomer! On location in downtown Syracuse! Areas south and east of Syracuse have experienced more than three inches of new snow in the past five hours!" Boomer Dougherty stared importantly into the Channel 14 cameras. A red watch cap was pulled over his ears, and his thick jacket was open to the mild breeze. He clutched his microphone. A few flakes swirled down Genesee Street. No cars were in sight. A few disgruntled-looking pedestrians edged past him.

Quill glanced up from her laptop. She'd brought the television into her small living room right after dinner, with the irritable conviction that at some point during the evening, a crowd of maddened Syracusians would descend on the Channel 14 studios and give Boomer his just desserts.

Quill paused in the composition of her letter to the all-new on-line Channel 14 web site. The laptop was propped on her knees, and her feet were on the coffee table. Max sprawled on the floor, his nose twitching in his sleep.

A nice, thin layer of new snow dusted the deserted grounds of the Inn. The dining room was closed. All the guests had checked out. The staff had scattered. Meg was at Andy's. John was in his apartment over the carriage house. Mike the grounds-keeper was playing poker at the Hemlock Falls village garage with the other volunteer snowplow drivers. There was no blizzard, of course. The storm—if indeed there had been a storm—was on its way to the vast, underpopulated plains of central Canada.

". . . sustained a loss of approximately four thousand dollars in room rental," Quill input crossly, "due to the irresponsible reporting tactics of your weatherman, which is not covered by our Acts of God policy, since there wasn't an Act of God."

"Well, folks," Boomer said engagingly, "it looks like the Boomer blew it this time."

"No *shit*," somebody yelled off-camera.

"And I have to say, better safe than sorry. If that blizzard *had* hit our fair city, and we were unprepared, goodness knows the toll of lives and property that would have resulted. Well, folks, if you're snug at home tonight, take advantage of the little holiday the Boomer's arranged for you, and log on to the City of Love, the Boomer's second favorite web site . . ."

Quill reached for the remote and clicked the television off. Boomer's first favorite, she had learned, was the very same online hot line to which she was going to send this letter. "Like the boy who cried wolf," she input, ". . . the kind of media irresponsibility . . ." She paused. She'd used irresponsible twice in the space of two sentences. She lifted her head, musing into the silence.

She was surrounded by silence. Utter, total, blissful silence. No phone calls to return, no kitchen quarrels to settle, no cranky guests to propitiate. "And no guilt, Max," she said. "There isn't a blessed thing I should be doing that I'm not doing." She stretched luxuriously. Even her arms and hands felt good.

She hit the delete key, sending the letter about Boomer into the cyber dump. Max flopped over on his back and regarded her upside down. He grinned. His eyes closed. He slept.

Quill looked back at the screen. The Go To feature blinked at her. There was another item she could delete, while she was at it. Quill pulled thoughtfully on her lower lip, then keyed in: www.CityofLove.com.

The site was simple to navigate. She tapped in "Art" in the space for her handle, then "stopit" for her password. There was a short pause, and the screen read: "Welcome, Art! You have 5 responses in your mailbox! Love Conquers All!" Right below the message were five beating hearts.

She squeaked. There wasn't any other word for it. She hadn't squeaked since she was eleven and Ernie Schofield dropped a worm down her back. Max raised his head and thumped his tail on the floor.

"Go back to sleep, Max."

He looked a question and then barked.

"Tell you what. You don't say a word, not a word to anybody, and we'll go out for a walk in the snow."

Max shambled to his feet, grinning. "Two minutes, Max." Quill scrolled down and tapped gingerly at the first heart. Joss Roberts, if it were he who had designed the architecture, certainly knew what he was doing. The messages downloaded like Superman, faster than a speeding bullet. All but one had photographs.

"I've shown you mine. You show me yours.—Don" The picture that accompanied this somewhat abrupt request was of a very good-looking man in his late forties.

"What would Miss Manners say, Max?"

Max, not hearing the word "walk" in this comment, merely grunted.

"Do I have to respond to this stuff?" She sighed, then tapped in: "Thanks. But I don't go out with guys prettier than I am. Sincerely, Art."

The second was from a man who described himself as "widower" looking for a woman five feet three, with blonde hair, who liked to cook and clean, and who wore a size eight dress and size six shoes. Quill replied sympathetically, but firmly. The third was from a manager who had just lost his job at Xerox, in nearby Rochester. He described himself as willing to relocate for the right woman, as long as she was financially secure. Quill suggested South Carolina. The fourth was an absolutely gorgeous guy in swimming trunks, whose handle was Adonis.

Quill looked for a long moment at Adonis. "Wow," she said. Adonis was a bodybuilder, looking for a female bodybuilder. It was a studio photo. "And he's a lawyer, Max." Quill read on, "And he likes to work out at the beach. I wonder which beach. No," she said firmly, "No and no." She wrote as much in her response.

The last message had no photo, but the single line:

"Is it you? After all these years, is it you? If it is, be careful!" Max growled.

"Hang on, Max." I'm sorry, Quill input, but no, it's not me. And yes, I'll be careful. "There. Finished." She deleted her profile, typed "Yes" when the dialogue box inquired reproachfully, "Are you sure you want to leave CityofLove.com?" and got ready to take Max for a walk.

Max bounced happily out the front door and into the fresh

winter's night. Quill shrugged her coat collar around her ears, pulled on her gloves, and followed him. Max rolled vigorously, and then dug his nose into the thin, powdery drifts. A light breeze puffed handfuls of snow along the asphalt drive.

The sound of the waterfall was a soothing counterpoint to the still air. Quill took a deep breath. Stiffened against the cold, she walked down the driveway and crossed into the park.

It had been too long since she'd been out on a winter's night. The moon was a thumbnail; the stars smudged points of light against the dark sky. Quill stretched her legs, taking longer and longer strides.

She hit an icy patch, and she fell hard. She lay for a moment, ignoring the ache in her hip. Max ran around in frantic circles, tugging at her boots, her jacket, wanting to play. She rolled over on her back and said, "Dammit." She got to her feet and walked on. She was leaning, herself, to a diagnosis of Lou Gehrig's disease. ALS. A perfectly healthy person wouldn't have slipped on the ice like that.

Unless it was just that her boot slipped, and that a whole month of inactivity had made her muscles liquefy into good old fat.

By the time she passed the statue of old General C. C. Hemlock, she'd walked herself into high spirits. She crossed Main and turned left, passing Esther's shuttered dress shop and the stone house that had briefly housed the restaurant she and Meg had opened that spring. A bright new sign hung in the front window: FOR SALE, COMMERCIAL SPACE, Marge Schmidt Realty. The property wouldn't be up long; space in the village was at a premium.

The parking lot of the Croh Bar was crowded. Quill paused outside. "What do you think, Max?"

Max, investigating the base of a fire hydrant, barked cheerfully, then took off around the building at a dead run. Quill looked at him with exasperated affection and trudged into the Croh Bar to warm up.

Most of Hemlock Falls seemed to be crowded into the dark room. There wasn't any music—Marge Schmidt, who had acquired the Croh Bar some months earlier—loathed too much noise. She'd gone to England in her youth, and had decided that the one thing the English knew was how to run a bar. "You oughta," Marge said frequently, "be able to hear yourself think."

Conversation was a cheerful rumble. The wood stove in the corner gave off welcome heat. Quill stamped her feet free of snow and zipped open her jacket. She edged her way to one of the few empty barstools and sat down with a grateful sigh. Marge herself was behind the bar, face flushed. "Well," she said by way of greeting. "Look what the dog dragged in. Where is he, by the way? Not in my dumpster?"

"Your dumpster's in the back?"

" 'Course my dumpster's in the back."

"Well," Quill said. "Then he probably is. I'll go get him, Marge."

Marge roared, "Betty!" Her partner pushed open the door from the kitchen and poked an inquiring face around the edge. "That damn dog's in the garbage!"

"Nope. He's in here," Betty said briefly.

"Oh, dear. I'll get him and take him home." Quill got off the stool. Marge waved her back. "Nah. We had a prime rib special earlier. Betty'll give him a bone back there."

"Thanks," Quill said, surprised. Marge, possibly the richest person in Tompkins County—certainly the richest resident of Hemlock Falls—stayed that way by practicing extreme thrift.

"Yeah, well, that Doreen gave Carol Ann a good smack in the jaw yesterday. There's a freebie for her, too, if she comes on in here tonight. Wanted to do that myself a couple of times. You tell her to keep it up. Besides, everybody else has showed up. You might as well stick around and wait for the snow." Marge never smiled, exactly, but her weather-beaten face sort of melted on occasion, like cheese on toast, as it did now. "Got a blizzard special on. Hot mulled cider."

Quill accepted the mug gratefully. It did look as though almost everyone in the village had taken the night off to spend it at the Croh Bar. Quill waved to Esther and the mayor and his wife and nodded to the notoriously taciturn Harland Peterson. A lone figure in the corner rose and made its way toward her. Quill squinted in the dim light.

"Joss Roberts," he said, extending his hand.

"Of course. You designed the web site." Freddie Bellini, who'd been sitting next to Quill at the bar obligingly moved one stool over, and Roberts settled next to her. "It's a terrific piece of work," Quill said. "I don't know a lot . . ."

". . . about computers, but you know what you like," he finished. A smile lit his face, making him look years younger. Quill was struck again with the sense she knew him from somewhere else. "I'll bet you get a lot of that."

"Me? Oh . . ." Quill felt herself blushing. "You mean my, um—er."

"I know a lot about art. And I like your work a lot."

"You do?" Quill glanced at his left hand. No ring. Rather nervously, she realized she was flirting.

"You signed up for City of Love, too, huh, Quill?" Marge, swiping down the bar with an extremely clean rag, gave Joss Roberts an approving nod. "You got yourself a nice little business there, Joss. I wouldn't mind learning about this Internet stuff myself."

"Just what," Esther said earnestly into Quill's ear, "*is* the Internet, Joss? And I'll have another one of those mulled ciders, Marge." She leaned across Quill, who found herself shifting off the barstool to let Esther by.

"Actually, we'd both like to learn more about the exciting world of cyberspace." Miriam Doncaster's elbow landed in Quill's ribs. "Oh! Quill! Sorry. I didn't see you there!" Then in a fierce undervoice, "Are you planning on grabbing *all* the single men in Hemlock Falls?"

Quill gave an indignant gasp and choked on her cider. She endured several obliging pats on the back, and ended up three feet from the bar with no empty seat in sight. She sat down next to Harland (who had a table all to himself) and nodded to him again. Harland smelled pleasantly of cows.

"How are you, Harland?" Quill asked.

"Good."

"And the cows?"

"Good."

"Seen any good movies lately?"

He nodded.

Quill raised her eyebrows encouragingly.

"Over to Ithaca."

"With Marge?"

He nodded.

"And how was it?"

"Good."

Quill gave up. Harland had never been big on social chitchat. She left three dollars on the bar for her cider, picked up her coat and boots, went into the kitchen to retrieve Max, and left the Croh Bar by the back door. A second light snow was falling.

Suddenly, she was exhausted. Her legs trembled. Her arms felt heavy. She was, she decided in a spurt of crankiness, too young to be this out of shape. She'd walked the two miles from the Inn into town, and she could damn well walk back. It was an easy walk, too, with a slow grade. Doreen and Stoke lived in the village and Doreen walked it every single day in the spring and summer and Doreen was seventy-two years old.

"Besides, Max, there is one, exactly one taxi in Hemlock Falls and he goes to Florida in the winter."

Max, with infuriating energy, was making wide circles in the road.

Quill put one foot in front of the other. It wasn't particularly cold, just barely below freezing. She trudged across the parking lot, and then turned onto the sidewalk.

She had to sit down.

She stopped, feeling herself sway a little.

"Or," she said to Max, "we could go over to Doreen's and get a cup of coffee."

Max sat down and looked at her. She felt his paw rake her boot, heard his whine, as if at a distance.

"Quill?"

She knew that voice, all too well. "Oh, no," she said. "It's you."

"You're sure you don't want me to call Andy."

"Very sure." Quill tucked her feet under her and smoothed the afghan over her knees. "He'll just tell me that he didn't mean that I should get *that* much exercise. I saw him yesterday. My annual checkup," she added airily.

Myles sat in the Eames chair opposite her couch. He looked as he always looked: solid and reassuring. But there was more gray in his hair, and the lines around his eyes were deeper. "And I've already told you, I don't know what the heck Marge put in that cider, but I'll bet half the village is snockered before the late night news."

He laughed. "You could be right."

"So. I haven't seen you for a while. Somebody told me you were home. It was a long assignment this time."

He nodded. "Yep."

"And you were successful?"

"More or less."

"You *are* related to Harland Peterson. No. No. Don't deny it. You two are brothers under the skin."

There was a long pause. She hesitated. "Are you back for a while, or off again?"

"I'll be here for a few months."

It was strange and uncomfortable to sit with him, as she had for years when they were together, the two of them in their accustomed places. "Well, thanks for the rescue."

"Any time."

Quill made a sudden movement to get up. "Would you like anything? Wine?"

"Relax, Quill." He clasped his hands and leaned forward. "What have you been doing to yourself?"

"I look haggard, don't I? No sleep. No time." Quill raised one arm and pointed back to the easel.

"Mind if I look?"

"No," she said slowly. "No, I don't mind."

She didn't turn around. But she heard the rustle of the drop cloth as he pulled it aside. He didn't say anything, but she could almost feel the intensity of his absorption. He let the cloth fall, and then she felt his hand on her shoulder.

"I don't want to say it. But it's worth what it cost you. If that's what this is all about." He grasped her wrist, thin, now that she'd lost weight, and then let it go.

"I don't know what it's all about." She bent forward so he couldn't see her face. "I don't know what anything's all about."

The phone shrilled through the quiet. Quill glanced at her watch: ten o'clock. Harker. She let it ring, three times, four, then reached to the end table and picked up.

"Quill?"

"Hi!" She turned slightly away from Myles. Her voice was at least three decibels higher than usual.

Harker didn't say anything for a moment. Then he said, "This your Bob Barker imitation. You're auditioning?"

"Oh, no. No." Her smile was plastered on; she could feel it. "But it's kind of a bad time. Could you call back?"

"That's a little difficult. There's a party at Fortesque. I promised to make an appearance. Everything's all set for the weekend?"

He could feel her hesitation. That was the thing about Harker. His intuition was almost spooky. She, in turn, felt his withdrawal. "Everything's *not* all set for the weekend," he said. "Are you rescinding the invitation?"

"It's just . . ." Quill cleared her throat. "It's going to be so busy, Harker. And it looks like we're going to be short-staffed. I may have to co-opt you into waiting tables."

"I see," he said shortly.

"Look," Quill said, "If we could talk a little later?"

"Tomorrow," he said. "Don't fail me, Quill. What we have . . ."

"Yes," Quill said. "Okay." She hung up, aware that her face was flaming red. She glanced at Myles. He gave her a rueful smile.

"You said you'd like some wine?"

"No, thank you. I'd better be going." He got up; he was tall, and Quill felt small on the couch. "You're sure you're going to be all right?"

"If I don't keel over in total embarrassment," Quill said, crossly. "Honestly, Myles, I'm behaving as if I'm sixteen years old. I'm sorry."

"A love interest, I take it."

Quill blinked. Love interest. It seemed a peculiar way to characterize Harker.

Apparently, her expression was sufficient response for Myles. "Is it serious?"

"Serious," Quill repeated, stupidly. "I thought so. It's the oddest thing, Myles. But I've been going up to New York to see him every weekend." She stopped, abruptly. "I hope it's okay to talk about this with you."

"I wouldn't ask if it weren't, Quill."

She thought about the slight edge to his voice. It wasn't jealousy. She knew for a fact Myles was seeing a woman in Syracuse. Miriam Doncaster's younger sister's best friend had seen Myles and his date in Syracuse a few weeks ago. It was the focus thing again. It annoyed everybody. Kath had been right. She wasn't clear enough with people. Not with the staff, not with Myles or Harker. Certainly not with herself. And Myles was the clearest thinker she knew. It was over between them. It'd been over for months. And they had agreed, she'd insisted, that they remain friends. And who better than a friend than help her sort this out?

"Quill?"

She'd been staring at him. She gripped the afghan. "I've been to New York every weekend for the past month. This man, his name is Harker, he's an artist, Myles. Oils," she added thoughtfully, "not my medium."

"No, your medium is acrylic," Myles agreed. Was there a hint of amusement there?

"At any rate. We just clicked."

"Clicked?"

"It was as if we knew everything about each other from the moment we saw each other." Myles raised his eyebrows. Quill scowled. "That's your skeptical look. I know it sounds like a Clairol commercial, but it's true. That's the thing about clichés, you know. They hang around because they're true."

"I wasn't aware of being skeptical. But it does seem a bit far-fetched. On the other hand, I've heard that these things happen. So. It's a perfect fit." He took a breath and let it out. If Quill hadn't known better, she would have called it a sigh. "And? What's the problem?"

"I need to be two people, I guess. I'm being pulled two ways. I feel like the baby in front of the king."

Myles cleared his throat. He was definitely amused. Quill relaxed a little. The atmosphere was lightening. "All right. I'll bite. Which baby? What king?"

"You know. Solomon and the two mothers that each wanted the baby?"

"And you feel like the baby. As if you should be cut in half to please both parties."

"I'm going berserk," Quill said gloomily.

That drew a genuine laugh. "You'll be fine."

For some reason, this made Quill crosser than ever.

"You have a big weekend coming up?"

"Yes. I mean, as far as bookings go. Boomer Dougherty. Meteorologists," she added, as if this clarified matters.

"No corpses this time?"

Quill hesitated. Decision time. "Well, actually, there *is* a corpse."

"George Nash?"

"You've heard about it, of course." Everyone always seemed

to end up telling Myles everything. "But there's something about George Nash I've never told you. I think I'd like you to hear it."

He listened well. That was another thing about Myles. He didn't override her, or make decisions for her, or tell her what she ought to do—unless it was to stay out of police business—and even then, he tended to a rueful kind of resignation. And he listened well.

"So," he said. "An unusual coincidence, you think."

"Don't you?"

"Hard to say. I've known stranger ones." He smiled. "But that's a good lead on the Honda. I'll make a couple of calls, see if I can pass it along to Syracuse. There haven't been any other—er—what did you call them? Anomalies?"

"Just . . ." Quill hesitated. If she mentioned the odd message on the computer, she'd have to explain about the dating web site and she'd embarrassed herself quite enough this evening. She had an idea about tracking that message anyway. And if she were right—then that was the time to tell him. "Nothing. I'm seeing connections between things that aren't there." She sneezed. "And this—whatever it is—is making my brain soggy."

"It is, is it?"

She grinned at him. "And don't you say any soggier than usual."

Myles crossed his legs and seemed to change the subject. "I've heard that business is going well."

"We've made a profit every month since we've reopened."

"Then, like Hamlet, your only problem is indecision. Not soggy brain syndrome."

Quill flung her arms in the air. "Well, Hamlet did eventually decide—and look what happened to him! The bloodiest fifth act in drama." Myles crossed the room to the front door, Max at his heels. "You're leaving?"

"Give me a call, Quill. When you've made up your mind."

He left, closing the door gently. Quill stared after him. The room seemed empty suddenly. Max thudded to the couch and looked up at her.

"So much for clarity, Max." She ran his floppy ears between her fingers. The phone rang, making her jump. She eyed it warily. Harker may have decided against the party. Meg wouldn't call this late. Abruptly, she was furious. She was right. She was going berserk. Even the simplest decisions were unmakeable. She grabbed the phone when it seemed as if the burring would never stop.

"Hello," she said. "Harker?"

A long, hissing silence, like a cold wind. And then, a voice, almost too faint to hear: Not Harker. Not Meg. Not anyone she knew.

"Is it you? After all these years, is it you? If it is, be careful. Be really careful."

Quill hung up the phone with a slam. She got up to go after Myles. She sat down again. "Give me a call, Quill. When you've made up your mind."

She'd wait. She could solve this particular problem herself.

# CHAPTER 13

The phone jerked Quill out of a sound sleep. She stared at it, confused, her heart pounding so hard she had to fight for breath. Had she dreamed it? *Is it you? After all these years, is it you? If it is, be careful!*

Suddenly angry, she snatched the receiver and shouted into it, "Who is this! How dare you! Who *is* this?"

No answer, just the hum of the equipment. Max, who'd been curled at the foot of the bed, hopped onto the floor with a thump. Then, a startled question, "Quill? Are you okay?"

"Andy." Quill fell back against the pillow. "Um. Sorry. I thought it was someone else. I was having a dream. I was asleep."

"Sorry, kiddo. Meg always said you were up before the roosters. I thought you'd be up and painting by now."

"What time is it?" Quill narrowed her eyes at her bedside clock. The numbers were fuzzy. Great. On top of everything else, she was going to need spectacles.

"Seven-thirty. Do you need a few minutes? Would you like me to call back?"

"No. I'm fine." She swung her feet to the floor and looked down at her toes. She'd fiddled a bit with the painting before she'd gone to bed last night, and it had been three o'clock before she'd gone to sleep. The fuzzy vision was clearing. "But you'd know better than I would. Am I fine?"

"I'd like you to run up to Ithaca for a few more tests."

Max shoved his nose into her knees and whined. Quill scratched his ears to give her time to control her voice. "What kind of tests?"

"A myelogram. It's a test to determine how well your nerves are firing. And a CAT scan. I'd like to know what's going on in your medulla oblongata."

"That sounds like the first line of a Cole Porter song."

"Hm. Anyway, the sooner the better. I've made a couple of calls, and I've set a few appointments up for tomorrow."

"Friday," Quill said. "That's awfully fast, Andy. We've got a full weekend here at the Inn. I don't think I can take the time right now. What about Monday?"

"What about tomorrow," Andy said firmly. "Is there someone who can take you up there? I'd rather you didn't drive right now."

Quill tugged nervously at a tendril of hair over her left ear. It came off in her hand. She stared at it numbly.

"Quill? I don't mean to alarm you with this at all. These tests are just a precaution."

"Yes," Quill said. The logical part of her brain knew this was true. There was no alarm at all in Andy's voice. If anything, he sounded obnoxiously chipper. He was always the kind of guy that double-wrapped his garbage and kept everything in his closets indexed. She let the red-gold pieces fall to her lap. "Andy . . ."

"The myelogram and the CAT scan are scheduled for the morning. Then you're to drop down to the lab. You're going to donate a little more blood to the cause."

"Andy, my hair's falling out!" Quill didn't know whether to scream or laugh. "Andy, what *is* this!"

"Take it easy, Quill. The preliminary blood tests tell me your white blood cell count is up a little, and your red count's down. We could be looking at a thyroid issue, or some other endocrine imbalance. Or just plain old stress. And most of us lose a little hair in the fall. It's normal. The myelogram and the CAT scan are just to rule out other major stuff. Unlikely stuff."

"For example." Quill ran her free hand through her hair. There'd been more than the usual hair in her brush and comb lately. She was positive of it. Oh, sure. Andy was right. Everybody lost hair when the weather turned cold. And when they were under stress. And when they drank too much coffee and didn't get enough sleep. "What?" she said. "What kind of unlikely stuff?"

"The unlikely stuff would be growths on the pituitary gland.

That sort of thing." He chuckled. "Of course, I'd say the chances of that were slim to none. I'm just being thorough. My best guess—and it's a very educated guess, Quill—is that your thyroid's a little wonky."

"Can I look that up in the *Merck Manual*? Wonky thyroid."

"You bet. Look here, Quill." Andy's voice was kind, and as far as Quill could tell, unworried. "Both you and Meg are bouncingly healthy. This is a glitch, probably a temporary one, but I'm not taking any chances. Mostly," he added cheerfully, "because Meg would kill me if I missed anything. So I'm being very thorough."

"I'm going bald," Quill said. "My hair's coming out. Just now. I can't stand being bald."

"Hair loss just reinforces my opinion that we need to rule it out. Thyroid."

"It's not your hair," Quill muttered.

"What?"

"I said it's not your hair. Men don't understand about hair. A lot of men look great bald. I can't think of one woman who looks good bald."

"Sinead O'Connor," Andy said promptly. "There's one. And you're not going bald, Quill. You'll get to those appointments tomorrow? The sooner we establish the problem, the sooner your hair will stop falling out."

"Ha, ha," Quill said. She stood up and craned her neck to look in the mirror over her dresser. Her hair was still there. "Okay, yes, I'll think of something to tell Meg and Doreen. You still haven't said anything to Meg."

"Scout's honor. But I want you to take someone with you. You've reported dizzy spells, it's right here in my notes. So here's the deal. I won't say a word to Meg if you get someone to drive you to Ithaca."

"I thought the Hippocratic oath barred you guys from blackmail."

"Nope. So, let me hear you say, 'You know best, Dr. Bishop.' "

Quill could count the times she'd used four-letter words on one hand. She used one now. Andy chuckled again and hung up.

Max looked up at her and barked twice. His tail wagged vigorously. He raced off to her small kitchen, and returned with his empty food bowl in his jaws.

"Fine," Quill said. "What kind of dog are you, anyway? I'm probably dying of a dread disease. At the very least, I'm going bald. And do you care? No. Lassie would be ratting on Timmy to his mom right now. Rin Tin Tin would be howling in sympathy. You, you want food." She marched to her front door and opened it. "Go find Doreen, or Meg, and ask them for breakfast."

Max, who liked going out even more than he liked to eat, gave an approving bark and disappeared down the hall.

Quill shut the door and went back to her mirror. She stared at herself. She was vaguely aware of the symptoms of thyroid deficiency. Dry skin, weight loss, hair loss. She was also pretty sure that thyroid problems were fixable, unlike, say, amyotrophic lateral sclerosis. Or a grade IV astrocytoma. Or a slew of a lot of other polysyllabic dread diseases, whose names, for some reason, she could readily recite. And she knew that Andy was right, she should go to Ithaca with somebody. Not Meg, who would fuss and drive her bananas. Not Doreen, who not only would fuss, but was more than capable of publishing the news in her "Folks of Note" column in the weekly *Gazette* with a plea to half the village to keep an eye on Quill's well-being. The trouble with the women she loved was that they would fuss.

Men, on the other hand, tended not to fuss. Asking John would send the wrong message. The logical choice was Harker. The romantic choice was Harker.

Quill made coffee, rather defiantly using the caffeinated French blend. It would be embarrassing to ask Harker. Thyroid problems were not romantic. Going bald was definitely not romantic. And for artists like Harker, who loved and admired the grace of the human body, skinniness was revolting and unhealthy.

Maybe she could avoid the stupid tests altogether. Quill glumly contemplated her bald and skinny future if she didn't go to get her thyroid checked out. She needed a friend who wouldn't make judgments. Who would take with equanimity the possibility that it couldn't be fixed. So, she needed someone practical, who'd put the whole dumb, annoying, scary problem in perspective, and who wouldn't be revolted if she were bald for the rest of her life, and who would feed her milkshakes to keep her from being skinny, and who wouldn't fuss.

She picked up the phone and dialed Myles's number.

"McHale residence," said an unfamiliar, unmistakably female voice.

"Um," Quill said.

"Hello? Hello?"

"This is AT and T," Quill said. "Would you be interested in changing your long distance carrier?"

"One moment, please. I'll check."

"Wait!" Quill shouted. And before she could hang up, Myles was on the phone, and she remembered, too late, that he had caller ID and would know precisely where this call was coming from.

"Quill?"

"Sorry," she said casually. "I dialed out of habit. Didn't mean to get you out of bed, but now that I did, have a nice day."

"Janice said she didn't realize it was you, but hello, anyway."

"Janice Peterson?" Janice made an excellent living as a cleaning lady. As a matter of fact, she'd been Myles's cleaning lady for years. She was also sixty-three years old and long-married. "You tell her hello right back," Quill said heartily. Then, because if she stopped to think about it, she'd dither and not ask him at all, she simply told him, and he said, of course, no problem, he'd go with her to Ithaca.

Quill said good-bye, and hung up. She was still staring at the phone when it rang again.

Ominous mystery callers didn't do it at eight o'clock in the morning. Quill picked up the phone with confidence. "Kimmie Bloomfield is here," Dina said. "She wanted to know if you could come down to breakfast so you could talk."

"Oh, man," Quill said, in a very cowardly way. "Is she upset?"

"Um—yeah."

"She's Meg's friend, Dina. Not mine."

"Meg's busy with the chutneys."

"Well, I'm busy with my canvas."

"She looks kind of, like, distracted," Dina whispered. "Like she's going to cry and whatever right here in the foyer. Want me to tell her to go away?"

"No. Just give me a few minutes. I have to make one more

phone call and get dressed. Put her in the dining room, would you, Dina?"

"Are you calling Harker?"

"Dina!"

"I just wondered, that's all. I kind of accidentally picked up the phone down here and heard you asking the sheriff to take you to Ithaca tomorrow, and everybody knows Harker's coming in on the train, and how can you meet him if you're off having lunch in Ithaca with the sheriff? I think," Dina added sunnily, "that you guys ought to try Elise's. It's a very romantic . . ."

"Dina, if you listen in on my phone calls one more time, I am going to kill you. And after I kill you, I am going to fire you. And after I fire you, I'm going to call your parents and after that—"

"O-*kay*," Dina said. "Jeez. I'm sorry. It was a mistake."

Quill banged the phone down and wished heartily for the days when people communicated by letters. Or even further back than that—smoke signals, maybe.

She called Harker, who turned out not to be there. She showered and dressed. She went downstairs to listen to somebody else's problems instead of her own.

"You look awfully tired." Kimmie Bloomfield drummed her fingers nervously on the tablecloth. "Are you sure I'm not imposing on you?"

Quill didn't say what she was thinking: that she couldn't possibly look as tired as Kimmie did. "I've been a little tired," she admitted. "But it comes and it goes. Shall we have some coffee? Or hot chocolate. Just the thing for a cold November morning." She looked over Kimmie's shoulder and wiggled her eyebrows at Kathleen, who was clearing tables nearby. She gave Quill a thumbs-up and disappeared through the swinging doors to the kitchen. The five temporary wait staff John had recruited from the Syracuse agency were all due for a training session in half an hour, and Kathleen's mood was sunny. A lot sunnier, Quill reflected gloomily, than her own, or for that matter, the weather itself. Where could Harker be before eight o'clock in the morning? Why wasn't he there when she'd called? He never rose before ten, if he could help it.

She looked out the windows, an activity that rarely failed to soothe her spirits. Gray morning light filtered through the dining room windows. The sky hung heavy over the icy falls. Last night's snow was a thin coverlet on the lawn.

"I really need the job," Kimmie said. Kimmie, who had nervously greeted Quill with a request "just to talk," was dressed for bad weather in a gorgeous thick sweater and Versace jeans. Quill, who'd thrown on sweatpants and a flannel-lined shirt, felt skinny, bald, and dowdy.

"So what do you think?" Kimmie prodded. "I'm very reliable, and I pick up things very quickly. I know I could do a good job. I mean, Meg and Doreen don't seem to think so, but honestly, Quill, don't you think they're being a bit elitist? A doctor's wife can be just as good a waitress as anybody else. I haven't always been a doctor's wife. And of course, I don't intend to be a doctor's wife much longer."

She said this with such an air of desperation that Quill couldn't refuse further confidence. Her day was already full— and Quill wanted to say that she was the last person in Hemlock Falls, or for that matter, the entire state of New York, qualified to give anybody advice about anything—much less problems with husbands. But she heard herself ask, "Did you have a career outside the home? Before you met Louis?"

Kimmie took a deep breath. "I certainly *did*." And the floodgates were open. Quill nodded sympathetically through the torrent of complaints.

Rescue arrived fifteen minutes later with Meg and the hot chocolate. She set the tray on the table, and then dropped cheerfully into the chair next to Quill. "Sorry this took so long, but some of the temps showed up early, and I sent Kath off to begin their training. And Kath said that you were out here with Quill, Kimmie, and she said if you still want a job, you should join them."

Kimmie, jerked from a somewhat weepy recitation of the miseries of her life, blinked rapidly. "You mean I'm hired?" She smiled in a bewildered way. "I mean, so it's okay if I come to work for you?"

"Sure," Meg said. "Right, Quill?"

Quill, who had already decided that Kimmie was far too volatile at the moment to shovel snow, much less serve a clutch of demanding meteorologists, decided to ignore Meg's interference in her, Quill's, managerial duties. She regarded her sister with a baleful eye. Bouncy. Meg was in a bouncy mood. And she'd done something weird with her hair again. "Was there a sale on mousse that I missed?"

Meg gingerly patted the top of her head. "What do you *honestly* think?"

"I honestly think it looks like Max's dinner."

Meg grabbed a tendril over her ear, and tried to look at it. Since her hair was as short as it always was, she succeeded only in looking cross-eyed. "Andy's getting close to setting a date for the wedding, Quill, and I've developed this kind of compulsion to fiddle with my hair. You've probably noticed."

"I've noticed."

"And I have to go to Joss Roberts's office this morning to get my picture taken with his digital camera, so I thought, gee, what a perfect time to try out this mousse Dina gave me. What do you think? Never mind. You've told me what you think."

"Why is Joss Roberts taking your picture? I thought he was a computer programmer."

"Architect," Meg said. "He's a computer architect. They're the ones who create the platform for the programmers."

Quill leaned across the silver chocolate pot. "I don't care."

"What?"

"I don't care what a computer architect does. I already know too much."

"Too much about what?"

Quill waved her hands rather helplessly. "About everything. I've decided I'm going to stick to finding out things I really do need to know. Like, why is Joss Roberts taking your picture?"

"It's for the Hemlock Falls web site. I'm going to judge that stupid dessert contest, and Joss thinks it'd be great if my face were on-line. I'm meeting him at his office at nine. Want to come with me?"

Kimmie, with a justifiably irritated look, stood up abruptly, dabbing at the tears on her face. "So I guess I don't get the job?"

Quill felt horrible immediately. "I'm sorry, Kimmie. Of course you can work for us if you like. But why don't you take a few days to think it over? I'm sure you'll be a wonderful waitress if you decide to join us," Quill added. "We'll be happy to have you on staff."

"And I want to *be* on staff," Kimmie said earnestly. She smoothed the sleeves of her elegant sweater. "I just hadn't planned to start right now. How long will the training session this morning take?"

"All morning," Quill said, who had no idea how far Kath had gone in her sessions the day before. "And probably after lunch."

"I have a few errands to run, Quill. It's not that I don't want to work. I do, I really do. I just hadn't planned on starting this morning. And I thought, you know, that we'd have a chance to talk a little more. But if you're going to see this computer guy, maybe we ought to put the rest of the interview off for another time. Unless you aren't leaving?"

"No, no." Quill rose to her, and so did Meg. "As a matter of fact, I have to ask Joss Roberts a few questions about another matter. So perhaps we can talk later in the week, Kimmie." She reached over and gave Kimmie's hand a gentle squeeze. "It'll work out," she said, meaninglessly.

"Do you think so?" Kimmie blinked back tears. "Do you really think so?"

"What exactly is she trying to work out?" Meg asked a few moments later. They were in Meg's car, a little Ford Escort that she rarely used, because, she'd told Quill crossly, there was no way to get the Honda out of the vegetable garden without wrecking the winter crop of Brussels sprouts. And she had and it did and Meg wasn't going to ride with Quill anywhere, anymore.

Meg downshifted to accommodate the icy driveway, and the little car bucked. "Kimmie's a little young for a midlife crisis, and how much of a crisis can she have with a great new house, and a nice guy for a husband, anyway?"

"If you're inferring that the success of a woman's life has to do with the state of her house and her husband, I'll put it down to wedding neurosis." Quill kept her feet firmly planted on the floorboards. She hated it when Meg drove. As a matter of fact, she hated it when anybody else drove. Except Myles.

"Divorce?" Meg said, loudly.

Quill jerked to attention. "Sorry. No, I mean, yes, she's talking divorce. They don't have any kids, he wants them, she doesn't think she should risk it after that miscarriage a few weeks ago and she needs something significant in her life. That's pretty much . . . Meg, the light's red."

Meg gunned the accelerator and swept on through the intersection, then turned onto Main Street. "The light's yellow. And we're late for the meeting."

"How come I get all the tickets?" Quill said. "How come you don't get tickets? You've never had a ticket in your life."

"I am a very good driver," Meg said seriously. She took one hand off the steering wheel and patted her hair. The Escort swerved suddenly, slamming Quill sideways. Meg recovered the wheel and straightened them out. "See that? Instant reflexes. If I didn't have such great reflexes I would have hit your dog."

"Max?" Quill leaned forward and looked out the windshield. Max shot across Main Street, then galloped behind the Croh Bar. "Darn it, if he's in the dumpsters again, he's going to be in big trouble when I catch him."

Meg pulled into the parking strip behind the store Roberts had rented. He'd taken space two stores down from Esther West's dress shop, and Quill noticed that Max the garbage hound had already made a visit to Esther's dumpster.

"Okay, how do I look?" Meg peered into the rearview mirror and patted her hair.

"Does Roberts use a digital camera? I understand you can edit photos with it."

"How *rude,*" Meg said cheerfully. "Are you coming in with me? Or was it a clever ploy to avoid the trials and tribulations of Kimmie Bloomfield?"

They got out of the Escort at the same time, and Quill avoided a response. She waved Meg into Roberts's office, then trudged down the walkway to Esther's dumpster. By the time she'd cleared up all the garbage and walked into Roberts's office, Meg was scowling at the results of her photo session in front of a large computer screen. Joss Roberts stood behind her, and turned as Quill came in. A melancholy smile split his thin face.

Meg didn't look up. "Why didn't you tell me my hair looks horrible?"

"I did," Quill reminded her. She smiled and nodded to Roberts. "Hello again."

"Oh, you two've met?" Meg grabbed her purse and pulled out a comb, a small can of mousse, and a brush. "You have a bathroom here, or something, Joss? I have to fix this hair."

"Sure." He nodded toward the back. Quill removed the can of mousse from Meg's hand as she sped by.

"I like your office," Quill said politely.

Joss blushed slightly, which charmed her. "Let me show you around. I haven't quite finished moving in, you know. The Chamber hit me with a whole load of work as soon as I opened shop, and a lot of my stuff is still in boxes."

Quill made admiring noises as he showed her large pieces of equipment manufactured from the mysterious and ubiquitous stuff that encased most computer equipment. She genuinely warmed to a series of photographs of a small baby lined up on a shelf on the back wall. She picked the largest one up with a smile. "What a beautiful baby," she said.

Joss took the photograph from her hands and set it back among the others. "He's gone," he said quietly.

Quill wasn't sure how to respond to this. The child in the photographs was no older than a year. A divorce, Quill guessed. "Do you get to see him often?"

"No." Joss touched the photographs lightly in turn. "No. He's gone. He'll never be older than this. Gone."

"I see." Quill touched him lightly on the shoulder. "I'm so sorry. Joss, may I sit down for a moment? I have a question to ask."

Joss shook himself slightly. The haunted expression disappeared from his eyes, and he gestured toward a comfortable-looking couch near his desk. "Sure. What can I do for you?"

They settled themselves, Quill on the couch and Joss behind his desk. "I registered for City of Love." She grimaced a bit at his grin. "I mean, I didn't. Doreen Stoker did. For me. You know Doreen."

Joss really was attractive when he grinned. Quill bit her lip ruefully. "It doesn't matter how I registered. Anyway, I received a pile of e-mail."

"I'll bet you did. You know, you'll get even more hits if you let me put your photograph on the site."

"No!" Quill winced. "I didn't mean to sound so—um—"

"Nervous?"

"Not nervous. Well, maybe a little nervous. Anyway, I deleted my profile."

"Oh. I'm sorry, was there something about the web site that offended you? Is there . . ."

Quill tugged at her hair. "No, no, it's a beautiful web site, Joss, but I don't want to be a member." She screwed up her face in sympathy at his obvious chagrin. "Maybe in the future.

At the moment, I'm . . . involved with someone. And I don't really need to look any further."

"I'm sorry to hear that."

Quill acknowledged the regret in his voice with an embarrassed nod. "Well. Um. The last e-mail message I had was from someone whose . . . handle? Is that the right term? Whose handle was Searcher, and the message was 'Is it you? Is it really you?' "

"Um. Yeah. Well, a lot of these guys are a lot more inarticulate with writing than they are with words . . ."

Quill, nodding in agreement, interrupted, "You don't understand. I responded to that message—to all the messages in fact—with a thanks but no-thanks sort of thing, and then I deleted my profile, as I said, and last night . . . last night . . ." She stopped, floundering a bit. How to tell this man, who she didn't know at all, who had a life of his own that seemed to have a disproportionate share of tragedy, that the phone call had scared her out of her wits. That the remembered echo of the ghostly, whispering voice had kept her awake most of the night. "I got a phone call from someone who used exactly the same words. Exactly. 'Is it you? After all this time, is it really you?' "

"You're kidding." He ran one hand over his face. "Man, I'm really sorry about that. And you think that the guy who sent you the message on the web site is the same guy who phoned you."

Quill, who was finding it hard to meet Joss's steady, dark gaze, had thought since last night at the Croh Bar that it was Joss himself. But she said aloud, "So my question is, I guess, I thought this dating site was secure? I mean, there are notices all over City of Love itself that users are anonymous, blah, blah, blah. And everyone in the Chamber seems to think that it's impossible for casual users to find out who the person behind the profile really is. But is it?"

Joss's dark eyes flickered at Quill's slight emphasis on the word "casual." A shout and a muttered curse from behind the closed bathroom door reassured Quill that Meg was within hailing distance. "Nothing on a web site is secure," he said soberly. "Not only that, nothing is for certain. You can pretend to be anyone you want. On the other hand, it's probably nothing. But why don't you let me check it out. Did you save the guy's e-mail address?"

"I deleted all of it. Including my profile."

"You never really delete anything on a computer." He smiled a little. "Casual users don't, anyhow. I can drop by and check it out for you."

"I'd appreciate it a lot," Quill admitted. "I'd just like to know who it is. It's probably just a crank, don't you think?"

"We'll find out." Quietly, he turned over the leaves of the calendar sitting on his desk, his face shuttered. He had a talent for stillness. So did John Raintree, but John's physical reticence was born of economy; he spent energy when he needed to. The man across the desk was . . . wary, Quill decided. Watchful. "I can come by tonight. I need somebody here all the time in case the server goes down. It's difficult in a town this size to find people interested in computers. But there's a kid called Arnie Peterson who's pretty good. I can get him to come in tonight to baby-sit."

Quill mentally ran through the members of the Peterson clan. There were a lot of them. "Arnie's Harland's grandson, through his middle daughter, Arlette. He's only fifteen."

"Any adult with a real computer background ends up in Rochester or at Cornell."

"You didn't," Quill said, with a slight upward inflection.

"No. I'm not much on big cities. Or medium-sized ones, for that matter."

"What did bring you to Hemlock Falls?"

Joss didn't respond for a long moment. Quill engaged in a brief struggle with her conscience: she and Meg were pretty good amateur detectives—just try, she'd demanded once of Myles, to find another gourmet chef and innkeeper who'd solved eight, count 'em, eight, murder cases—but she never was comfortable with the fact that good detecting required lousy manners. On the other hand, she didn't want any more mysterious phone calls in the middle of the night. So she pushed a little. "I think Doreen told me that Boomer Dougherty invested in this. Do you know him well?"

"Boomer?" Joss looked momentarily confused. "Oh, yeah. The guy who predicts the weather. And yeah, he agreed to hire me to create the web site and maintain it. I heard about it through a friend of a friend."

Something about this answer was evasive. And it didn't quite jibe with what she'd heard about Boomer's investment from Doreen and Sylvia Prince. Quill tugged at her lower lip, but before she could ask what friend of a friend, Meg banged crossly into the room. Her hair was damp and flat.

"I've had it. I'm not a picky person, but I refuse to look like this in public. I'm sorry, Joss. I've wasted your time and mine this morning. Can I come back this afternoon? No, I can't come back this afternoon. What about tonight? No, I can't do it tonight. Aaagh! I look like a toad!"

"Let the computer fix it," Joss advised. "It'll take me five minutes to give you a new hairstyle. The wonders of digital technology, you know." He regarded Meg thoughtfully. "You might look pretty nice as a blonde. Would you like to try that?"

"I don't want a new hairstyle," Meg said. "I want my good *old* hairstyle. I want to look normal!"

Joss's cell phone shrilled, cutting Meg off in midshriek. Meg scrambled into her coat and boots as he answered it. Quill zipped up her winter jacket, her eyes on Joss. She heard his quiet "hello," then saw him start and turn to look out the front window at Main Street. "You're kidding," he said. "What? What?" The phone still to his ear, he went out the front door.

"Let's go," Meg said. "I can't believe I wasted everybody's time. I've got a ton of stuff to do back at the kitchen."

Joss stepped off the curb into the street. The phone was at his ear and he was listening hard, his face pale. He seemed oblivious to the cold. The set of his shoulders was tense. He turned and looked north, toward the train station.

He didn't hear the Honda as it roared out of nowhere behind him. And if he felt the tremendous blow that threw him three feet into the air, or the sickening crack as he landed, he wasn't able to let anyone know.

He didn't hear Quill's horrified "Stop!" And he wasn't aware of the two of them, Meg and Quill, racing into the street and kneeling by his limp and broken body.

By then he was dead.

# CHAPTER 14

"My car," Quill said. "I can't believe it. Somebody murdered Joss with my car."

"Have another glass of wine." Meg grabbed the cabernet and refilled both their glasses. The Honda had been confiscated by the Tompkins County sheriff's department and taken to the forensic lab in Syracuse. Joss Roberts's body was at the morgue in Ithaca. Meg and Quill were in the Tavern Lounge with John and Doreen. It was late.

"Just came out of the blue, like?" Doreen said. "I heard that Honda come barreling down Main Street at a hundred miles an hour. And you didn't see nothing? 'Course, you got the license plate number." She smiled, grimly.

Quill shook her head. "I kept telling Dave Kiddermeister whoever it was was in a ski mask. At least, I think it was a ski mask. It could have been a crazed Samoan who was heavily tattooed with red, green, and white stripes."

Doreen frowned disapprovingly at this attempt at humor.

"It all happened so fast," Meg said. She was pale, but her hands were steady. "The impact made the Honda swerve and almost tip over."

"Them SUVs," Doreen said darkly, "I told you they aren't all that steady."

"The Honda fishtailed on the street with this horrible, howling squeal. But the driver got it under control and *phuut!*" Meg motioned like a plane taking off.

The car had been found abandoned in Peterson Park. Myles had organized a search party, and they were in the park now, equipped with flashlights, searchlights, and for all Quill knew, candles.

She nibbled on a piece of Gouda. No one had had much appetite for dinner, so Doreen had insisted on putting cheese and crackers out for them. "It doesn't make any sense, guys," she said suddenly. "A Martian would know that a forensics lab can pick up all kinds of evidence from the car. Fiber samples, hair samples." She tugged cautiously at a curl over her ear. Some of her hair came away in her fingers. She took a healthy sip of wine.

John ran one hand through his own thick hair. "The entire murder doesn't make sense. Broad daylight, and a murder method that's chancy at best."

"That's true." Quill stared at John thoughtfully. "So the murderer was desperate."

"The murderer had a lot of guts," Doreen said bluntly. "I don't know about desperate. But it takes a lot of nerve to try something like that in broad daylight. And in front of witnesses."

"Experienced witnesses," John pointed out with a small grin. "All of us have had experience with murder before, but especially Meg and Quill."

"I don't know," Quill said doubtfully. "I've never actually seen a murder before."

"Yes, we have," Meg said quietly.

Quill put her hand on Meg's arm. "The Ross baby," she said. "Oh, lord. I'd forgotten about that."

Doreen raised an interrogative eyebrow and Quill shook her head slightly. She would tell both John and Doreen about that long-ago case another time.

"You had no idea who was on the phone?" John asked.

"None," Quill said flatly. "Were there two of them, in it together?"

"That's fruitless speculation," Meg said sharply. "So is Meg asking why someone would want to murder Joss. What do we know about him? Where did he come from? How long has he been in town? Who does he know? We don't know anything about him."

"Boomer Dougherty hired him," Doreen said. "And he's coming in tomorrow. Maybe he has some information."

"Maybe," John said. "But this whole web site business was put together in a highly informal way."

"It must have been," Quill said. "I asked Joss about how he ended up here, and I think he met Boomer once or twice. It didn't sound as if they knew each other at all."

"Why did you ask Joss all that?" Meg demanded.

"Because I've been getting weird phone calls, and I thought it might be him. He. Him. Whatever."

Meg ignored this flailing at correct grammar. "Weird phone calls? You never said a word about weird phone calls."

"It was just one, actually. A weird phone call and a weird e-mail."

"Obscene, like?" Doreen asked.

"No. It started with that stupid web site, Doreen," she added crossly. "There were five responses to the ad you made me post, and I answered all of them."

"You what!" Meg yelled.

"To say thanks, but no thanks," Quill said patiently, "honestly, Meg. Anyway, that same night, yesterday, actually, I got a phone call with the same words as the e-mail. Anyway," she took a breath, "I figured that the only person who could have known enough to track down our phone number was Joss. I mean, he handles all the computer stuff."

"What was the message?" John asked, frowning. "You should have said something before this, Quill."

"It didn't seem very ominous, at first. 'Is it you? After all these years, is it really you?' Then something about being careful."

"Hm," Meg said. "There's nothing really creepy about that."

"Not about the e-mail, no. But e-mail leaves out the way people say things. And the tone of the phone call . . ." Quill bit her lip. The day was catching up with her. She was tired, and her hip hurt from slipping in the snow, and her arms were trembling with fatigue. "I don't know. The phone call was very creepy. Ghostly."

"Ghostly," Meg repeated, skeptically. "Sounds like a sick joke, to me."

"Exactly. I thought it was just random foolishness, but then, this is going to sound really weird, I kept getting the feeling that I'd known Joss Roberts from somewhere before. And then he was sort of flirting with me at the Croh Bar the other night . . ."

"You've been going out to the Croh Bar at night?" Doreen said.

"The night of the nonblizzard," Quill said, "Honestly, Doreen. Anyway, I put the kibosh on the flirting, you know, the way you do, but when I got home there was the phone call." Quill slumped against the back of the chair. "Now that the poor guy's dead, it's probably moot."

"Coulda been somebody else, easy," Doreen said. "Want me to take a look?"

"Yes," Quill said firmly. "Yes, I do. It might have something to do with why he was killed."

"How in the world could it have something to do with why he was killed?" Meg looked troubled. "How could you be involved in all of this, Quill?"

"Beats me. But if we don't follow up all the leads, we may never know why Joss Roberts was murdered this afternoon. So, if we can trace who sent me that message, we'd at least have one question answered."

"Yuh."

"Could you do it?"

Doreen shook her head. "Haven't learned that much about it yet. But I can find out who can help you. You want me to set something up for tomorrow morning?"

Quill hesitated. "I have a couple of errands to run tomorrow morning."

"Andy sending you out for some tests. I forgot. Goin' down to Cornell? I'll take ya."

Quill closed her eyes. "Dammit, Doreen."

Meg glared at her. "So, what's going on with you, Quill? Everyone knows you're sick but me? I don't know whether to scream or cry."

"Prob'ly not much," Doreen said gruffly. "My guess is thyroid. I mean, look at her. She's skinnier than ever, her hair's fallin' out . . ."

"It is?" Meg leaned forward and peered into Quill's face. "No, it's not."

"Not so's just anybody would notice," Doreen said matter-of-factly. "I mean, she's still got mor'n enough to lose."

"Excuse me!" Quill shouted. "Hello? I'm sitting right here!

Would you *please* leave me some privacy?! And who told you all this anyway, Doreen?"

"Nobody," Doreen said with satisfaction, "has to tell me nothin'. My eyes are as good as ever. Besides," she added, "I grabbed that Shirley Peterson, Andy's nurse, Meg, and shook it out of her."

"So how serious is it?" Meg asked. "Quillie, you should have said something."

"It's not serious at all." Quill stood up and brushed cracker crumbs from her sweater. "What it is is slightly ludicrous. And yes, if you two insist on being nosy, yes, I am going down to Cornell tomorrow, and yes, I have a ride, and no, I don't want you guys smothering me with attention and I will be fine! It's just a little thyroid problem."

"Well, it's not just a little thyroid problem." Aaron Goldman clicked the mouse, and the lab results on the computer screen scrolled down. He and Quill were standing at a computer kiosk in the hall just outside the outpatient clinic. "Your thyroid level's fine." He was thin, with a narrow, intelligent face and a receding hairline.

Quill, who hadn't been near a huge urban hospital in years, felt slightly intimidated by all the equipment. Despite the staff's friendly behavior and the warmly efficient atmosphere of the hospital itself, she felt like a carburetor. Or maybe it was an engine cylinder. Some piece of machinery, at any rate, that was going through mechanical diagnostics. She'd slid through the CAT scan on a conveyor belt, then had been hooked up to a series of leads on a computer and had her arms and legs tickled with current. The only process reminding her she was a human being and not a faulty piece of equipment was having blood drawn. And there, she felt like the victim of a vampire bat.

"Ms. Quilliam?"

Quill recalled herself with a jerk. "Sorry. If it isn't . . . I mean, what is it? Not—" She tried a light laugh, which sounded more like a gargle. "—not amyotrophic lateral sclerosis? Or an astrocytoma? Or lupus erythematosus?"

Dr. Goldman looked startled. "By any chance do you have a copy of the *Merck Manual*?"

Quill blushed.

"Well, throw it out. I don't think you have a collagen disorder, or a brain tumor, or a demyelinating disease. I grabbed a quick look at the CAT scans and the myelogram, and *at the moment*—" He tapped his forefinger on his desk to underscore his words. "—*at the moment* everything looks fine. But Neurology's got to review the results."

"So am I just going bald?" Quill wanted to burst into tears. She liked her hair. "Or maybe I'm just crazy."

"Hair loss is normal in the fall," Dr. Goldman said in a very uninterested way. "I'm perplexed, Ms. Quilliam." He sounded pleased. "Andy wanted me to give him a call after I'd seen you, and I'll tell you right now, I'm perplexed. This is a nice little problem. Yes, a nice little problem."

"I see."

"I wish I did." He scribbled on her chart, tapped a few keys on the computer, and then offered her a smile. He put his hand under Quill's elbow and began to walk her back to the waiting room, where Myles sat reading a three-year-old *Newsweek* magazines. "We'll get to the bottom of this. Let's wait for the full results of the lab work, okay? Some of the tests I've ordered take a few days. We'll get back to you the first of the week. In the meantime, avoid caffeine, get plenty of sleep, and exercise at a comfortable level. And don't worry about it. Worry is just going to exacerbate your symptoms."

They both stopped in front of Myles, who rose with an easy grace. Dr. Goldman shook hands with Myles, nodded to Quill, and left before she could ask him anything else.

"Well?"

"You must have been bored sitting here. Sorry."

"Not a problem." He scanned her face, his eyes narrowed. "Anything?"

"Just a lot of stuff it isn't." She pushed her hair away from her face. "You know what I'm going to do if I go bald?"

"Quill, you're not going bald." He draped Quill's coat around her shoulders. "And even if you do, it won't matter."

Quill wanted to shout, what do you know, but decided against it. She didn't speak until they were well out of Ithaca, headed north on Route 15 back to Hemlock Falls. "Goldman says he's perplexed."

Myles's hands tightened on the wheel. "Did he know how long he's going to be perplexed?"

"Early next week. In the meantime, he said not to think about it. So I'm not going to think about it, and I don't want to talk about it. I'm going to think about Joss Roberts's murder instead."

A series of conflicting expressions crossed Myles's face. He didn't like her involvement in murder investigations. Crime wasn't, he insisted, for amateurs. On the other hand, it was clear to them both that a significant distraction was in order if Quill was going to get through the next few days without tearing what remained of her hair out. He cleared his throat. "We don't know much at this point. It might not even be murder, the way you and Meg define it. It certainly is vehicular homicide. It's possible someone was joyriding."

"The call on the cell phone," Quill insisted.

"But neither you nor Meg know who the caller was or what the caller wanted."

"True. But, Myles, whoever it was talked Joss right onto Main Street. The cell phone wasn't in the car."

Myles shook his head. "The scene of the crime technicians didn't recover much from the Honda." He was silent for a long moment. "But what they did recover was fairly interesting. The car was used to transport George Nash."

"What!?" Quill shrieked.

"I'm afraid so. Tell me again where you were when Petey and Harland discovered Nash's body."

Quill's memory, for everything except Chamber of Commerce meetings, was actually excellent. She ran over the events of that morning.

Myles nodded. "So someone could have stolen the car and returned it."

"I'll have to make up a list of who was where at the relevant time," Quill mused. "Good god. This is awful. Myles, I don't even know how to make up a list of who was where at the relevant time. I mean, there aren't any suspects!"

"Not at the moment," Myles agreed. "We can start with when and where you bought the Honda. How long have you had it?"

"A few weeks," Quill said glumly. "And it only has a few hundred miles on it, because I've been taking the train back and forth from New York."

The silence between them was loaded. All thoughts about Joss Roberts dropped away.

Quill took a deep breath. Goldman didn't know; he'd dismissed her dread disease as an interesting problem. Andy Bishop didn't know; he thought it was mildly funny. She said, casually, "I could be facing death, you know, as well as baldness."

Myles laughed, a deep, spontaneous laughter that made Quill laugh, too.

"Okay, so I'm probably dealing with a little-known endocrine imbalance of some kind. Or maybe Andy's right, and this is just stress, stress, stress. Anyway, what I meant to say was that I've been thinking a lot, the last few weeks, and I've decided. The hell with diplomatic silence."

"Oh?"

"You," Quill said, with more than a little asperity, "may engage in as much laid-back cool as you want to. I, on the other hand, have come to value directness."

"You have." This wasn't a question; it was an observation.

"I have. And because I am now, officially, unafraid of emotional issues, no matter how fraught they may be . . . don't you laugh again, Myles, or you'll set me off, too. I just want to say I've decided that Harker's not coming up here this weekend."

"And your plans for the future? Since you're now officially unafraid of emotional issues?"

So. Here it was. Quill stared straight ahead.

Myles cleared his throat, in an uncharacteristic way. "I'm afraid I haven't been forthright with you, either. We've been friends for a long time, Quill."

Quill thought if she heard one word about this *person* he'd been dating in Syracuse, she would get out of the Jeep and walk home.

"But it's occurred to me that we don't talk a lot."

"We don't talk a lot?"

"I don't talk a lot. About how I feel." His hand reached out and covered her own; warm and strong, she thought, but didn't say so. "I miss you."

"Even skinny and bald?"

"Especially skinny and bald." He glanced over at her. "You're a beautiful woman. You're warm and intelligent. And talented. I don't know that I've ever told you that." A muscle jumped in his cheek. "Are you crying?"

"No," she lied. "I'm sneezy."

"Well." He released his hand and returned his attention to the road. "This is what I'd like to do. I'd like to start seeing you again."

"Harker," she began, and stopped.

"You'll have to make your own decision about that."

"This—um—person in Syracuse."

"A nice woman. But I've made my decision about that."

"Okay," Quill said.

"Okay." He reached out and her took her hand again.

They drove in silence for a while. As they turned off Route 15 to Hemlock Falls, Quill pulled restlessly at the seat belt. She needed time, alone, to sort out the confusion of feelings. Most of all, time to examine the happiness bubbling inside her throat. "Myles? What do you think about Joss Roberts's death?"

"To soon to say. We found a cell phone in the woods about a half a mile from the Honda."

"You're kidding. That could be a clue."

"Well, it could. Except that it belonged to Andy."

"Andy? Andy Bishop?"

"He misplaced it a couple of days ago. And he carries a beeper, which he prefers to getting phone calls since he can control when and where he returns calls, so he didn't cancel it or get a new one. But he's not sure when it disappeared. And he has no idea who took it. And of course, there aren't any fingerprints of any kind on it."

"I'll bet I know whose would be," Quill said. "It's been obvious to me from the beginning, actually. Although this is intuition, Myles, and I know how you feel about intuition. Kimmie Bloomfield killed Joss Roberts." She glanced at him. His right eyebrow went up a bit, but otherwise he didn't react. "She was at the Inn, she knew Meg and I would be gone, and she had every chance in the world to steal my Honda."

"Where were the keys, Quill?"

"To the Honda?" she asked innocently. They'd had some sharp discussions about this before.

Myles, with admirable forbearance, merely nodded. "I've mentioned it before. Keeping the keys in the car is a bad habit."

"Everybody does it. Nobody locks their house doors either. Myles, this is Hemlock Falls."

"So it is. But with the keys at hand, anyone could have stolen the Honda. And did Kimmie Bloomfield know Joss Roberts well?"

"Well, she's met him at a Chamber meeting." Quill thought back. They hadn't paid any attention to each other at all. As a matter of fact, if she looked back, it seemed that they had made a deliberate point of avoiding each other. And that in itself was significant. "I mean, I haven't seen them speak to each other, but she knows who he is. She's thinking of divorcing Louis, you know. And Joss was single. Divorced, I mean, he has a picture of whom I think is his little boy in his office . . ."

"Quill."

"So maybe they were having an affair, and he dumped her."

"The Bloomfields have been in Hemlock Falls two weeks, Quill."

"So? They were back and forth this summer, making arrangements, weren't they? Or maybe she and Joss met on-line. She could have been signed on City of Love just the way everyone else in town seems to be."

"Quill! For God's sake."

"Well?" The familiar exasperation in his tone was long missed, she realized. There was nothing dishonest about Myles' reactions. Ever. And he never pushed. "Well," she repeated, happily. "Even you have to admit Kimmie would have had a good chance to swipe Andy's cell phone. Her husband's Andy's new partner, for goodness' sake."

"Pretty thin, Quill, if you'll forgive me saying so. Andy doesn't lock his car either. In the absence of a motive, I think Kimmie can drop to the bottom of the suspect list."

"Joss was new in town," Quill mused. "And as far as I know, everyone who lives here liked him. What about the guests? We've got quite a few people checking in tonight, but as of this morning, we had six overnights: a family of four, a salesman who stays here every month while he's servicing his accounts in the area, and a retired lady who's related to one of the Nickersons. She's here for the holidays. Maybe it's someone to do with the resort."

"Why don't we wait until the facts are in, Quill. The background check on Roberts will be in sometime tomorrow. Dave will get the results of the forensics investigation early next week. The motive for Joss Roberts's murder probably lies in Syracuse, or wherever he lived before he moved here."

"You're forgetting George Nash," Myles continued. "Now

that is interesting. But I won't know any more until I drive up to Syracuse."

"You're right, you know," Quill said after a long moment. "Maybe this is one set of murders I won't have time to solve. And there aren't any *clues!* I mean, I don't even have my Honda back, for Pete's sake." She settled into the seat. "I'm not even sure how I'm going to feel about driving it now. Poor guy. Poor guy. Both of them."

Myles visibly relaxed. "It might," he said, "be a very good idea to let this—er—case go by the board for now."

Quill, alert to the tentativeness in the current state of their relationship, decided not to push it. She glanced at the clock on the dashboard. "Three-thirty. I told Meg I'd pick up the actors at the train station. You wouldn't mind a quick stop there, would you? There's more than enough room in the Jeep."

Myles didn't mind at all. Neither did any of the men at the Inn who came into the director's orbit. The director, who doubled as the lead actress, was a drop-dead gorgeous brunette: the glorious, magnificent Kate.

# CHAPTER 15

"What's Kate's last name?" Meg asked, in an undertone.

"Something German-ish," Quill said. "Dina checked them all in." Meg and Quill sat in the Tavern Lounge watching the frenetic rehearsal activity with awed incomprehension. The tables were squashed to either side of the long room, and a wide space had been cleared in front of the long mahogany bar. Kate and her troupe were in the middle of rehearsal. Boomer, his round face sweaty, rolled flat-footed around the improvised stage. The cast was doing the final scene from *The Merry Wives of Windsor*. This involved a great deal of boisterous shouting and a lot of complicated blocking.

Kate leaped onto mysterious staging and acting problems with bewildering efficiency, flying around Boomer and the five professional actors like a seagull diving for clams. She was short, not as tall as Meg, who was five two in her stocking feet—and built along the generous lines of 1880s beauties like Diamond Lil. She had a gorgeous bosom, a wasp waist, curvy hips, and perfect dancer's legs. Her dark-brown hair cascaded in a riot of curls down her back.

Meg and Quill watched for a moment in silence.

"Is more of my hair falling out?" Quill asked anxiously.

Meg cocked her head. "I know you told me your hair's falling out, but honestly, Quill, I can't see it. You look fine."

"I feel skinny."

"You do look a little thin," Meg admitted. "But that thyroid medicine will fix that. If it is thyroid."

Quill felt doleful. "I feel skinny and bald. And too tall."

"Quill," Meg said in a flat, listen-up-kiddo sort of way. "You are beautiful. You have always been beautiful. You look like Katharine Hepburn only with a prettier face and a nicer voice."

"Katharine Hepburn is ninety-four years old."

"A thirty-six-year-old Katharine Hepburn. And your hair is a *gor*geous red. Even if there isn't as much of it as there once . . . ouch!" She rubbed her arm where Quill had punched it. "Just kidding."

"Darlings!" Kate cried in her actor's voice. "From the top! Once more unto the breach, my friends. I know, I know, wrong play! Boomer, darling! Your cue."

Quill recalled the final act of the *Merry Wives* dimly, but she remembered it was the scene where Sir John Falstaff was pinched by cuckolded husbands disguised as fairies. There was a song in it, too, and a lot of rocketing about while Falstaff declaimed.

Quill leaned over and whispered in Meg's ear, "I don't think Boomer is very good."

"Boomer stinks."

Perhaps it was Kate's trained bellow, honed in countless theaters with poor acoustics that served to diminish Boomer's not inconsiderable presence. Because, try as he might, his voice sounded weak and watery, a thin stream among the rich cascade of sound from the others. And although he was the center of the action—and bigger than any two of the other actors—the eye tended to drift away from him and settle on whomever he was talking to. Kate, as Mistress Ford, had a particularly compelling stage presence.

The fairies pretended to burn poor Falstaff with imaginary brands, then pinched him as they broke into song: *"Fie on sinful fanta*sy! *Fie on lust and luxury."* Boomer roared, rolled his eyes, and walked like a duck.

Kate stood with her hands on her hips and watched Boomer dash around the stage pursued by the fairies. At last, she threw her hands up in the air. "Stop!"

Everybody stopped. Boomer wiped his face with his handkerchief and beamed.

"Boomer, darling," Kate cooed. "Why are you walking like a duck?"

Boomer's lower lip protruded; he looked like an injured baby.

"I asked you not to walk like a duck in New York. I'm asking you not to walk like a duck now. I. Don't. Like it."

There was a heavy silence.

"Take five, darlings!" Kate yodeled, spinning to the bar and the dazzled Nate. "May we have some seltzer please, you gorgeous man?"

Nate, who had been standing behind the bar, his mouth slightly open and his face flushed with excitement, sprang into action. Two of the male actors sank thankfully into chairs next to Meg and Quill.

Quill looked at them with an odd mixture of pleasure and nostalgia. Nothing recalled the excitement of New York City like stage actors. Artistic circles are small there, and Quill had made a lot of friends in the business. She smiled warmly at the athletic blond who was playing Master Ford. "You're just terrific," she said. "All of you. Have you worked together before the Showcase in September? Even in rehearsal, the performance seems so polished." She reached across the table and extended her hand. "I'm Sarah Quilliam. And this is my sister, Meg."

Instead of shaking her hand, the actor kissed it gently. "Michael Burns. And yes, we've worked together before. We did *The Winter's Tale* as an Equity Showcase in September and October the year before."

" 'Exit, pursued by a bear.' " Quill recalled Shakespeare's notorious stage direction with a pleased air.

"Exactly."

"I'll bet the reviews were terrific," Meg said. "I suppose the critics reviewed Boomer, too?"

"Oh, yes." Michael's eyes were a pale blue, and slightly protuberant. As Ford, the cuckolded husband, he used them to great comic effect. They widened impishly, and he drawled, "Oh, yes." Nobody said anything for a moment. Then Michael added, "Having people like Boomer isn't really copping out. It's good for the Showcase, you know. To have a name draw. Nobody gets paid for Showcases and it's hard to get reviewed if you don't have something of interest for the critics. And a TV personage turned Shakespearean actor is of great interest to the critics. Ah! The mistress calls!" He leaped gracefully to his feet.

"Lines!" Kate commanded in a melodic shout. "Lines, lines *lines,* Boomer darling! You must place the emphasis like this: *'Now the hot-blooded gods assist* me! *Remember Jove, thy wast a bull for thy Europa!'* You're horny, Boomer, horny!"

The rehearsal swung into full gear.

"I suppose I'd better make sure all the others have checked in," Quill said reluctantly. "Boomer mentioned he was bringing his crew and a few other people from the TV station."

Meg looked around Quill to the Lounge's entrance. "Looks as if they're here."

Quill swiveled in her chair. Three guys in denim shirts and jeans were walking in. Sylvia Prince was with them. Quill waved them over to the table. "Would you like to join us?" Quill asked them. "We're just watching the rehearsal."

"Oh, God," Sylvia said. "As if we didn't get enough of Boomer back at the station. No, I didn't mean that, did I, guys?"

A chorus of yesses from her companions made her laugh out loud. "So, Quill. Can we get a drink?"

"Of course."

"And we haven't met yet," Meg said. "I'm Margaret Quilliam."

"I've met your food," Sylvia said. "And I'm hooked for life. Guys, this is the chef. I'm seriously considering adopting her."

The TV crew nodded, then settled into morose silence around Quill's table. In front of them, the scene stopped, started, and stopped again. Sylvia ordered a round of martinis, and sipped hers glumly, her eyes on Boomer.

"No, darlings, no!" Kate shouted, with great emphasis. "We will begin again! From my entrance." Instantly, she assumed a sexily flirtatious stance and whirled gracefully across the floor. 'Sir Jo-ohn. Yoo-hoo! Art thou there, my deer? My male deer?' "

Boomer narrowed his eyes and stared across Kate's head toward Quill's table. "Hang on a minute, Kate. I see my guys there."

"We're in re*hear*sal, Boomer," Kate said dangerously.

"Just want to arrange a little something." Boomer was apologetic, but firm. Kate backed down. Boomer came to Quill's table and stood over them like Mount St. Helens looming over Seattle. He addressed the crew, his voice menacing. "When did you guys get in?"

"We were right behind you on the Thruway, Boom." The guy who responded to this was thin, with the concave chest of a smoker. From the way his fellow crewmembers looked at him, he was clearly the lead tech.

"You pulled off, Tommy," Boomer said.

"We stopped for coffee."

"I thought I told you I wanted a couple of shots of me getting out of the Channel 14 van here at the Inn. You know, background for the spot we're going to run on the conference."

"We can get those anytime, Boom. We'll get it tomorrow." Tommy grinned, showing tobacco-stained teeth. "If we're not under two feet of snow. What d'ya think? Got a blizzard coming tomorrow?" He snickered.

To Quill's surprise, Boomer didn't respond to this provocation. At least not directly. He glared at Sylvia. "You. I told you to keep on top of things here. I stopped at the Croh Bar before I came up to the Inn, to make sure their kitchen was set up for me tomorrow morning. Place was full of yak about the wetbacks these people here—" He jerked his thumb at Quill and Meg. "—got to wait tables tomorrow night. This was supposed to be a first-class place. You don't have wetbacks serving my guests in a first-class place."

Meg gave Quill's hand a warning squeeze. Quill raised a reproachful eyebrow at her sister. "After all these years, Meg?"

"What the hell are you going on about?" Boomer demanded. "I'm paying for the best. I expect the best."

"I'm not going on about anything, Mr. Dougherty. Meg knows by now that with all the guests we've had over the years, I'm used to dealing with all kinds of people."

Boomer's eyes shifted uncertainly from Quill to Sylvia and back again. "What?"

"Bad temper. Bigots. Bullies." Quill's voice was cool. "Yes, you've paid for the best. And yes, you'll receive the best. And Sylvia has already expressed concern that the wait staff be fully trained. So I wouldn't be concerned. If I were you."

Someone from the TV crew let out a low whistle. Sylvia, who was grinning from ear to ear, said, "Just like the Incredible Hulk, isn't it, Boomer? The beautiful Miss Quilliam! The elegant Miss Quilliam! The polite Miss Quilliam drops the disguise."

Boomer's face was pale. "You watch it, Syl. I made you, I can break you."

The challenge in Sylvia's eyes was unmistakable. So was the hate.

Quill, whose temper was rapidly subsiding, got a strong sense that something other than the immediate problem was going on.

Sylvia paused a long moment. Then she asked in a friendly tone, "Did the 'yak' you heard at the Croh Bar come from a squeaky-clean blonde with a voice like Gummi Bears?"

"Uh."

"Thought so. Bad source, Boomer. You've been suckered. Again."

"Sir Jo-ohn!" The command in Kate's voice was clear. Boomer shrugged, and without a word, turned and marched back to the rehearsal.

"She's got a voice like a saxophone," Sylvia observed. She caught Quill's eye.

Sylvia drained her martini. "I like the saxophone, don't you? It's a shame that television's shelved the need for trained voices. You don't hear them all that much in the legit theater anymore, either. Microphones," she added darkly.

"Your own voice is lovely," Quill said.

"Thanks. Took a lot of work. I majored in radio at Columbia. Thought about the stage, but I can't sing, which puts me out of the running for big budget musicals. And if you can't sing, forget making any money. Thought about politics, too. But twenty years ago, I wouldn't have been able to get elected dog-catcher. It's a big world out there, and it's not kind to ambitious women."

"Not yet, anyway," Meg said. "But it's getting better, don't you think? Twenty years ago, there were maybe two women master chefs in the U.S., and both were Julia Childs. It's easier for me, now, anyway."

They exchanged conspiratorial grins.

"You don't like TV?" Meg asked.

"Oh, TV's okay. It's just that the competition is incredible. And Boomer's so paranoid about his own career that he's not about to give anyone else a hand up. You really need a mentor in this business."

"That's true of art, too," Quill said absently.

Sylvia looked interested. "Do you have a mentor? Wait, that was stupid. You're Quilliam, right? Even if I don't get your art, I know that a lot of other people do. You're probably mentoring somebody, right now."

"He took her in his arms and mentored her until dawn," Meg muttered.

Quill kicked her ankle under the table.

Sylvia continued, "Although I heard you've retired."

"Not really," Quill said.

"That guilty look you see on my sister's face is because she should be upstairs working on a new piece right now," Meg said. "And Quill's mentoring a fine newcomer from New York. At least I think he's got talent. I don't know. Not having met him myself. Yet."

"O-ho." Sylvia raised her eyebrows in mock alarm. "Don't want to bring him home to the folks, huh?"

Quill bit her lip. She'd been very certain about not wanting Harker to come to Hemlock Falls this weekend. She'd been very very certain about seeing Myles again. Slowly. One date at a time. But here she was, surrounded by the excitement of all that she'd left, and she missed Harker. He would enjoy this. "I don't know what I want."

"Hamlet," Meg said succinctly. "Like the infamous Prince of Denmark, my beloved sister can't make up her mind."

"Well, no harm done, I suppose," Sylvia said cheerfully.

"You're kidding, right?" Meg said. "Even I remember the fifth act of *Hamlet*. Nobody gets out alive."

"Laertes gets out alive," Quill said crossly.

"Horatio," Meg said. "Laertes comes in *Romeo and Juliet*."

"Oh, he does *not!*" Quill said.

"Well, he's not in the last act of *Hamlet*," Meg said. "Or if he is, he's dead."

"Sylvia?" Quill had been vaguely aware that one of the TV crewmen was on his cell phone. He snapped it shut and nudged Sylvia again. "That was the newsroom. Had a murder up here today. Same guy who's been working with Boomer on that damn web site."

Sylvia's eyebrows arched. "Really?"

"News desk wants to know if we can pick up some local color on it. If we get something in the can quick, I'll feed it back for the ten o'clock slot. Good chance for you, Syl."

"Thanks. It is." Sylvia turned her violet-blue eyes on Quill. "Do you know anything about this murder?"

"God, yes," Meg said. "We saw it."

"You *saw* it?"

Quill hesitated. "Well, yes. But I don't think . . ."

"Could we get an interview on tape?"

"No," Quill said.

"Sure," Meg said. "You'll mention the Inn, won't you?"

"Meg!" Quill glared at her.

"Sorry, kiddo. Why do you think we've been doing so well the past few months? Sure, it's my fabulous skills in the kitchen. And sure, the economy's doing pretty well at the moment, but mostly, *mostly*, Quill, it's because Boomer's been mentioning the Inn a couple of nights a week on Channel Fourteen. We owe them."

"Not to mention Lally Preston's TV show, the *Rusticated Lady*," Sylvia said. "To be totally fair, a lot of people see that show, too, Meg, and you're great on it. But gee, if you guys actually saw the murder, that'd give me a great scoop. I'd like nothing better than to get out of producing just the weather slot. I mean, half the time, Boomer's predictions are just plain wrong . . ."

"Like yesterday," one of the crew muttered. "Man, you should have heard my wife rag on that idiot."

"And the other half of the time they're *absolutely* wrong," said the camera guy who'd been on the cell phone. "Come on, let's shoot it. The sooner we roll tape the better."

Quill agreed, reluctantly. It was stupid to hate publicity. It was un-businesslike to loathe public attention. "Okay, but you do it," she said to Meg.

"You both saw it, didn't you?" Sylvia asked. "So we'll interview you both."

"No," Quill said. "I'm having this hair problem. And I look like a toad."

"You've got great hair," Sylvia protested. "You have no idea how much I wanted curly red hair when I was a kid. And there's tons of it."

"At the moment," Quill said gloomily.

"Come on. Where did this murder happen? And *how* did it happen?"

"A man named Joss Roberts was run over by a car on Main Street," Meg said. "It looked like the driver called him on his cell phone, got Joss out into the street, and then, *pow!*" She shuddered. "It was awful."

"God. I'll bet. Did they catch the guy?"

"No."

Sylvia's eyes lit up. "Huh. Means there's potential for more story."

"Car crash, was it? Then we'll want to shoot outside," the cameraman said laconically. "Let's shoot it in the parking lot. We'll use the Channel Fourteen van as a backdrop. It'll look like we were on the spot."

"Great."

Quill, dubious about the ethics of implying on-the-spot reportage some ten hours after the fact, nonetheless let herself be dragged outside.

Sylvia insisted that she and Meg keep their winter coats open, and their hair free and blowing in the slight breeze. "More viewer-friendly," she said. "Just don't shiver, okay?"

Quill and Meg both backed against the Channel 14 van outside in the parking lot. It was cold, and a few flakes of snow were in the air. One of the tech crew made a crack about the weather—Boomer had predicted clear and sunny skies for the weekend—and Sylvia swung into action.

Bright lights switched on in Quill's face. The cameras rolled. Sylvia shed her easygoing charm as fast as the skin off a parboiled tomato. Her voice was crisp and decisive as she spoke into the handheld microphone. "Special correspondent Sylvia Prince here on location in Hemlock Falls with two eyewitnesses to today's brutal murder of . . ." She consulted a slip of paper shoved into her hand by one of the tech crew, and continued without a noticeable break. "Computer expert Joss Roberts. With me tonight is Sarah Quilliam, the world-renowned artist, and her sister, Master Chef Margaret Quilliam. Sarah, can you tell our viewing audience what you saw this morning?"

"What in the hell is going on here?"

Boomer Dougherty, his face flushed with rage, snatched the mike out of Sylvia Prince's hand and glared angrily at them all.

# CHAPTER 16

"What a jerk Boomer is." Meg wound her legs around the stool at the kitchen prep table and stirred a bowl of cranberries. The pungent scent of freshly grated horseradish tickled Quill's nose. She sneezed, and agreed that last night, yes, Boomer had been a flaming jerk. Despite everything, Quill's mood was problematic. She'd had a long talk with Myles the night before, about nothing in particular. She'd had a long talk with Harker, too. Friendly, with just the right amount of distance. Maybe, she'd suggested, they'd gotten involved too quickly. Maybe they needed a little time for reflection. She was, Quill thought, getting better and better at managing her emotional life.

So why didn't she feel better about it?

She sneezed twice.

"Bless you, Quill, and the horse you rode in on, too." Meg ate some of the cranberries from the wooden spoon. "This is terrific. It's sensational. I'd enter this recipe in Boomer's stupid contest, if he hadn't banned pros. 'My Kingdom for a Horseradish' cranberry chutney. What do you think?" She held a spoonful out to Quill, who declined with a shake of her head. "What? Turning down my food? Are you sure you're okay?"

"I'm fine. My stomach's a little wonky."

"After the scene last night, whose stomach wouldn't feel wonky? What a temper tantrum. You'd think Sylvia was after his firstborn." She peered at Quill. "Uh-oh. I recognize that expression. It's the 'It's all right, Ma, I'm only bleeding' expression." She pointed the wooden spoon. "You, my friend, are upset. You, pal, are in denial about being upset. It wasn't that creep, Boomer. We've had worse jerks stay here."

Boomer hadn't upset her. Harker hadn't upset her. And her wonky stomach would go away once she ate some dry crackers, or whatever.

She had been wakened by another phone call. The same eerie whisper. *Is it you? After all these years, is it you? If it is, be careful.*

And poor Joss Roberts was dead. And George Nash, as well. There had to be a connection. There had to be.

Quill cleared her throat. "We should have guessed how Boomer was going to feel about Sylvia doing any kind of broadcast without him. Remember? He told us when we were planning for the menus. He thinks everyone's out to get him."

"Well, I'm out to get him after that tongue-lashing. He deserves a couple of good smacks in the kisser. Where's Doreen when we need her? The guys in the studio aren't dancing on air, either. Did you see the look on Sylvia's face? She was ready to turn him into pâté."

Boomer had staged a tantrum remarkable for its inventive invective. Sylvia had stamped off in a flood of angry tears. Then a suddenly affable Boomer had interviewed Meg and Quill himself. The clip had just made deadline for the eleven o'clock news the night before. Quill had stared hard at herself on-screen. So, she didn't look bald. Not yet.

She'd spent a restless night, troubled by a dream about Joss Roberts. In her dream, she arrived too late to push him out of the way of the oncoming car, over and over again.

And then the phone call, before the dawn broke. She had risen to work a little on the canvas, and quit in frustration after several hours. She felt rotten. Her arms and legs were shaky. Her head hurt. She had wandered down to the kitchen for an early lunch. Meg and the staff were in full battle readiness, preparing for the evening's banquet. Boomer and the meteorologists who were entering the dessert contest had left for the Croh Bar.

"Well," Quill said with a sigh. She got up and took the remains of her turkey sandwich to the sink, then settled into the rocking chair by the kitchen fireplace. Meg's herbs were strung along the mantle. The scent of thyme and sage drifted among the other odors of the kitchen: roast pork from the suckling pig, mince, apple, and as always, fresh bread.

Soothing scents. She usually loved them.

Quill's stomach flipped, and she closed her eyes for a brief minute until it settled down. She'd decided this morning that there was something worse than going bald. Being sick to your stomach was definitely worse than going bald. She could always get a wig. It was a lot of trouble to get a new stomach.

Meg darted a shrewd glance at her. "How'd the painting go this morning?"

Quill shook her head.

"Sorry I asked. Well, you'll be glad to know everything's well in hand for tonight. And guess what? Kate needs more fairies for the scene where Boomer gets pinched and kicked, so she asked for volunteers. Not a speaking role, you know. You just get to dress up in a buskin or whatever and hit Boomer."

"I take it you volunteered."

Meg grinned. "Of course. I told her I could memorize the song the fairies sing by tonight, and she said fabulous."

Quill made a face. "She hasn't actually heard you sing, Meg."

"Phut," Meg said airily. "Anyway, guess who else is going to be a fairy?"

"Doreen," Quill guessed obediently.

"Nope. The horrible Carol Ann."

"Carol Ann Spinoza? How did she horn in?"

"I told you," Meg said patiently. She had set aside the horseradish chutney and was doing something with oranges and cranberries. Quill usually loved the smell of oranges. She swallowed hard. Maybe a cup of tea might help. Maybe putting absolutely nothing in her stomach ever again would help.

Meg, oblivious, went on. "A lot of the Chamber members are after that thousand bucks, and some of them brought in their desserts this morning. Partly because they were finished, and partly to get a jump on what everyone else was bringing, some of them," Meg added gravely, "to see if they could bribe me. Carol Ann," she continued, making free with he nutmeg and grater, "brought in Othello Jell-O. Those little nugget things, you know? You make them out of gelatin."

Quill groaned. "What makes the dessert Othello Jell-O? I mean, rather than just plain old Jell-O nuggets?"

"Well, it's two colors, for one thing, pineapple and blackberry, and they're all shaped like camels." Meg set the grater down and tested the cranberry-orange mixture with a thoughtful air. Quill stared at her accusingly until she added, "Camels are the only beasts with two backs. You know that scene, Iago's driving poor old Othello mad with jealousy and says . . ."

"I remember the line. It's a wonderful speech. That woman is a menace to the living, now she's a menace to literature. *Ugh!*" Quill wanted to grab her hair and pull it, but she stopped herself just in time. She was going to save every precious bit of hair she could. "That's the most tasteless thing I have ever heard in my life." Then with a kind of horrible fascination, she asked, "There were other desserts? With other awful names?"

Meg nodded vigorously. "Oh, yes indeedy. None as gruesome as Carol Ann's, though. Actually, most of them were kind of cute. Dookie Shuttleworth brought in Midsummer Night's Dream Coconut Cake, and Miriam Doncaster made Scottish Play Shortbread, and Howie Murchison contributed Yorickshire Pudding. Boomer himself," she concluded, "is making Hamlet Omelets. Out of egg whites and oranges. He says. If he's not too exhausted after the performance." She rolled her eyes.

"I'd better go see how everything's going." Quill got to her feet a little shakily.

"Sit down."

Meg's voice was so commanding Quill found herself back in the rocking chair.

"I told you two days ago you were going to have time to paint, Quill. John's on top of everything. So's Doreen. So, for that matter, am I. Got it?"

Quill thought that nothing would be better than to lie down and think about nothing at all until she felt more like commanding the troops and less like she'd been through a mangle. "I can't just go up there and paint while the whole Inn's turned upside down," she said.

"Sure you can. Oh. Hot news. Dina was here early to take care of all the check-ins, and Davey Kiddermeister is all of a doodah because she's developed an amazing crush on that guy Michael, the one who's playing Master Ford in the play. Who appears to be in love with Kate . . ."

"Oh, dear. Why was Davey here, anyway?"

"Glad you reminded me. You're supposed to give him a statement about the accident."

"It wasn't an accident," Quill said. "It was murder. Or at the least, Myles says it was vehicular homicide."

"I know that. You know that. Davey's gotten some idea that it was kids, skylarking around with your Honda."

"I don't think it was kids. Neither does Myles."

Meg's eyebrows went up. "Myles doesn't, does he?"

"Don't use that ooky tone of voice with me, Meg."

"Ooky," Meg said thoughtfully. She had a third bowl now, filled with more of the apparently inexhaustible supply of cranberries. She started shredding beef into the chutney with expert hands. "So. What about Myles?"

Quill ignored the invitation to confide details of her love life. "I had a few things to talk over with Myles, and besides, he offered to drive me to Cornell to get those stupid tests, and of course we talked about the murder on the way there and back. Who wouldn't?"

"I wouldn't talk about murder," Meg said frankly, "not if I wanted Myles back. What kind of lover's conversation is that? I'd talk about him. Or me. Or if I'd just been through a raft of tests at Cornell, I'd talk about that, unless, of course, I was saving that information to discuss with my beloved sister."

"Hm."

"Just 'hm'?"

"They'll let me know, Meg. And when I know, you'll know."

"You aren't dying."

"I'm dying. My proof will be my death and then you'll be sorry. Anyway. About Joss Roberts. So Davey thinks it's kids. How does that explain the cell phone call? We were there, Meg. Someone wanted Joss smack in the middle of Main Street so they could run him over. And they did. That doesn't fit with Davey's joyriding theory. Davey talks to Myles. He knows Myles thinks it's murder."

Meg shrugged. "I think Davey's out to impress Dina with his manly independent attitude. Especially now that there's a rival in the offing. So Myles thinks it murder. You and I know it's murder. And of course, Boomer just told the entire population of Syracuse that it's murder in that broadcast last night, so Davey's in the minority. It'd be a real poke in the eye if he were right, Quill."

"I don't think so. There's something I haven't told you."

"There's a lot you haven't told me," Meg said tartly. "But what specifically is it you've been holding back?"

Quill told her about the second phone call. Meg's eyebrows went up again. "That sounds perfectly horrible. Here, Bjarne! Take these chutneys, will you?" Bjarne took charge of the cranberries. She washed her hands in the vegetable sink, and then came to sit by Quill. "Wow, Quill. This has not been your month. Who could it be? And why? I mean, we discussed this. We thought it was Joss Roberts. Why did we think it was him?"

"I thought it was Joss Roberts, not you. As to why." Quill hesitated, conscious that her cheeks were red. "I thought it was a flirtation gone sour, sort of."

"You mean Joss Roberts was flirting with you and you turned him down and he was sort of harassing you?"

"Something like that."

"He didn't seem like that kind of guy to me at all."

"We don't know what kind of guy he is at all, Meg. How long had he been in town before he died? Two months?"

"Yeah."

"And in that time he'd taken Esther West out and she went wiggy over him, Carol Ann Spinoza was absolutely wiggy over him, and Doreen told me he's been calling Miriam Doncaster, and she probably liked him, too. I mean, he didn't look like much, but he had charm, Meg. And he liked women. He kind of expected them to fall all over him, and when I didn't . . ." She made a face. "I guess I thought he was miffed."

"You know what? You've just given us about three good motives for someone to murder Joss Roberts *and* make harassing phone calls to you," Meg said.

"No. I can't see Esther killing anyone. And Miriam? Never."

"Howie?" Meg suggested. "Because he and Miriam have had this thing for a while?"

"It's been kind of a tepid thing, Meg. Easygoing."

"True."

They looked at each other.

"I *wish*," Meg said fervently. "Man, oh man, do I wish it was Carol Ann Spinoza. I can't tell you how much that woman scares me."

"We'd be heroes," Quill said. "To the rest of Hemlock Falls. And wouldn't it be just like Carol Ann."

"Hm. Well. First, what were you planning to do about the phone calls?"

"Trace them. I'm pretty sure we can trace the calls. But Joss was killed before I could ask."

"Well, he can't help us now, poor soul. I wonder who could?"

"Arnie Peterson," Quill said. "The kid who helped Joss on the web site. That's who."

# CHAPTER 17

Meg bodily shoved Quill out of the Inn to interview Arnie Peterson. Quill had appreciated the first part of her speech: the phone calls had to be stopped. The second part, which had to do with Quill's current enfeebled, (possibly) thyroid-deficient state and the total inconsequence of her contribution to the day's activities in light of her (Meg's) superior skill at arranging to have Quill's duties taken care of, made her feel unwanted and incompetent. *Those* feelings she put down to her current enfeebled, (possibly) thyroid-deficient state.

Except that it wasn't thyroid, according to the efficient, depressingly well-informed Dr. Goldman. Quill pushed that unwelcome fact to the back of her mind and pulled Meg's Ford Escort into the main parking lot of the Hemlock Falls High School. It was noon. She hoped Arnie would be at lunch.

Quill's acquaintance with Hemlock High was limited to interviewing students for summer help with the grounds at the Inn, and a passing acquaintance with the athletic coach and the school superintendent, both members of the Chamber of Commerce. But walking into the school was like walking into any high school in any state of the Union, including Litchfield High, where she and Meg had gone in Connecticut. The disinfectant smell was exactly the same: pungent and piney, with an odd underlay of shellac. The indoor-outdoor carpeting was the same, and so was the green paint on the walls and the apathetic trophies in the glass case and the posters. She smiled at it all, fondly.

Quill pulled open the door to the Administration offices, overwhelmed by nostalgia. Yes, the school secretary said, Arnie's lunch period was at 12:20, and yes, Quill had to wear a hall pass, and wasn't Quill supposed to be meeting her friend from New York on the train this afternoon? She'd heard *that,* she said in response to Quill's heated inquiry, down at the Croh Bar.

The total population of Hemlock Falls—despite the incursion of flatland foreigners due to village expansion—was still well under four thousand, and Hemlock High's student body was correspondingly small. The first teenager Quill met pointed to a tall, painfully thin kid with the distinctive Peterson chin (large and jutting). He was wearing a Hemlock High school jacket (purple and black) and carried a large paper bag and a stack of books. Quill introduced herself and found her hand engulfed by Arnie's large, red-knuckled one. "Oh, yeah. How're you feeling, Ms. Quilliam? M'mom says you maybe got a thyroid deficiency."

A day might come, Quill thought, when the entire village knowing the state of her health and her love life wouldn't rattle her. She hoped it was soon. "I'm fine, thank you, Arnie."

"M'mom thought maybe I had a thyroid problem." He grinned down at her from his gangly, skinny height. He had very beautiful skin and glossy brown hair. "But it was the Gunderson side coming out. You know, m'mom's a Gunderson."

"No, I didn't know that," Quill said. Arnie looked surprised. "Arnie, you worked for Mr. Roberts on the web site, didn't you?"

"Joss? Sure. Awful what happened. M'mom said . . ."

"Yes. My sister and I saw it happen."

He looked sad and his nose dripped. Quill had used up all her Kleenex, but she patted her sweater pocket anyway. "It all happened so quickly." She was about to add the standard, "I'm sure he never felt a thing," but something in his eyes—skepticism, perhaps—made her add, "He knew, of course, that he'd been hit. But it was so fast, Arnie, he only knew for a few seconds, if that."

He nodded once, awkwardly. Then, he said, "Thanks."

"My sister and I think Joss was murdered deliberately." Students swirled around them like ducks circling a whirlpool in a pond. They glanced sideways, curious, then swept off.

"You're gonna find out who did it? Like with my uncle Gil?"

Quill grimaced a little at this mention of her and Meg's very first murder case. "We'd like to try. There's not a lot to go on. But there is one faint possibility."

"Can I help?"

"I hope so." Quill explained the mysterious phone calls, and the preceding e-mail. "Would you need to—um—access the web site server in order to track where the e-mail came from? And maybe find out how that person—if it's the same person, got my private phone number?" She liked the casually competent way the computer jargon sounded.

"Oh, yeah. Either that or hack into it from home, which would be a pain. M'mom's been promising to get me more ram and a sneezer . . ."

(That's what it sounded like, Quill told Meg later.)

". . . but with Christmas mor'n a month away, we better use Joss's equipment. I go there right after school since the Chamber's keepin' me on to maintain the web site. Want me to try it now?"

"Now?" Quill looked at her watch. "You have school until two or so, don't you?"

"Study hall, is all. I just have to tell Mrs. Houlihan."

"You know much about computers?" Arnie asked her as they settled themselves in front of an ominous array of equipment some twenty minutes later. Arnie adjusted the height of the office chair without looking, his eyes glued to the screen. A bright-red banner scrolled across: BLUE COW COMPUTING . . . WHEN YOU'RE ON THE MO-O-O-VE.

"That's a screen saver," Quill said brightly.

Arnie's fingers began to move with the frenzy of Horowitz in the grip of the fourth Hungarian Rhapsody. "Uh, yeah. What's your handle, Miss Quilliam?"

"I'm really sorry. All that stuff's been deleted."

"It'll be there, ma'am."

"Call me Quill, please. And I know about the TRASH icon, Arnie. I deleted it all permanently."

"Nah. Unless you scrubbed the hard drive. Then I gotta take it to Syracuse. Nothing's ever really gone on a hard drive. Unless maybe it's been sitting for, like, a hundred years or something. So what's your handle?"

"Art."

"Art. Got it. And your birthday?"

"My birthday?"

"Didn't you use that for your secret password? Almost everybody does." His fingers were poised. "Unless you used something else."

"No," Quill admitted, "I didn't. I used STOPIT."

At first, she watched Arnie pull up information from the hard drive with admiring interest. It was always pleasant watching an expert, and Arnie clearly knew what he was doing. First, a series of little boxes appeared on the screen, then a whole line of names and what looked like e-mail addresses, then Quill's own profile. "Huh," Arnie said. He sat back, his lips pursed. "Okay, this is what I'm doing here, Miss Quilliam. I have the time and the date. We have to contact two servers to get the address: the ISP and IP. We're the ISP here—so I'll just . . ." He hunched forward and attacked the keys so intently that Quill felt tired just looking at him.

She got up and wandered restlessly around the office. The photographs of Joss's baby still lined the bookshelf. Where was his family? She knew that Myles would see that they were notified. And even if he'd been unable to find them, the previous night's television spot had made Joss's death public. She wondered how old the baby was now. How long Joss had been divorced. Whether he missed his wife and his child.

"Huh," Arnie said. "You were some kind of pissed at Mr. Dougherty, Quill."

Quill peered over his shoulder. Her letter to the Channel 14 news line was on screen. And she hadn't even sent the damn thing.

Arnie renewed his attack on the keyboard with one hand, the other scrambled in the brown paper bag he'd brought from school, and emerged with a huge sandwich.

She was hungry. And her stomach was feeling a lot better. She always felt better when she was moving toward something.

"Whoa," Arnie said. "Here it is, Miss Quilliam. The guy who answered your ad, anyways. Now, just let me find out if he got your phone number from here."

"My phone number?" Quill said, outraged. "How did my phone number get on there!"

"Hacked into the billing database," Arnie said around a mouthful of ham. "Yeah. Same guy."

"What guy!?"

"Jeez, Miss Quilliam. It's that weather guy who's been calling you. Boomer Dougherty."

# CHAPTER 18

Quill left Arnie at the Blue Cow computing offices just after four o'clock, intent on cornering Boomer Dougherty to discover what the heck he meant by scaring her half to death. The thick, dark clouds hanging over Hemlock Falls had become thicker and darker as evening crowded in. A few fat flakes swirled lazily past her nose and stuck in her hair. The streetlights were coming on, and the window of Esther's dress shop glowed with bright fluorescent light. Boomer's storm seemed to be showing up after all.

The snow thickened alarmingly in the short time it took Quill to get to Meg's Escort. In the few minutes it took to go up the hill to the Inn, the snow increased to an opaque shroud of glaucous white. Max met her at the kitchen door, his fur fluffed out in reaction to the rising wind. Snow powdered his back and ice balled in the feathers on his legs. Quill let him precede her and apologized in the general direction of the shrieks of dismay from the kitchen staff. (Max always chose the most central spot to shake himself.) Quill stepped around the bits of snow and ice Max had left on the floor and sat down in the rocker next to the cobblestone fireplace. The kitchen was hot from the stoves, and Quill took a minute to let the warmth sink in.

It didn't fit. Boomer's arrogant, overbearing personality just didn't fit with the desperate tone of the e-mails, the panic in the phone calls.

It'd be easy enough for someone to hack into Boomer's mail; that was obvious. What wasn't at all obvious was why. Even less obvious was who.

Doreen, seated at the prep table, set down her coffee with a thump. "Snowin' somethin' awful, is it?"

Quill, jerked from her absorption, agreed. "It just came up."

A rising wind rattled the windows, and the fire in the fireplace whooshed with a sudden updraft.

"Shoulda guessed it," Doreen said sourly. "Himself called for fair skies and forty degrees tonight."

"You mean Boomer." Quill shook the damp snow off her hair, thinking. Then she asked, in an offhand way, "Where is he?"

"In the middle of one of them seminars. It's called Investing in Beachfront Property in Arizona."

"Global warming?"

"Yep. They wrap up at five. Potty break, or whatever. Then cocktails at six."

Quill glanced at her watch. "I want to talk to Boomer."

"You can catch him in the Tavern Lounge in a bit, I expect. He's a backslapper from way back, that one. Never misses a chance to stick that big, fat face of his into folks' faces."

"You don't like him, Doreen."

"Out for himself, is all. The kind that walks right over anybody in his way."

No. Those calls just didn't fit Boomer's personality. Quill ran her hands absently through her hair. Then who? And why?

"Better get a move on," Doreen advised her kindly. "You have just enough time to go up and change before you come on down for the banquet *and . . .*" She paused.

"And what?"

"The sheriff called."

Quill decided she didn't want to guess wrong this time. "Which one?"

"Sheriff McHale," Doreen said distinctly. "And you're supposed to call him right back. And that Harker called, too. So which one are you going to call back?" She slapped the pink message slips into Quill's hand.

"Sometimes, Doreen, I feel like a sacked quarterback when I talk to you."

"Well?"

Quill blinked innocently at her. "I'll go call him right now."

Doreen didn't react for a minute. Then she shouted. "*Ver*-y funny, missy!"

Quill moved at a dignified walk through the dining room,

partly because the room was a whirl of activity as the wait staff set up for the banquet and she didn't want to bump into anyone, but mostly because she could feel Doreen's steely gaze in her back and she refused to behave as if she'd been routed.

In the foyer, Dina was busy with a few late check-ins for the banquet. Quill recognized the meteorologist from the Ithaca television station and stopped to welcome him. "Glad to get here," he said, shaking her hand. "We've got a real nor'easter out there. My guess is, anyone who isn't here now isn't going to make it."

"How much do you think we're going to get, Alan?" the woman behind him asked.

"I was thinking ten, maybe twelve inches. Although my last look at the radar tells me twenty-four. And the rate's pretty impressive: two to four inches an hour."

"Wow," Quill said. "I thought we were going to have nice weather for the weekend."

"You watch Channel Fourteen?" Alan asked.

Quill nodded.

"Well, don't."

Quill paused at her office door. "Alan? Why is Boomer wrong so often?"

Alan shrugged. The woman behind him craned her neck around his bulky form and smiled at Quill. "Alan won't say a thing out of professional courtesy. But I'm just a researcher at Cornell, and I don't have to be discreet. I have no idea where Boomer Dougherty got his training. But it wasn't from any reputable program, I can tell you that right now."

Alan nodded in quiet agreement. "Celia's right, Quill. But there's no law that says a TV weatherman has to be licensed. Sorry, Celia—or weatherwoman."

"Pros like Alan have only gotten into the media thing in recent years," the woman named Celia said. "So professional meteorologists can't legitimately complain about people like Boomer. But he drives us all crazy with his grandstanding and his opportunism. He's a rank amateur, no, make that a bad rank amateur. No respect for the profession at all. And, you know, there's a real responsibility to report the weather as accurately as we can. People die in this kind of storm, if they aren't prepared for it. People die."

"But why does Boomer have the job?"

Celia raised her eyebrows cynically. "Ratings, dear. Ratings."

Thoughtfully, Quill went into her office and pulled aside the drapes to look outside. The snow came down with determined intensity. The wind gusted unpredictably, shoving the snow in random billows. When she and Meg had decided to buy the Inn ten years ago, they'd had long discussions about the pros and cons of giving up urban living. The one thing they hadn't considered was the weather. A city blizzard was a nuisance rising to major inconvenience when heavy snow shut the roads down. But nothing lasted more than two or three days, and almost everyone in the middle of a city blizzard loved the time off, the camaraderie, and the enforced leisure time. There was always a building to duck into, water, lights, food, even when the power went off—and you never lost your way.

A blizzard in the rural areas was deadly. Those caught in their cars in a whiteout could freeze to death before rescue crews found them. Huge drifts could bury cars, whole houses, barns, and factories. And there were no grocery stores to slog to when you lived miles from anywhere.

Quill let the drapes drop back into place. Later, when the winds died down and the snow stopped, the village and the land would be beautiful, wrapped in white like a gift. Right now, she was really glad she was inside, and that the weather wasn't.

She sat at her desk and picked up the phone. There was an extension listed after the number Myles had left; it looked as if he were calling from a hotel.

"So you're at the Hyatt," Quill said when he picked up. "Are you stuck?"

"Well, Quill," he said. "I've missed you. And yes—we're snowbound. I'm not getting back to Hemlock Falls anytime soon."

"Are you really snowbound, Myles?"

"All of Syracuse is snowbound," he said. "The roads are closed, so I'll be here until morning at least. How is it up there?"

"I have it on good authority that we'll be snowed in by supper if not before. And that's from Doreen. Not Boomer."

"You are back at home, aren't you?"

"Yes. I spent the afternoon with a computer whiz from the local high school. There's something funny going on, Myles. Joss Roberts didn't make those phone calls to me. Boomer Dougherty did."

Myles didn't say anything. Then, he said, "Hm."

"Hm? That's it? Hm? But it doesn't fit, Myles."

"We were both pretty certain the calls came from someone directly connected with the web site. And Boomer certainly is."

Quill liked the sound of that "we." And she could hear the warmth in her own voice when she said, "I know. But the e-mail and the calls—no. Boomer's arrogant. Self-involved. There isn't room in Boomer's universe for anyone but Boomer. And if he made the calls to scare me, that doesn't make any sense. Why would he want to scare me?"

Myles didn't say anything.

"Hello? Are you there?"

"Yes. Sorry, Quill. This surprises me. I don't like it."

"I don't like it either, Myles. But the phone calls are an annoyance. That's all. The first one took me aback, but I'm not exactly quivering in my shoes." She sighed. "Anyway, the banquet's tonight, and it'll be tough to catch him alone. But when I do, I'll just ask him why, and then I'll tell him to stop."

"I don't think I want you to do that."

"Excuse me?" Quill said icily. "Did I miss the election? You know, the one that left you president?"

"The background check on Joss Roberts came back this afternoon, Quill. He petitioned the courts for a name change in 1989. He was born Carl Ross."

"Carl Ross," Quill said. "The name's familiar. Was he a criminal? He didn't seem the type, somehow. Or in the Federal Witness Protection pro . . . oh my lord. Oh my god." Quill was so shocked she couldn't move. "That baby. The two men who killed that baby. Joss Roberts was the *father*? Oh the poor man. He must have changed his name because of all the publicity. Damn the media anyhow, Myles." She remembered the photographs of the little boy in Joss Roberts's office and blinked back tears. "What a terrible thing. And someone killed him, Myles. Why?"

"I've got a call into Will Gardner. He was the lead detective on the case."

"George Nash," Quill said. "And I was a witness. Myles, this is all connected."

"Yes. I'm afraid so."

Quill stiffened as an idea took hold. "Do you think. Myles. Do you suppose that Boomer is Franklin Overmeyer?

"We don't have any facts to support that, Quill."

"But he must be. He has to be. And he's killing off the people who could recognize him."

"You're theorizing in advance of the facts, Quill. Just like Nero Wolfe always warns Archie."

"I know, I know. But it's the only thing that makes any sense."

There was a faint undercurrent of laughter in Myles's voice: "Murder doesn't have to make sense, Quill. But it's a plausible theory."

"Fingerprints," Quill said with some excitement. "I'll get his fingerprints. The police have them on file, don't they? From all those years ago. Myles, Boomer's murdered three people. That poor child, George Nash, who must have called him once he was out of prison, and tried to blackmail him. And poor old Joss Roberts, too."

"Let's think this through. First, why would Boomer murder Joss Roberts now, Quill? And why set Joss up in business in Hemlock Falls?"

"Well," Quill said. "That's a point."

"Second, where was Boomer when Harland Peterson saw your Honda driving away from the Gorge the day Nash's body was dumped?"

"I'm sure he'd claim he was in Syracuse," Quill said. "But maybe not, Myles. It's only an hour's drive. But I can check that out with Sylvia Prince. And I suppose you're going to ask where Boomer was when Joss was killed. I can check that out with Sylvia, too.

"As a matter of fact, I do know where he was the day Joss Roberts was run over—he was taping at the studio. So no, I don't think Boomer's our killer.

"Maybe there's a conspiracy?" Quill said with hope.

"And maybe you're theorizing ahead of the—"

"Yeah, yeah, yeah." Quill sighed and then sneezed, twice.

"What is it? Are you all right?"

"I'm fine. Go on."

"I don't suppose Goldman called back."

"The neurologist? Um."

"Just 'um'?"

"If I were terminal, I'd tell you back like a shot."

"Have you spoken with Andy? Are you feeling any better?"

"Much better. Myles. I'm *fine*. What ever this is, it's just making my life miserable. It's not ending it."

"Oh, Quill." The love in Myles's voice was clear.

Quill didn't know what to do with her hands. She couldn't, wouldn't tug at her hair. She'd never bitten her nails in her life, and she wasn't about to start. She beat her free hand softly against the desk edge.

"I really don't want to discuss it right now, Myles."

"I thought we'd agreed to talk more."

"We should. We will. But there's a blizzard outside, and you're stuck in Syracuse, and this whole weekend is fraught with the usual obnoxious personalities careening into each other, and I don't think I can take it. I'm so tired, Myles."

"Get a grip, Quill."

"You're right."

"You're one of the strongest women I know."

"I am?" She said, more firmly, "I am."

"And you were going to take it easy this evening, stay away from the guests, maybe spend the night with Meg or Doreen in your room, and not pursue this investigation any further until I can get back."

"I was?"

"You were."

"But, Myles . . ."

"But, nothing, Quill. We don't know enough. Not yet. As it happens . . ." He hesitated, choosing his words. "It may be that Overmeyer is behind this. And it makes sense that both Joss and Nash were killed because Overmeyer's in the Syracuse area, and he was afraid of being recognized. I'm not certain about why Nash's body was dumped here before Roberts was killed— but I have some avenues I want to pursue there. But we can't do anything definitive right now, Quill. And these warning phone calls to you mean something. So, for the moment, do the sensible thing. Take some precautions."

"Don't go in the basement." Quill hated the kind of novels where the heroine in jeopardy went flying to the basement when she and the reader both knew the villain was lurking there. "Okay. I won't go into the basement. I'll make sure that I'm with someone all the time. And Myles! I could tape-record the phone calls. If I get any more of them, I mean. The answering machine will do it."

"Good idea. Just hang tight, Quill. I'll be back as soon as I can."

"I'm glad," she said simply. "I'm glad you're coming home."

She hung up the phone, lost in thought.

The wait staff. Overmeyer had to be with the wait staff.

The new wait staff from Syracuse.

Roberts had been with her in the train station when she'd picked them up. And a temp agency was just the place for a man on the run. Overmeyer must have spent years moving from city to city, living from hand to mouth through temp jobs.

Quill had a good visual memory. She had just glimpsed the back of Overmeyer's head as he'd jumped into the old Plymouth Fury, but she still recalled the nape of his neck, the way his hair trailed over his T-shirt, the shape of his ears. And of course, that picture had been in the newspapers.

She would recognize the back of his neck twenty years later. She had no doubt about it at all. Meg. Meg had interviewed the temporary workers. Could she have looked Franklin Overmeyer right in the face and not recalled that sultry afternoon?

Meg, almost five years younger, had been terrified. Quill had pulled Meg's face against her own chest and held her tight, terrified that her little sister would see what she shouldn't see.

And Meg wasn't good at recalling faces—Quill had gotten all those particular genes.

Yes, Overmeyer could have slipped by Meg.

The phone rang a second time. Quill stabbed at the record button on the answering machine and picked up the receiver, heart beating quickly. It was Myles.

"Quill? I just got another phone call from one of the guys I know at the Syracuse PD. I've been thinking. I don't like this. I don't like any of it. I'm coming up there."

Quill rose, the phone still at her ear, and pulled the drapes aside once more. The snow was ankle high, now. Another inch had fallen during their conversation. "You can't make it home through this, Myles."

"I can if I requisition some equipment."

"Please don't," Quill said. "I don't like it when you push, Myles. I don't like it when you come all overprotective. I can handle things myself. Mostly."

"We'll see."

"Look, if Overmeyer is here, he's done what he's meant to

do." She frowned. "But, Myles, why did he come back? Joss was killed two days ago. What would he come back for?"

Myles swore. "I'm going to tell you why. But you have to promise me something. You stay out of this, Quill."

"Out of what?"

"I'm calling Kiddermeister as soon as I finish speaking to you. I want Kimmie Bloomfield put into protective custody."

"Kimmie? What? Why?"

"Louis is her second husband. Joss Roberts was her first."

"No." Quill sat back in shock. Kimmie? The mother of the baby? "Oh, no. So you think that Overmeyer came back to kill her?" She cut herself short. "That doesn't make any sense. None of this makes any sense."

"I don't know anything, Quill. Remember the—"

"The facts," she interrupted. "Yes, but, Myles. Kimmie! That poor thing. What a tragedy. You never get over that kind of tragedy. No wonder she's so . . ." She bit her lip. "I feel awful about how much I disliked her."

"Well, make it up to yourself. The snow's a good thing, Quill. With any luck, she'll be snowbound at home with Louis. Now, I've got your promise, don't I? You aren't going to go haring off trying to find Overmeyer. You're going to leave it up to the police. This is a police matter, Quill."

"Sure," she said. "And the agreement's on both sides. You're not going to try and get through six feet of snow."

"No," he said reluctantly. "Probably not. Where's John?"

"Taking care of the wine," Quill said.

"Good. I'm going to call the sheriff's office now and let David know what I've scraped up here. With this kind of weather, he's going to have his hands full with highway problems, but I'm going to see if we've got a trooper free to check on you once in a while. And he's going to have to find a way to protect Kimmie."

"Do you really think Overmeyer's here, Myles? That he killed Joss Roberts?"

"I don't think it's probable. But it doesn't mean it isn't possible." His voice lightened. "Keep to the lighted areas. And lock your doors. Good night, my love. I'll talk to you later."

"What did you say?"

"I said I'd call later."

"Myles?"

"Yes, Quill."

She could hear the impatience in his voice. He had things to do, people to call. "What about Boomer?"

"Why don't you just ask him why he made the calls?"

"Just plain out ask him?"

"Ask him what the hell he's after and tell him to cut it out. You're a brave woman, woman. It's one of the things I like about you. Anything else?"

"Nope. Good-bye, Myles. And thanks." Quill cradled the phone. Then she leaned back in her chair and closed her eyes. She needed to make sure that Kimmie was safe at home. And she was going to find Boomer and confront him. She shivered, suddenly.

All that happened when you behaved like a tough guy and said "fine!" when people asked you how you were was that certain people stayed in a nice, safe Hyatt instead of riding to the rescue, letting a mere six feet or so of snow act as an insurmountable obstacle.

The phone rang.

Her private line, which meant that Dina had put through a personal call.

Myles. Myles was calling back. The hell with heroics. Quill picked up the phone and said pitifully, "Hello?"

"Quill."

"Harker!" Quill sat up, her queasy stomach momentarily forgotten.

"Called to see how things are going. When we last talked, Quill—you worried me. No. You scared me." There was a short, heavy pause. Quill, irrationally irritated, decided that Harker's conversational pauses were different from Myles's. Myles paused when he was thinking about something else and not paying attention to you. Harker paused when he was waiting for you to say something significant. Quill didn't feel like being pressured into saying anything at all.

"Now's not a good time, Ben. It's been—it's been kind of fraught here. There's been another death."

"You're kidding." Harker's tones went up a notch. "Jesus. It's worse than New York." Then, in an absent way, "You're okay, aren't you?"

"I'm fine."

"Well, forget about it. It doesn't have anything to do with you."

"I wish it didn't have anything to do with me," Quill said crossly. "Honestly, every time we have a little corpse problem in Hemlock Falls, the whole blooming media seems to show up and we keep making the national news."

"That's true," Harker said thoughtfully. "As a matter of fact, that's where I first saw you, Quill."

"I thought you saw my work!" Quill said. "You said you loved my work."

"That was after I saw you on the late-night news," Harker said smoothly. "And when I saw your work—well, you know what happened." His voice dropped and he added huskily, "Now, look, I called because it's snowing like hell and the train's probably going to be late tomorrow. I don't want you to say a thing to the media without me, Quill, not a thing. I should be by your side when the interviews are done."

"That's okay," Quill said hastily.

"Quill." His voice dropped. "You're not questioning our love?"

That final phrase set Quill's teeth on edge. Sentiment made her itchy. "My hair's falling out," Quill said. "And my arms and legs are so shaky . . ." She decided, defiantly, on a little exaggeration here. She hadn't had the shaky part since she'd dropped her coffee consumption. ". . . sometimes I can barely walk. And now I'm sick to my stomach. I hate being sick to my stomach. So, no, Ben, I'm not questioning our love, as you put it. I've been sick. And there's been two murders here."

Harker's voice dropped into something that sounded suspiciously like belligerence. "You aren't . . . I mean, you *were* taking precautions, Quill. In addition to the condoms, I mean."

"This is *not* what being pregnant feels like," Quill said. "I've been to Cornell for tests and nobody knows what it is." She added coldly, "I'm probably dying."

"What do they think it is, Quill? I mean, Cornell's got an international reputation. They must have some idea."

Quill looked at the *Merck Manual* on her desk. "They don't know. Amyotrophic lateral sclerosis. Or an astrocytoma. They don't know."

"An astro-what?"

"It's a brain tumor. Possible brain tumor."

"Oh my god, Quill." Then, he asked, "Is it catching? Not the brain tumor, but that other stuff you mentioned?"

"No."

"Oh my god. But they never know, do they? Quill, you were absolutely right. I had no business coming up to see you this weekend."

"Actually, I could have used some help," Quill said craftily.

"Your sister's there, isn't she? Family's really the best in circumstances like these, Quill."

"And you aren't?"

"Aren't what?" he asked uneasily.

"Family."

"God, Quill. I mean, a few weeks together, that's what we've had."

"So far," Quill said dryly.

"Of course. So how well do we really know each other?"

"Not as well as I thought, obviously."

"I mean, we've shared at the very deepest level."

"But not that deep."

"Quill!" His voice was wounded. "And I wouldn't be any help at all. Didn't you say one of the symptoms of this brain tumor was going bald? I had a friend that went through that. Believe me, you don't want anyone around when you're going through stuff like that."

"So," Quill said cheerfully. "Sorry to dump all this on you. And I'm even sorrier I didn't tell you before." She nibbled at her thumbnail. She was pretty sure about Harker now. But not totally. Not yet.

"Harker? So you're coming, right? To be by my side through this . . . um . . . ordeal. Not the media part—they probably can't get up here anyway . . . but my dread disease. You don't want to be by my side when I'm possibly, probably dying? And it can't be too infectious. I mean, Meg's fine. So far."

"You say there's a lot of snow?"

"More than a lot." Quill leaned forward and twitched the drapes aside again. "There's a bloody ton. But the trains run, even in weather like this, don't they?"

"Not this weekend," Harker said smoothly. "You know me, Quill. You know me." His voice dropped to the vibrant level that had literally made the back of her neck tingle. "I would be there. For you. But there's a gallery opening here tomorrow, an important one . . ."

Quill pulled at her lower lip. She was a chump. A perfect chump. Her office door burst open with a thump. Doreen stood there, hands on her hips. "Here's where you're at. You're needed, Quill. In the kitchen."

Quill put her hand over the receiver. "Just a second, okay?"

"It's herself," Doreen said. "Meg. That Kate heard her sing and she won't let her in the play."

"Meg," Quill interpreted for Harker. "And the Magnificent Kate is going to kick her out of the show. Will you call me later?"

"I have to be honest," Harker said. "Not tomorrow. But keep safe, my darling. Get some sleep. I'll call you soon."

"I've got a banquet for forty people, a dread disease, and a murderer in the wait staff . . ."

"What?!" Doreen shouted.

"So I've got no hope of sleep."

"Then treat yourself well, my darling, until I can be there to do it for you. And *call me,* promise?"

"I will," Quill said. She hung up the phone and regarded Doreen with a smile.

Doreen scowled back. "So?" she demanded.

"My friend Harker has feet of clay."

"And?"

"And you know, Doreen. I liked him. For a while I loved him. But it's not a good fit, Doreen."

"Good. So you can get on with it. You gotta do something about Meg."

"And Meg is where?"

Doreen cocked her head kitchen-ward. Quill followed her through the dining room, which was looking splendid in its banquet garb.

They both paused in front of the swinging doors to the kitchen and listened before entering. Two voices soared over the evening cacophony within: Meg's, raised in polite (for her) protest, and another, dulcet and stentorian at once, raised to reach the back row of Yankee Stadium. "No-no-no," Kate said.

Doreen swept the doors open. Kate, dressed as Mistress Ford in a bodice, long skirt, and jerkin, stood with arms akimbo, facing Meg. Meg, in her sweatshirt and jeans, had a mutinous look on her face.

Doreen and Quill ducked simultaneously to look at Meg's socks. The color and style were an invariable indicator of her temper for the workday.

"Red," Quill said.

"Yuh."

"But I've memorized all the words," Meg said to Kate. "*All* of them."

"No," Kate said. "You cannot sing. And you poked Boomer too hard in rehearsal. He squealed. Like a pig. And he wasn't supposed to. Even though he is a pig. Meg, darling. I love you. I love your food. I love your Inn. But you're fired. And dammit, I'm down one fairy."

"I," Meg said evenly, "know the damn part by *heart!*"

"No-no-no-no-no," Kate said. "Darling."

Meg scowled and opened her mouth. Quill leaped forward and grabbed both Meg's hands enthusiastically. "Meg! The chutneys! Fabulous! But Bjarne was just telling me he's not quite sure about the horseradish. And to be frank . . . I think you ought to talk to him yourself." She dragged her sister to the Sub-Zero and flung open the door. The chutneys sat in serried ranks on the shelves. "Bjarne? You were saying?"

A Finnish expletive from the neighborhood of the sink reminded her that Bjarne would eventually make her pay for this diversion. Quill turned back to Kate, who had settled morosely, if somewhat theatrically, next to Doreen.

"How are things, Kate?"

Kate held up one hand in a gesture of command worthy of Charles DeGaulle at his most French. "No jokes, please. None. But I'm a fairy short. You," she said critically, looking at Quill sideways, "are green enough to be a fairy, but you look a little tottery to me. Are you sick?"

"She don't have time to be sick," Doreen said, to Quill's outrage. "Look here, you need more actors?" Doreen straightened up to her full height. Her head poked forward like a rooster after a worm. "Thing is, I might be snowed in here tonight, and I done a bit of acting in my time. What I mean is, I might be free."

"Oh, yes?" Kate's eyebrows climbed almost to her hairline. "We'll see. But first? Tea!" Kate ordered. "And perhaps a bit of bread. If you please."

Quill drew hot water from the kettle on the Aga and brought

out the tea. She dragged a loaf of prune-walnut bread from the fresh bin and cut several thick slices.

While her tea was being readied, Kate held her head to one side and regarded Doreen. "Have you been on stage before?"

"*Oklahoma*, chorus, Kansas City, 1954, or somewheres about there. And one of the madwimmin in *Marat/Sade*, in the '70s . . ."

"*Marat/Sade!*" Quill said. "My goodness!"

"Character parts," Doreen said. "Non-speakin', but I know a flat from a round."

"Do you sing?" Kate asked with deep suspicion.

"Chorus. Pinafore."

Kate gulped her tea, shoved a slice of the prune bread into her mouth, shook Doreen's hand, and mumbled, "Come wif me."

Meg, finished with a surprisingly placid exchange of views with Bjarne, watched the double doors swing shut behind them. She tilted her head back. Barely moving her lips, she said, "And I coulda bin a contender."

"Not if you had to sing, Marlon," Quill said brutally. "Honestly, Meg. Although I wish I'd been there to see Kate's face when you *did* sing."

Meg ignored this with aplomb and turned to survey her kitchen. Except for the side dishes—the squash soufflé and the cranberry chutneys—the banquet was the kind of cooking she usually left to Bjarne, and it was clear from her expression that things were going well. She gave the under-chef a cheerful nudge and undid her apron, a clear signal she was leaving the field of battle and retiring with honors to her tent. "So, how'd it go with young Peterson?"

"Oh my god," Quill said. "That was only what, an hour ago. You won't believe what's happened since then."

"I believe it's snowing fit to bust outside. It's a good thing we're stocked up on food. Tell you what. I've got to do a quick taste of the desserts in the Lounge so I can decide the winner, and then we can sit down with a cup of tea."

"I'll walk with you. I feel as if I've abandoned the deck of the ship in the middle of a typhoon."

"Everything's under control, Captain. John and Nate went over the wines this afternoon. And Kathleen's pretty happy with the wait staff for tonight."

Quill, her long legs keeping her ahead of Meg as they walked through the dining room, stopped suddenly. "Meg. There's a lot to tell you as soon as you're ready. But I just want to confirm something for my own peace of mind. Kimmie is not here tonight, right?"

Meg nudged her forward. "Don't worry about Kimmie. She showed up just after you went down to the school and said that they'd made an appointment with a marriage counselor. She said that *he*," Meg added, "wasn't all that keen on going. But Andy told me Louis's been trying to get her to see a counselor for months."

"So she's at home with him, right?"

"Sure. I guess."

Quill, listening with half an ear, stepped into the Tavern Lounge and looked at the area in front of the bar. Kate and her troupe had been hard at work; floodlights were rigged to illuminate the flooring in front of the bar, leaving the area behind in shadow. Pots of philodendrons were placed strategically around the "stage." It looked quite authentic. Elizabeth I had commissioned *Merry Wives* from Shakespeare; he, too, had staged it at Hampton Court with a minimal set.

"Quill?" Meg stepped around her, still chattering. "Anyway, Andy says physicians spend all their time telling people what to do and it's hard for them to . . ." Meg grabbed her arm so hard it hurt. "Oh, no! Quill! No! No-no-no-no! Not another body!"

Quill turned and looked at the dessert table. Kimmie Bloomfield lay sprawled across Dookie Shuttleworth's Midsummer Night's Dream Coconut Cake.

# CHAPTER 19

"The ambulance is stuck at the bottom of the drive," Meg said. "Andy and Louis are walking on up." She shut the cell phone with a decisive click and went to the French doors leading to the flagstone patio. Drifts of snow piled waist-high against the glass panes. "I hope they have their snowsuits on."

Kimmie lay on a quilt on the floor. Quill knelt at her side. She was breathing normally, as far as Quill could tell, and although she was pale, she didn't look deathly ill. Doreen sat nearby, her legs akimbo, a damp cloth at the ready. She'd emptied the Lounge of curious guests with her customary gusto. Quill was thankful she hadn't been armed with her mop.

"How is she?" Meg paced restlessly back and forth. "Dammit, I don't like those guys out in this stuff. You can't see your hand in front of your face."

"She's just the same," Quill said dubiously, "unconscious. But her pulse is normal, according to Andy, and her respiration is slow, but low normal. Also according to Andy. I think she's been drugged."

All three of them turned to look at the cake. Doreen had cleaned the cake off Kimmie's face, but when Quill forced Kimmie's mouth open to make sure she wasn't going to choke, there'd been coconut on her tongue.

"Seen it before," Doreen said.

"Seen *what* before?" Quill asked crossly. "Poisoned coconut cake?"

"Dieters. They lose their minds. Never know what's gonna set 'em off. See, I think Ms. Bloomfield saw that cake and just couldn't help herself. The pieces were all cut ready for Meg to judge, and she just grabbed a piece and stuffed it in her mouth and there you go."

"There *I'd* go," Meg said. "I was the only person supposed to eat that cake. If you're right, and Kimmie was just sneaking some, it should be me on the floor." Meg seemed thoughtfully pleased at this piece of deduction. She stared at Kimmie for a moment, and then said, " 'O, what can ail thee, maid at arms, alone and palely loitering?' "

Quill stood up to relieve the ache in her knees. "We'd better bag it for evidence," she said. "The cake, not the Keats. Or at the very least put something over it to protect it before the sheriff gets here."

The French doors rattled with a violent gust of wind.

"*If* they get here," Meg muttered. She walked restlessly to the doors again, and then gave a whoop. "The knights have arrived!" She pulled the doors open and fell into the embrace of a bulky figure in a snowsuit.

Quill, who didn't know how Meg could tell Andy from Kimmie's husband since they were both cocooned in dark-blue down and black artic masks, stood protectively in front of Kimmie's body. "Shut the doors, guys. The snow's going all over."

"Hell of a storm out there," Andy said. "The big plow's coming down the drive, but I don't think it's doing much good."

The figure Meg wasn't hugging pulled his arctic mask off and took three long strides across the floor. "Has she regained consciousness?"

"Her eyes were fluttering a few minutes ago." Doreen got up with a grunt and came to stand beside Louis Bloomfield. "There, see? I think she's waking up."

Louis dropped to one knee, felt for Kimmie's pulse, and then peeled one eyelid back with his thumb. Andy, with Meg at his side, came up and knelt beside his partner. Standing over them both, Quill noticed that Andy was balding. She stopped herself from patting her hair. She caught Meg's eye.

"Stop that," Meg whispered.

"You three want to give us a little room?" Andy's voice was mild, but Meg and Doreen withdrew to a nearby table. Quill went behind the bar to search for something to cover the cake.

"What's this stuff in her hair?" Louis called roughly.

"Coconut cake," Quill called. "What is it, Louis? Could she have been drugged?"

"Maybe," Louis said. "It's not a coma. That damn diet she was on. Damn it, Andrew. I don't want to give her a shot of adrenaline. I need a blood scan."

"She's not diabetic, is she?"

The two men exchanged looks. "Hypoglycemic shock?" Andy offered. "I had a case earlier this year."

"Couldn't be. Look at her. She's what, a hundred and thirty, hundred and thirty-five pounds?"

"If she had a predisposition to diabetes, could be."

"This looks like a drugged sleep to me, Bishop. Her vitals are good. But we've got to get her to the clinic where I can run some lab tests."

"You could draw some samples. I can run it down the hill for you. If she's not in any immediate danger, she'd be better off here than taking a stretcher out in that storm."

Louis didn't answer. Andy got to his feet and came to the bar, where Meg joined him. The tips of his nose and ears were red and his eyes were still watering from the cold. He slapped his hand on the mahogany top. "Whiskey for me. Fresh horses for my men. And where's my woman?"

Quill rolled her eyes as Meg, the fool, responded to this with a truly odious giggle. "Scotch or bourbon?"

"Just coffee, if you've got some."

Quill nodded and switched on the Bunn coffeemaker. "So you don't think she was drugged?"

"Too soon to say. But you might save those desserts, in case we need to run some tests."

"She was drugged," Meg said with conviction. "Only it wasn't Kimmie the murderer was after. It was me."

Andy accepted the coffee Quill handed him, and took a cautious sip. "Um," he said, skeptically.

"Tell him, Quill."

"Well, Meg was the only person who was supposed to taste those desserts," Quill said. "So if Kimmie ate the cake, and if there was poison of some kind in it, then the poison was meant for Meg."

"My life," Meg said dramatically, "is clearly in danger." Andy was annoyingly unperturbed. Meg's lower lip jutted out. She drew her eyebrows together. "Andy!"

"I don't know of any substance that causes unconsciousness that doesn't have a strong, distinctly unpleasant taste," Andy said. "And furthermore, if she did happen to eat a piece of cake dosed with a drug strong enough to put her under, she'd throw it up before it got into her bloodstream. So no, Meg, I don't think the cake was poisoned."

"A lot you know about it," Meg scoffed.

"I do know a great deal about it." He said this with such an amiable, rational air, that Meg subsided immediately. Andy never took umbrage. Quill had long ago decided it was the secret to their relationship.

"Bishop. Take a look at this." Louis's voice was peremptory, reminding Quill of everything negative people said about doctors. They all responded to Louis's command, however, and clustered around Kimmie's still-unconscious form. Louis took a penlight from his shirt pocket and pointed it at Kimmie's nose. Quill found this detachment off-putting. She was developing a lot of sympathy for Kimmie's marital difficulties.

"See here? The reddened area around the nostrils?"

"Cocaine?" Quill said before she could edit herself, and clapped her hand over her mouth. Louis gave her a long, disparaging look before glancing at Andy Bishop. "Did anyone touch her face?" Louis asked icily.

"I did," Doreen said. "She was all-over coconut, so I cleaned her up."

"How hard did you scrub?"

Doreen's face turned pink.

Quill, deciding she *really* didn't care for Louis Bloomfield, said hotly, "Doreen's as gentle as a lamb," which made even Doreen laugh.

"I din't scrub," she said. "I wiped. That there's a scratch under there."

"Right. And the nasal passages are reddened, too. And see here?" The penlight moved impersonally down to her mouth. Louis took his thumb and turned her upper lip outward. "There's abrasions on the underside of her lip, from her front teeth." He stared up at them, his face hard.

Kimmie's eyelids fluttered, and she moaned. She opened her eyes, coughed, and then closed them again.

"See? She's coming out of it." Louis stood up and pocketed the penlight. He looked down at his wife. His face was totally expressionless. "Someone forced her to inhale something."

"An anesthetic?" Andy frowned. "I don't know, Bloomfield."

Louis Bloomfield's eyes swept the four of them. "Someone here tonight tried to kill my wife."

Except she wasn't his wife. She was someone else's wife. Before.

And for whatever reason, Kimmie hadn't told this husband about the first.

Quill looked at Louis Bloomfield. Like Andy, he was neatly made and fit. He had medium-brown hair and wore glasses. He didn't look like the kind of passionate man who would kill his wife's former husband.

Or poison his own wife.

Quill recalled the Chamber of Commerce meeting. Kimmie's bright, artificial chatter. The absolute nonrecognition of Joss Roberts, who wasn't Joss Roberts, but the grieving father of a baby dead and buried twenty years before. She remembered Louis himself, a little stiff, but surely, surely if he'd known Joss was Kimmie's first husband, he would have betrayed himself in some way. Surely, if he'd known about that first, lost child, he would be treating her with more kindness now.

What did they know, any of them, about Louis Bloomfield?

Kimmie was half conscious, her voice high and querulous. Andy was helping her sit up, while her husband watched, arms folded. Meg reached over the bar and tugged Quill's sleeve. "What are you doing?" she hissed.

"What do you mean what am I doing?"

"Stop staring at them like that. I think we should leave them alone."

"I have to talk to you," Quill said abruptly. "Let's go to my office."

"We can't just leave her in the middle of the floor!" Meg said.

"What's going on?" Doreen nudged Meg aside. "We gonna look for the person who tried to kill Mrs. Bloomfield?"

"Yes," Quill said to Doreen, and "You're right," to Meg. "We'll stay here and bag up those desserts. And we'll get Kimmie settled. Are there any spare rooms, Doreen?"

"Not a one. We're full up."

Quill looked at her watch "They should be serving the first course right now. Okay, we have, what, an hour before the meal's finished. Let's see what we can get accomplished before we have people swarming all over the place. Doreen, can you help the guys get Kimmie settled in your room? And would you tell John I don't want any of the wait staff to leave the Inn for any reason."

Doreen made a widely expressive gesture toward the blizzard raging outside the French doors.

"I know. But the guy we're after has got to be desperate."

Doreen grinned widely. "Should I call Stoke? Tell 'im to bring up my gun?"

"For heaven's sake, no!" Quill took a breath. "You wouldn't want Stoke out in this, Doreen."

"The doc said how's the plows are out already. Plus we got a snowmobile."

"For all of that, *we've* got a snowmobile. All the more reason for John to keep the wait staff together. Tell John that we're going to give them a bonus for their hard work tonight. Tell them anything, just get them all together right after the banquet, okay?"

"Got it."

Andy had come as fully equipped as a backpack would allow. He and Bloomfield unfolded a portable stretcher, and in less than a minute, Doreen led them out of the Lounge and up to Quill's rooms. In the interim, Quill found a box of plastic bags under the bar. She shoved a handful at Meg, and they began to wrap up the desserts.

"Why are we doing this?" Meg demanded. "And do we want the name tags with them?"

"Because I'm paranoid. Because I need to do something with my hands. Because there's a murderer running around the Inn, and I don't understand what's going on."

"So, we bag up all the food in the kitchen, too?"

Quill set down a dish called Chicken Macbeth, which appeared to be chicken-shaped meringues. "You're right. I'm overreacting."

"What exactly are you overreacting to? I don't understand why anyone would want to asphyxiate Kimmie Bloomfield, for one thing. Do you?"

"I think she recognized someone," Quill said. "I think she recognized Franklin Overmeyer. And he tried to shut her up."

"Overmeyer . . ." Meg's eyes widened. "What are you talking about? Not that murder? Not that horrible murder!"

"Myles called. Do you know who Joss Roberts really is? And do you know who Kimmie Bloomfield really is?"

Quill sat the both of them down at a table and told her. "And," she said, "Myles and I think that George Nash got out of prison and was one of the few people able to identify Overmeyer, and that's why he was killed."

Meg took two long breaths. She struggled for speech. "But *why*? Why kill Joss? Why try to kill Kimmie?"

"Who knows, Meg? Murderers are twisted people. Maybe Nash's release from prison brought it all back. Maybe Nash was blackmailing him, and Joss and Kimmie were going to be witnesses."

"Myles thinks this, too?" Meg radiated skepticism.

"Well . . . some of it, he does."

"Jeez." Meg ran both hands through her hair. It stood up in spikes all over her head. She looked around a little nervously. "So. He's here, do you think?"

"I do."

"Yeah, yeah, yeah. So which one is it?"

"You interviewed the wait staff, Meg. Not me. Which one could it be?"

Meg pressed the heels of both hands against her eyes.

"He'd be thirty-eight, now," Quill said. "Or thirty-nine. And cons have a certain look, Meg."

Meg glared at her between her fingers. "Oh they do, do they?"

"Yes. They do. Their body language is different." Quill thought a moment and then said sadly, "They have sort of a duck and run look. A beaten look."

Meg said, "Phut!" Then she looked at the ceiling. "None of the temp staff is Franklin Overmeyer."

"One of the wait staff has to be Franklin Overmeyer."

Meg ticked off the names on her fingers: "There's a guy who worked 30 years for Xerox and got laid off. There's two women who are earning money for Christmas."

"Could they be disguised?"

Meg blinked. "What? Don't be ridiculous. Then there's two kids, *kids*, Quill. Two guys. In their twenties."

"They could be disguised, too. And it's hard to tell how old people are, Meg. I'll have to see them. I know it's been twenty years, but I don't forget a face, or bone structure, or the shape of a person's ears. If I see Franklin Overmeyer, I'll know him."

Meg gave her hand a gentle squeeze. "Mom and Dad were worried about that. I remember. That we'd both never forget."

Quill, lost in the past, said, "I haven't. I haven't thought of it for years, but now that we're in the middle of this, I can remember it all. Every detail."

"Well, I can't, thank god." Meg sank back into her chair. "You know, all I can really recall is you grabbing me and smashing my nose in your T-shirt." She shuddered, suddenly. "That and the baby screaming. You remember faces, Quill. I remember sounds."

"I didn't remember Joss Roberts," Quill said.

"You never really saw him. We both scrammed out of there. And Mom and Dad were pretty good at censoring the news, if you recall." She leaned forward. She looked tired suddenly. "Quill, if we do find Franklin Overmeyer, what do we do with him?"

Quill blinked at her.

"Tie him up? Point a gun at him?"

"We don't have a gun."

"In all our cases, Quill, we've never really arrested anyone. How do we do it?"

"I guess we get John and Andy and some of the other guys to surround him and lock him up somewhere. Until the storm's over."

"What if he has a gun? He has chloroform, or whatever it was that almost knocked Kimmie into kingdom come. What if he has a knife?"

"Maybe we can get Boomer to sit on him."

Meg gave her a "that's not funny" frown, then tilted her head, listening. "Hear that?"

"Hear what?"

"The snowplow's stopped outside. Didn't you hear the smash and grumble as it went up and down the drive? Maybe we could get the crew to go on down to the village and get Davey Kiddermeister."

Quill had been aware of the snowplow then, and was aware now, that it had stopped. Both of them went to the French doors and peered outside. The snow piled in gigantic humps across the grounds. The yellow of the snowplow's headlights was fuzzy, blurred by wind-whipped swells of white.

"The guys are coming in," Meg said. "Look. They're probably frozen. Maybe I better see to something hot for them."

Quill waved at the shapeless figures through the glass. She thought she recognized one of the guys as the crew came closer to the doors: Harland Peterson. She wasn't sure about the others.

"What are they dragging?" Meg asked.

"I don't know. Poor guys. You couldn't pay me enough to freeze out there." Quill pulled the doors open and the crew began to file in through a blast of arctic, snow-laden air. There were three of them, Harland Peterson in the lead. The other two left the bundle they were dragging just outside the doors.

"We are really glad to see you," Meg said. "We think we're going to need the sheriff, and we hoped we could find a way to get him."

"Del Stuart's already took the snowmobile down there to find Davey," Harland said. He pulled his watch cap off and rubbed his face with one gloved hand. "We gotta problem."

"What is it, Harland?" Quill stepped forward. Except for the frostbitten pink of his cheeks, the elderly farmer was gray with distress. He put his hand out to keep Quill from stepping outside, but she shook it off.

"Some poor guy got caught up in the blade," Harland said. "Damn it. Damn it. We dragged the poor son of a bitch up and down your drive before we knew what was going on. Gee. I feel like hell. Don't go out there, Quill."

Quill stepped into the snow. They had wrapped him in a blanket, but there was no disguising the bulk. If it hadn't been snowing, they never would have been able to use the blanket as a sledge, and he would still be there, on the driveway: Boomer Dougherty.

# CHAPTER 20

The next morning, Quill woke to a world made silent by snow. She lay perfectly still in bed and looked up at the ceiling. The light from her bedroom window was brilliant with sunshine. The storm had gone, leaving close to two feet of snow in its wake. It'd be several days before the village was dug out. But it could have been worse.

Max was a solid lump at her feet and she wriggled her toes under the blanket. He grunted, yawned, and jumped onto the floor. "You ready to solve a murder today?"

Max panted and looked worried. This, Quill knew, was not out of any superdog empathy for the current circumstances but because she hadn't dashed out of bed to feed him.

The corpse of Boomer Dougherty lay in the equipment garage behind the Inn. The discovery of the body had resulted in chaos. Boomer had been tied behind the snowplow. How the murderer had gotten him there—and how Boomer, whose bulk alone made the idea that one person had done it problematic at best, had let himself be subdued—were yet to be determined. The body had been so mangled by the dragging that any preliminary deductions had been impossible.

Myles was on his way, with a team of forensic police from Syracuse. She'd called him, late. And he had some unsettling news. So there would be answers, soon.

"You know what, Max? I have a theory about this murder."

Max thumped his tail.

"The Ross baby was dragged to death. Boomer was dragged to death. Joss Roberts is dead. Kimmie's been poisoned, we think. George Nash is dead. There's all these little pieces, Max.

And right now, none of them fit together. I mean, what does Boomer have to do with all this?"

Max yawned.

"There's a question all great investigators ask themselves, Max. *Cui bono*? Who benefits?"

Me, Max's expression said. I should benefit. With breakfast, please.

"There are quite a few people who benefit from Boomer's death. The whole crew, who hate his guts. Even Kate, whose play he wrecked with his lousy performance. Of course, Sylvia most of all."

Sylvia Prince, of all people, had pitched a hysterical fit at having the body in the building, and the snow had been too monstrous to get him to the village municipal building (where he could have stayed in the cell) much less the Tompkins County Morgue in Ithaca.

"But who connected with the carjacking could benefit from Boomer's death?"

Quill had interviewed each of the wait staff, in person, John and Harland Peterson and Davey Kiddermeister within shrieking distance, and none of them had been Franklin Overmeyer. Not even the suspiciously angular lady with the prominent Adam's apple and the bad perm who'd waxed big time indignant when Quill had asked for a closer look at her ears.

All of this detecting activity had been wasted.

Max whined and pawed at her: breakfast!

"I didn't get to bed until three o'clock, you wretched hound." Max responded to this with a bark.

"All right, all right." Reluctantly, Quill sat up and put her feet on the floor. She couldn't even think of painting this morning. The Lounge was still a mess of desserts. The dining room had been cleared of the banquet dishes before Boomer's body had surfaced, but the Inn was full to the rafters with stranded guests, and the entire staff was exhausted. And at least when she didn't paint, she felt better. Her head didn't hurt, her arms didn't hurt, her stomach was fine.

She realized after a moment that her mouth was open.

The paint. Her tubes of paint.

"Oh, Max," she said. "Oh, no."

Who benefits? Who would benefit from Quill's own demise? Who hated her enough to send her to a skinny, bald death? Carol

Ann Spinoza, that was who. In her very own living room. Sneaking around her paint. Messing with the tube of azure, and the color hadn't been right, after that; it had an awful grayish undertint.

Carol Ann, the meanest woman in Tompkins County if not the entire umpty-ump thousand acres of upstate and central New York.

Quill leaped for the *Merck Manual* and paged through the back for poisons. There it was, heavy metal poisoning: headaches, shooting pains, upset stomach. "Oh, damn!" she shouted. "That miserable witch!" In a cold rage, she grabbed the tube of azure. The same color Carol Ann had on her finger when she'd been messing in Quill's paints.

Fingerprints. There must be fingerprints. Hers certainly, but Carol Anne's had to be on the tube, too. Quill grabbed a Baggie from her kitchen drawer and dropped the paint in it. Max raced excitedly around the living room. Quill tripped over him once, inadvertently stepped on his tail, and rather crossly banged two handfuls of kibble into his dog dish. She couldn't decide what to do with the tube of azure, to keep it safe, so she ended up putting it back in the chest.

She sat down on her couch and thought. Tests. She needed proof, so she'd ask Davey to send the tube off to the forensics lab and . . . No. She had to have tests, first. She'd call Dr. Goldman and make another appointment and take the tube to Cornell.

"And then, Max . . ."

Max wagged his tail hopefully.

"Then, we'll see. But I can tell you this, dog. She's had it."

Quill showered and dressed with a feeling that this, at least, was one mystery she'd be able to solve. "And it's a better start to the day than I could have hoped for, considering. Max."

Max cocked his head sorrowfully. Quill sighed, her high spirits evaporating as quickly as they'd come. She'd like nothing better than to spend the rest of the morning in bed, with the covers pulled over her head.


Quill passed through the dining room and on into the kitchen with little of her usual enthusiasm for her guests. The meteorologists were quiet, eating with subdued faces. Boomer's TV crew was sullen. Kate and the other actors weren't at any of the tables. Nobody was eating much. She stopped at Sylvia Prince's table. She stared out the window at the waterfall. Abstracted, Quill thought, but not grief-stricken.

"Hey," Sylvia said. "Have a seat."

"There's a lot to do this morning. Maybe later. Are you checking out?"

"Soon as we can." She stretched restlessly, and her smile was grim. "I've done a broadcast on Boomer's murder already. Not much of an investigation, yet. Didn't get squat from that sheriff of yours. He is dumb, Quill."

Quill suppressed her irritation. "We're a small town, Sylvia. We aren't exactly set up for homicide investigations."

"Oh, I wouldn't say that. Somebody told me Myles McHale is on his way here. Isn't he the guy with the rep in New York City? The one that had the highest number of homicides solved when he was a detective on the NYPD?"

"Yes," Quill said. "All that was a long time ago, though."

"And you and your sister have quite a reputation. Maybe we should have interviewed you instead of that dolt Kiddermeister. What's your take on this?"

Kathleen rudely slapped a plate of scrambled eggs in front of Sylvia and marched off. Sylvia raised her eyebrows, questioningly.

"The sheriff's sister," Quill said, unapologetically. Sylvia deserved to be embarrassed. "And I don't have a take on this. I'm as confused as everyone else. How in the world did Boomer get caught and tied behind the snowplow? Was he drunk?"

"Couldn't have been liquor. Boomer didn't drink. Ate like a pig, as you can tell from his size, but no, he didn't drink."

"When did you see him last?"

Sylvia shrugged. "He was supposed to give the after-dinner speech and announce the first prize for that stupid contest, but no one was especially interested in it, mostly because we'd stuffed ourselves with Meg's food. So when the sherbet and the coffee were served, we all just sat around shooting the shit. And then, of course, that dishy manager of yours came in. What's his name? John Raintree? He came in and told us what had happened and we all went up to our rooms until the sheriff got around to asking us the who, where, when questions. Well, most of us. I hung around trying to get a story, as you know."

"Yes." Sylvia had been an unobtrusive, but definite presence last night. "Was Boomer here for the whole meal?"

Sylvia shook her head. "He wasn't at the meal at all. Weren't you listening? I told that du . . . that sheriff that no one had seen him since the end of the last seminar at four-thirty."

Quill frowned, trying to get the timetables straight. If Sylvia were correct, Boomer could have been dead for a long time. "Where were you at four-thirty?"

"In the seminar, of course. Where were you at four-thirty?"

Quill put this down to Sylvia's natural aggressiveness, but she answered anyway. "I was coming back from the Blue Cow."

"The what? Oh. That computer office that poor schmuck Joss Roberts ran. So?"

"I'd just discovered Boomer had been making weird phone calls to me."

"Boomer?" Sylvia's eyebrows lifted. "That is weird. Why?"

"I don't know. You knew him. You've known him for a long time."

"What kind of phone calls were they?" Sylvia looked peeved. "You don't have to tell me. I can guess. I could never understand why he picked Hemlock Falls, of all places, to set up this conference. No offense, Quill, but it's the back of beyond. And if he wanted visibility, there's lots more glamorous places. But I got an inkling, when we were here in September."

"You were here in September?"

"Yeah. You were in New York with this guy. But Boomer wanted to see your work, kept talking about it. As if . . ." Sylvia looked at Quill through half-closed eyes. An odd, secretive smile crossed her face. "As if he knew you, almost. Or wanted to know you. We even went up to your room. Dina showed us the piece you were working on. He poked around your paints, too. Wanted to know all about you."

Quill stared at her.

Sylvia made a dismissive gesture. "Price of fame, kiddo. You ask me, I think Boomer had a bit of a thing for you."

Quill shook her head. "No. I would have picked it up."

"From Boomer? Not likely. Man had more secrets than the guys who ran the Spanish Inquisition. Trust me. I knew the guy all too well."

Quill's head was stuffed with too much information. "But why would he . . . it doesn't make sense."

Sylvia patted her hand. "It will, cookie. All things come to he who waits. Look at me. I'm about to become a weather girl.

And from there, who knows? Now, about the last time I saw the big, fat jerk. It was just when the snow started to get really bad. He wasn't at the cocktail hour in the conference room, and he wasn't at the dinner, and the last time I saw him, he was talking to Alan, over there." She jerked her thumb in Alan Simpson's direction. "Hey! Alan!" she shouted. "Come on over. Ms. Marple here wants to ask you some questions." She turned back to Quill and lowered her voice. "He's one of the contenders for Boomer's spot, too. Watch. He'll be here in a flash. He's been keeping an eye on me ever since this happened. Wants to know what I'm going to do, but hasn't had the guts to ask." She showed her teeth in a brief smile. "Alan's not tough enough for the big time."

"The big time," Quill said. "How tough do you have to be for the big time?"

Sylvia smiled unpleasantly. "As tough as I am, cookie. As tough as I am."

Quill couldn't think of a response to this that wouldn't sound actionable or rude. ("Tough enough to kill Boomer?" or "You don't have to work at it very hard, do you?") So she excused herself and went into the kitchen.

Despite the scent of baked breads and fresh oranges, the kitchen had an air of gloom and disarray. Everybody looked tired and unkempt. Doreen had broken out the guest emergency kits the night before, and there had been enough toothpaste, toothbrushes and razors to go around, but sleeping accommodations had been a problem, and nobody seemed to have had enough sleep anyway. Bjarne stood over the Aga, half awake. Meg looked pale, and there were dark circles under her eyes. She also looked cross. Quill craned her neck and took a quick look at her socks: an acid green. So Meg was going to be balky. Quill settled onto the stool in front of the prep table with an air of unconcern and Bjarne gave her a cup of coffee.

"Why aren't you in bed with the covers pulled over your head?" Meg stuffed croissant dough with chocolate rather listlessly. She put a fresh croissant in front of Quill. "I've decided that's the best reaction to a suspicious death in a snowstorm. Retreat until the cavalry arrives. I'm going to finish here, get rid of those desserts in the Lounge and go back to bed. What's the matter with you, anyway? You look suspiciously chipper. How are your aches and pains?"

"I'm feeling a lot better this morning." Quill reached over to take a croissant. "As a matter of fact, I'm feeling fabulous this morning."

Meg looked at her and smiled. "Good. Andy thinks it's just a matter of time before they find out what you're allergic to, but you're certainly suffering now, poor baby."

"I told you, it's not allergies." Quill smiled. She'd be less than human if she didn't take some satisfaction from the vision of Carol Ann Spinoza in jail. But that could wait. Who was it who said revenge is a dish best served cold?

"You told me it was a dread disease. You've told everyone it's a dread disease. Boy are you going to be embarrassed when Andy turns out to be right."

Quill decided to let this drop for the moment. Meg was not in the mood for detection this morning. And Quill had a suspicion that her sister was going to be very skeptical about Carol Ann until the facts were in. She was going to have to present the facts carefully.

"Quill?"

"What!" Quill choked on the croissant and Meg came over and pounded her back.

"Sorry. You were drifting again." She dropped the last of the dough into the trash can underneath the prep table and dusted her hands briskly. "There. I'm finished. No more cooking or baking today for me. We've got soup and chili on for lunch, and we put a couple of the Thanksgiving turkeys in for tonight and that's it. People will just have to lump it."

"Fine," Quill said mildly. "Is the snow over? How much time have we got?"

"How much time have we got for what? If you mean how much time have I got for a nap, the answer is, more than enough. I just have to get those desserts cleared up, and I'm gone."

Quill raised one finger after the other: "You're not interested in solving these murders?"

"No," Meg said. "I am not."

"Not even if this is the only chance we have to find out who did it?"

"This is not the only chance to find out who did it."

"With all the suspects shut up in the Inn while we dig out of the blizzard?"

"What makes you think whoever killed Joss Roberts is here?

And as for Boomer . . . well, I'll grant you that. Whoever killed Boomer probably is here. I mean, most of his colleagues appeared to have wanted to kill Boomer. But let's let the police take care of that, okay? Anyway, it looks to me like at least two different people did it. Somebody killed Joss and somebody killed Boomer. I'm too pooped to find out one murderer, much less two. And besides, Quill, every time we solve a case, it turns out to be dangerous. I'm about to get married, we're even thinking about having a family in a few years. I think I want out of the detective business. I mean, I don't even get a paycheck for it."

"You're just tired," Quill said kindly. "Let's look what needs to be done. One, find out what happened to Kimmie Bloomfield. Two, find out who killed Boomer Dougherty. Three, find out who ran Joss Roberts over. And four, who killed George Nash. And with *my car!*"

"That's two different cases, Quill. Maybe three."

Quill shook her head. "The cases are connected. They have to be."

"Why?"

"Why?"

"Yes, why?"

"They have to, it isn't logical if they aren't."

Meg dug her hands into her hair. "Who says murder has to be logical? I'm getting very confused."

"It's only confusing if you refuse to step back and look logically at the facts."

"Facts," Meg said. "What facts have we got? Three bodies. A poisoned doctor's wife. No evidence. Guesswork."

"Logic," Quill said firmly. "We just have to be logical. Here's what I think. Let's go through it logically."

"I hate that word already," Meg said. "Don't use it anymore."

"Okay, rationally. How's that? Rationally, Kimmie's poisoning, and George Nash and Joss Roberts's murders are definitely connected. It's Boomer's death that is the confusing part."

"I *told* you this was confusing," Meg muttered.

Quill conceded this, reluctantly.

Meg pressed the advantage. "We don't know that Kimmie was poisoned. I think Doreen was right. I think Kimmie's nutty diets put her into hypoglycemic shock or something. You're making a lot of assumptions here, Quill. It's just like your dread disease. You won't wait for the tests to get back and you refuse to believe your headaches and muscle aches are allergies of some kind, and you're coming to the wrong conclusion *as usual!*" This last comment, shouted with some of Meg's old preblizzard enthusiasm, made Bjarne drop a platter of sausage. "That twenty-year-old case," she added calmly, "*is* a connection. I'll grant you that."

"Hang on a minute about my dread disease. First, I'm not making assumptions. I'm just looking at the facts log . . . I mean, rationally. Joss and Kimmie were married at one time. The two of us actually witnessed the tragedy that broke their marriage apart, although Meg, and this is important, you were too young to have been a factor."

The revelation hit Quill with the force of a two-by-four. "Oh, no. I was wrong."

"So what else is new. Quill? Quill? What is it? What do you mean, too young to have been a factor? A factor in what?"

"In the murders that are happening right now." Quill waited a few beats and then said slowly, "Hmmm."

Meg stared blankly at her.

"Bear with me. George Nash has been dead for three days. You know who had the opportunity to kill Nash and Joss and Boomer?"

"Who?" Meg asked, in a fascinated way. "And Boomer is *not* connected to this. How could . . . ?"

"In a minute. There's something you don't know. There's something I don't know. I mean, I suspect it, but I don't have the facts. Not yet."

Meg ground her teeth.

"We need to go into Doreen's office for a second and look at the computer."

Meg made a face. "Forget it, Quill. This is too complicated for this early in the morning. Besides, I told Doreen I'd help her clean up the mess in the Lounge. Those desserts are all over the place, still, and she's afraid we'll get bugs."

"We won't get bugs in November."

"I don't want to go into Doreen's office and look at the computer. I want to finish cleaning up the Lounge and go take a nap."

Quill got up and grabbed Meg's arm. "Boomer was trying to warn me. I want you to see it."

"Boomer was trying to warn you about what?" She followed Quill with the same kind of reluctance she exhibited as a little kid when they did the dishes, stamping her feet and muttering under her breath. Quill pushed her into the chair next to Doreen's desk and set the *Merck Manual* and Arnie's instructions down next to the desktop. She booted the computer up, then logged on to CityofLove.com. Using Arnie's instructions, she found the delete file and brought up the e-mail from Boomer.

"Look at this."

Meg, slumped back in the chair with her eyes closed, snarled no, then reluctantly stirred and looked over Quill's shoulder.

"Yuck. 'After all these years, is it you? If it is, be careful!' "

"From Boomer," Quill said, "See?"

"I see. I don't understand it, but I see."

"Now, what does this sound like?" Quill flipped open the *Merck* and read aloud the symptoms of heavy metal poisoning.

Meg frowned. "That sounds like what's happening to you."

"Not allergies," Quill said, "Poison."

"You've been poisoned?"

Quill nodded. With a pleased sense of how dramatic the gesture was, she took the tube of azure from her sweater pocket and held it out. Meg took her hands, her face white. "Someone's been trying to kill you? Why!"

"The Ross baby," Quill said simply. "This is all about the Ross baby. And all the people who were there."

"But lots of people were there. The police. The ambulance people. The reporters."

"Not at the crime scene," Quill said. "They were there after the crime was committed."

"But why Boomer? He wasn't there."

"Oh, yes, he was. I told you about the ears," Quill said. "I know I'm right about the ears. But there's a way to prove it. I hope. Look." She tapped away quickly at the keyboard, saving the peg file of Boomer at his outsize weight from the City of Love promotional material. She spent several long, impatient minutes finding the Syracuse Herald's photo of the getaway car. She saved the peg file of the back of Franklin Overmeyer's head. She put the two of them together on the spilt screen.

Meg stared, her mouth open. "Boomer was Franklin Overmeyer," she said. "Oh my god. And I thought he was that fat out of greed. He was that fat to conceal his identity."

Quill told her about Boomer and Sylvia's visit to her room in September.

Meg tugged thoughtfully at her lower lip. "But I don't understand, Quill. If anyone wanted to get rid of all the people concerned with the crime, it'd be Boomer himself, wouldn't it? I mean, I can understand George Nash. He's out of prison. And Boomer was back in Syracuse three days ago, so Boomer could have run him over. Nash could have been a blackmail threat to Boomer when he got out of prison. And I can see that Boomer would want to get rid of Joss Roberts, and even Kimmie, if somehow they recognized him after all these years. I mean, I'm willing to concede that maybe someone did try to kill her last night. And now you. And the poisoned paint. You did start to have those symptoms right after Boomer first came to the Inn. And Dina did take him up to see your work, Quill. She said he was very interested. But why now, Quill? Why not long ago? And if Boomer did commit all these crimes, *who killed Boomer?*"

Quill shrugged. "First of all, I don't think Boomer committed these crimes. As for why now, and not long before this, I haven't quite figured all that out, yet. I think it may have to do with the fact that all of us are together, in the same place. As for who killed Boomer, I think it was the same person who killed Joss, who killed George Nash, and who tried to kill me and Kimmie Bloomfield."

"Well, we'd better figure the 'why' out right this minute. The case depends on it. And who did kill Boomer?"

"That's the easy part," Quill said confidently. "Sylvia Prince."

"Sylvia Prince?"

"The woman in the car. The third person. The one the police never even identified. The accomplice."

"No," Meg said.

"You didn't see her. I caught a glimpse, no more than that. So did Joss Roberts. But Boomer and George certainly did. And the guilty, Meg, have a heightened sense of, well . . . guilt."

"Sylvia Prince? Sylvia Prince?!"

"It has to be. She's the right age. Boomer practically accused her of blackmail—he was neurotically afraid of her, at the very least. Boomer got her the job. It's obvious they hate each other, but they've worked together for years. And there's more than that, Meg. You know that we solve many of our cases by intuition—" She ignored Meg's derisive snort. "... But intuition is nothing more than being able to put little pieces of information together into a whole. Just like putting these pictures together."

"Good grief," Meg said. "Maybe you're right, for once."

"When I look back on all my conversations with Sylvia—well, she dropped hints all over the place."

"Yeah?"

"Yeah."

Meg shook her head. "No. I don't buy it. She killed Boomer after all these years because of why?"

"We'll ask her."

"What? Just march up and accuse her of all these killings, not to mention being an accomplice in a twenty-year-old horrible crime, and you expect her to say, yes, you're right, I give up, I did it? We have no evidence, Quill. Listen to me." She leaned forward and shouted into Quill's ear. *"No evidence!"*

"There's evidence," Quill said. "This tube of azure is evidence. I'm going to send it off to the lab right now."

"You are, huh. What lab? Where?"

"Andy can send it. We can say we suspect it's the source of my . . ." Quill laughed lightly. "Allergies."

"Yes," Meg said. "We can do that."

"But there's even better evidence, Meg. Right up in Doreen's room."

"Kimmie."

"Kimmie. And we have to interview her now. In the best Agatha Christie tradition. Sylvia's here. Snowbound. We have to solve this before she leaves the Inn."

Meg cocked her head. "And before Myles gets back?"

"Absolutely before Myles gets back. We will mightily impress him, Meg."

"We will, huh?"

"First, where is everybody? We have to be orderly about this."

"Everybody who? You mean our everybodies or Sylvia?"

"Sylvia's in the dining room." Quill looked at her watch. "She was, anyway. She's probably somewhere else by now."

"Well, Davey was here to sequester the snowplow. Louis still wouldn't let him interview Kimmie, and he didn't think it was important anyway, so he left it for later, which means we have a chance to solve this ourselves. But, Quill, if she knows anything, don't you think she would have said something by now?"

"She may not know she knows anything," Quill said.

"Uh, whatever. Doreen's cleaning up the Lounge, where I'm supposed to be right now, giving her a hand. And I know that every able-bodied person was supposed to go outside and give John and Mike a hand in digging us out. I don't know how enthusiastic everyone was about that, but even the kitchen crew was supposed to lend a hand."

"Then let's talk to Kimmie. Now."

"No."

"No?" Quill resisted the impulse to whack her sister over the head. "What, do you want time for a nap?"

"We need to check out the Lounge, Quill. Even as we speak, Doreen may be destroying clues."

"You're right. I mean, what if Sylvia did put something in the cake? She was talking to Kimmie about coconut, remember? This is a subtle set of murders, Meg. Sylvia's as wily as they come."

"I still think you're making far too many assumptions," Meg grumbled.

"I was just determined to be thorough. The last place anyone saw Boomer was in the Lounge, where he was rehearsing. And Kimmie collapsed there. It may be a crime scene. And Kimmie will wait."

"Unless Sylvia tried once, and is going to try again."

They stared at each other. Quill was the first to move. They raced into the kitchen, which was empty. Quill pushed open the doors to the dining room. That was empty, too. Meg followed her into the foyer. Dina was not at her desk, and the front door was halfway open. Snow had been tracked in, and puddles were all over the floor. Meg went to the door with an exclamation of annoyance. She looked out and down the driveway. "They all seem to be down there," she said. "My goodness. I had no idea we had so many snow shovels."

Quill peered over her shoulder. A huge crowd of people had formed a work party, although from her and Meg's vantage point, it looked as if it was more party than work. A couple of the meteorologists were in a snowball war with the camera crew. Kate's clarion tones soared above the shouts and laughter. She had apparently organized her actors into making a snow fort.

Someone had unearthed a snowblower, and the stuff sprayed in a crystalline waterfall, sprinkling in the sun. Mike, the grounds-keeper, had attached the snow blade to the Inn's pickup truck, and was making cautious headway against the huge mound of snow that had piled at the top of the drive.

"Do you see Sylvia?" Meg asked anxiously. "Your eyes are better than mine."

"I do," Quill said in surprise. "See? She's in the truck with Mike."

"That looks like the warmest job out there," Meg said. "I feel guilty. We should be helping."

"We should be solving this crime," Quill said. "Come on, let's make sure Kimmie's all right."

"She's sleepin'," Doreen said from behind them. Quill jumped and turned around. Doreen clumped down the stairs. She was dressed in farmer's coveralls and rubber boots. Her gray hair frizzed out from beneath a knitted hat. She addressed Quill with a flinty eye. "You ain't goin' out in that, are you, missy? Not in your condition. You—" She swiveled her beady gaze to Meg. "—are supposed to be in the lounge cleanin' that stuff up. We're gonna get bugs. You just let me get out there and stop all that horsin' around and I'll be back in to help you."

"They look like they're having fun, Doreen," Quill said.

"Huh. We got a crisis and those damn fools are out havin' a party. I don't think so."

Quill and Meg moved aside to let Doreen thump out past them. "Don't hit them with anything," Quill warned. And Meg added, "You're sure that Kimmie's all right? You saw her your-self?"

"I did. Sleepin' like a baby. I made her eat something," Do-reen added. "And put a flea in her ear about diets."

"I don't think it was dieting," Meg said.

"Keep an eye on Sylvia," Quill added. "If she comes back into the Inn, don't be obvious about it, but come with her. Okay?"

Doreen looked at the two of them from under lowered brows. "Yeah? That Sylvia up to something?"

"Yes," Quill said.

"We're not sure," Meg said.

"Just watch her." Quill put her hand on Doreen's shoulder. "And watch out for her, Doreen. She may be dangerous."

"I knew it," Doreen said in satisfaction. "I knew there was something up around here. You go to it. I'm on her like an oil slick on a duck."

Meg closed the door carefully behind the wiry housekeeper. "Lounge first, Quill. Facts first."

The Lounge was still a mess from the night before. The props used in *The Merry Wives of Windsor* were tumbled every which way in front of the Tavern bar. It occurred to Quill that the plot of the play—which involved disguises for nearly all the principal actors—bore more than a passing resemblance to the mystery she was so close to solving.

"Yuck." Meg poked her toe at the smear of coconut cake on the floor.

The Inn was eerily quiet. Somewhere in the distance, a door slammed. Meg took a fistful of plastic bags from her pocket and carefully scraped the cake into one. The rest of the desserts sagged on their presentation plates, and methodically, one by one, Meg put them into bags, too. Quill looked at the labels in front of them. The Macbeth meringues were a sorry puddle.

"That one I don't get," Meg said, coming up behind her. "It's a gruesome play, and what does this dessert have to do with chickens, anyway?"

Quill stared at the label. She cleared her throat. "Who made this dessert?"

"What's the matter?"

"Meg. Who made this dessert?"

"I don't know. Hang on. There's a list of the entries somewhere." She scrabbled through the stack of detritus at the end of the table. "Well, nuts, is it so important? We can ask Marge if we have to, I suppose. The outsiders used the Croh Bar kitchen to make their desserts. But if it was one of the people from the village . . . oh. Here it is."

" 'What?' " Quill quoted. Her voice sounded distant to her ears. " 'What? All my pretty little chickens?' " She turned to Meg. She could feel the tears in her eyes. "It's the line from the Scottish play, Meg. The saddest line in any play, anywhere. Macduff discovers the death of his children. And he takes his revenge.

"You were right, Meg. I was wrong. Sylvia didn't do this."

"Oh, no." The voice behind them was a whisper, no more. "Oh, no. I had just the one, you know. And they took him. All of them. Ross left him in the car. And those bastards. Those bastards. But I got them. I got them."

Kimmie Bloomfield was dressed in an old nightgown of Quill's. And she looked eerily like Lady Macbeth herself. Her curly hair streamed over her shoulders. Her eyes were soft and distant. She looked—peaceful.

Quill didn't know where Kimmie had gotten the gun. Quill started toward her, one hand out. Meg clutched her shoulders and pulled her back.

"It's the anniversary, you know. He would have been twenty-one today, my Evan.

"My one chick.

"My only chick."

She fired, once.

*And the rest is silence.*

# CHAPTER 21

"It was the miscarriage, I think." Andy spoke directly to Myles, as if not looking at either Meg or Quill would spare them grief. "Louis said she really took it hard."

Myles walked to the fireplace and shoved the poker between the flaming logs. Sparks whirled up the chimney.

"But she could still have had children," Meg said. "I mean, there's all kinds of ways to have children, Andy. There's tons of infertility clinics."

"Logic must not have had much to do with it," Quill said. "She just never got over Evan's death?"

"We'll never know, will we? Not for certain." John sat with his hands clasped and stared into the fire.

The five of them were alone in the Tavern Lounge. The roads were open. The ambulance had come and gone, Kimmie's body a silent mound on the stretcher. The Inn was empty of guests. Meg had sent the exhausted staff home. Even Doreen's incredible energy had flagged, and Stoke had bundled her home. Her protests were perfunctory at best.

"I think we should close down for a week," Quill said. "Reschedule the bookings for some other time. Just—disappear for Thanksgiving."

"Somewhere warm," John said.

Quill opened the door to her rooms with a nudge of her shoulder and dropped her luggage to the floor. Max, looking fatter than he should, bounced in after her, and then tore madly around her living room, barking at the top of his lungs. He was making so much noise she didn't hear Meg's light tap at the door.

"Hey!" Meg hugged her hard. "Did your plane get in early?"

"Yes. But Mike was early to pick us up, too. When did you guys get back?"

"What?" Meg yelled over the frantic dog.

"Will you *hush*, Max?" Quill went to her cupboard and tossed him a rawhide bone. "Mike feeds him too much when we're away." The dog settled happily and sloppily to the floor with it. "I asked when you guys got back."

"Last night."

"Skiing," Quill said. "I can't believe you and Andy forked over cash for more cold and snow."

"We had a great time. So did John. He met a really nice girl there, Quill." Meg curled into the corner of the couch. "So. How was Bermuda?"

Quill stretched lazily. "Warm, rum-filled, and fabulous."

"You've put on five pounds at least."

"So did Myles."

"And the sneezes and the muscle cramps and the dread diseases?"

Quill scowled at her. "Okay. So you were right. Stress. And inactivity. And no sleep and too much coffee." She added, carelessly, "And I suppose I missed Myles. And yes, I had an allergic reaction. To that new perfume Hark—I mean, that you-know-who gave me. But I was partly right, Meg. All those symptoms were related to painting."

"Sentiment," Meg said. "My very own sister getting sentimental on me." She tilted her head critically. "You don't look bald, either. What about the heavy metal poisoning part?"

Quill tugged at her hair a little nervously. "Well, that disappeared, too, of course," she said nervously. "I was wrong about that."

"You thought Boomer was poisoning you."

"Somebody could have been poisoning me," Quill said indignantly. "And I had a very good suspect. As a matter of fact, once we established it wasn't Kimmie or Boomer, I pursued another suspect."

"Who did you suspect?"

"Never mind," Quill muttered. "I may, however, have been too hasty about that. My hair's just fine."

"About what?"

"It doesn't matter," Quill said evasively. "The thing is, the hair-falling-out part was related to the stress. Or the allergies. Whatever, it's over. It doesn't," she repeated, "*matter*."

"Of course it matters," Meg hooted. "Honestly, Quill. You really think I want to give up this kind of ammunition? No way. It's too good. I want to know." She thumped the couch cushion with one small fist. "I need to know. Every time you get a little touch of the flu and decide to remake your will I can remind you that you thought someone was poisoning you to make your hair fall our and go totally bald."

Quill thought about throwing a couch pillow at her, but didn't. "Just shut up," she said amiably. "If you must know, I thought it was Carol Ann."

"Carol Ann? The tax assessor? That Carol Ann?"

"Yes." Quill thought about telling Meg that she'd given Davey Kiddermeister the tube of azure to test—and told him of her suspicions—but she didn't. The tests had come back negative, and though Davey had been oddly silent when she'd called from Bermuda to apologize for wasting his time, as far as she was concerned the episode was over.

"So," Meg said. "Andy and I just tried to put the whole thing out of mind while we were gone. But I'd like to know now, I think. Did you learn anything? I mean, I know Myles has a lot of contacts."

Quill nodded. "I'm going to make some tea."

"Okay." She looked around Quill's rooms. "Where is Myles?"

"At his place. He'll be over later."

"And Kimmie Bloomfield was behind it all."

"Yes." Quill plugged the kettle into the wall. Meg didn't press her. Quill herself had shrunk from the details when Myles had brought them to her. The memory of the shot, and the quick fall of Kimmie's body to the floor—like a stone, Quill thought, like a stone; the cliché was right—was still fresh and painful. The kettle whistled. Quill took out the green tea, and then brought the steeping pot to the coffee table.

"It started last year. Her plan. She'd gone to see George Nash in prison. He wrote to her, to apologize for his part in Evan's death, he said. But what really happened, nobody knows. George died with a total of four hundred thousand dollars in savings. Boomer suffered a series of "financial reverses" about that time, according to his broker, and lost about that much. Myles thinks that somehow, George saw Boomer on television and discovered who he was. It could have been a trick of speech, or even the ears, Meg. Ears are as good as fingerprints. Whatever happened, George found Boomer out a year or so ago, and has been blackmailing him ever since.

"Then Nash wrote to Kimmie. He tracked her down by logging into the city records, and discovering that she remarried after Evan's death.

"Kimmie wanted revenge."

"So she tracked down Nash, killed him with your car. Nailed Roberts with your car . . ."

"She was at the Inn at the relevant times, Meg. We just didn't put it together."

"And Boomer?"

"He'd been in touch with Nash. When Nash was found dead—he knew something was up—he just didn't know what. He did his best to warn me without revealing anything of who he was. I guess I have to give him credit for that."

"She waited all that time to murder?"

"Myles doesn't think she meant to kill them initially. But she started blackmailing Boomer, too. Only we think her scheme wasn't for money—it was to set up this meeting of all the people concerned with Evan's death—you, me, her ex-husband, and, I suspect, Sylvia Prince, although we'll never know that for certain. She—well, you know what she did."

"And all this because Evan would have been twenty-one?"

Quill bit her lip. "Because Evan would have been twenty-one."

"And the miscarriage?"

"Everyone seems to think that pushed her over the edge. It was then she decided to kill. The autopsy on Boomer showed he'd been given a dose of barbiturates in the coconut cake. Kimmie walked him out to the equipment garage, at gunpoint, probably, and then shot him. She tied him to the bulldozer—Myles doesn't think I know that Boomer was still alive when they pulled the dozer out of the garage, but I do—and you know the rest.

"Kimmie got a dose of insulin—you know you can just buy it over the counter, Meg? Anyway, she swiped a syringe from Louis's bag, gave herself an injection in the Lounge, which was where we found her."

"For an alibi?"

"Yes. She wasn't thinking at all clearly at that point. We both saw that."

"You did," Meg said glumly. "I didn't."

"Anyway, there you are. That's pretty much all of the story Myles was able to piece together."

"That's enough." Meg sipped at her tea. "Well. It's over, thank goodness. And peace and harmony are restored. And Christmas will be on us soon." She glanced sideways at Quill. "I take it Myles will be spending it with us?"

Quill nodded.

"And Harker?"

"The last I heard, he was partying it up in New York."

"If you miss it there, Quill, why don't you come down with me when I cook at La Strazza? It's a nice train ride. You can bunk in with me at the restaurant. And you can kind of, you know, keep up with things."

Quill looked at her canvas, draped in the south corner of her room. Her fingers twitched. Perhaps it was time to get back to work. "I don't know, Meg. How do you think the Inn will get along with both of us gone?"

"John can handle it, as long as it's only a day or two a week. And Bjarne," Meg admitted, grudgingly, "is learning his stuff. Still has a heavy hand with the spices, but I have to admit he's learning his stuff."

Quill wiggled her toes. She and Myles had taken long walks on the beach and long swims in the ocean. She felt fine. She felt fit. She hadn't sneezed once she stopped using the perfume Harker had given her that had been the whatever-Andy-had-called-it that made her allergic in the first place. She'd have to look the term up in the *Merck*. Allergenisis, or whatever.

She glanced at her desk, where she'd kept it out and handy all the months she'd been convinced she'd had a dread disease. "Hey!" she said. "What happened to my *Merck*?"

"Threw the sucker out." Doreen, who had entered, as usual, without knocking, stumped into the center of the room. "We need you downstairs."

"It's good to have you home, Quill," Quill said to the air over Doreen's head. "I missed you. Max missed you. Even Stoke missed you."

"Yuh," said Doreen. "Well, the great state of New York missed you, too. That there Carol Ann Spinoza's suing us for false arrest, or some such garbage. There's one of them process servers downstairs right now."

"Oh, hell," Quill said. "I knew Davey Kiddermeister wasn't telling me the whole truth."

"I'll go down and take it." Meg grabbed Quill by the shoulders and made her face her canvas. "You go paint."

So she did.

———————

Meg—when she could stop giggling—made nice, comforting desserts for Quill for the duration of the lawsuit *Spinoza v. Quilliam.* This is one of them.

# POACHED PEARS A LA QUILLIAM

2 cups water
4 cups cheap red wine (*not* cooking wine; there's salt in it)
1 stick cinnamon (Bjarne puts in two; that's way too much)
1 teaspoon nutmeg
Orange peel
8 Bosc pears, peeled and left whole

Bring the wine, spices, and water to a boil. Poach the pears whole for twenty minutes. Remove from the liquor. Chill pears for four hours or so.

1 cup softened cream cheese
1 cup black walnuts, chopped fine
1 tablespoon orange liqueur

Split the pears carefully in half. Core the halves. Mix cream cheese, walnuts, and orange liqueur and fill the halves with the mixture. Press halves together and chill until ready to use. Garnish with whole, chilled mint leaves.

CLAUDIA BISHOP, the author of nine Hemlock Falls mystery novels, is the pen name of Mary Stanton. She is at work on the tenth novel. As Mary Stanton, Bishop is the author of eleven novels for young adults and two adult novels. She divides her time between a cattle farm in upstate New York and West Palm Beach. She can be reached at mstanton@redsuspenders.com.

And now
an exclusive preview of

*Savage Run*
the new Joe Pickett Novel
by acclaimed mystery writer
C. J. Box

# 1

On the third day of their honeymoon, infamous environmental activist Stewie Woods and his new bride Annabel Bellotti were spiking trees in the Bighorn National Forest when a cow exploded and blew them up. Until then, their marriage had been happy.

They met by chance. Stewie Woods had been busy pouring bag after bag of sugar and sand into the gasoline tanks of a fleet of pickups that belonged to a natural gas exploration crew in a newly graded parking lot. The crew had left for the afternoon for the bars and hotel rooms of nearby Henry's Fork. One of the crew had returned unexpectedly and caught Stewie as Stewie was ripping off the top of a bag of sugar with his teeth. The crewmember pulled a 9MM semi-automatic from beneath the dashboard and fired several wild pistol shots in Stewie's direction. Stewie had dropped the bag and run away, crashing through the timber like a bull elk.

Stewie had outrun and out-juked the man with the pistol and he met Annabel when he literally tripped over her as she sunbathed nude in the grass in an orange pool of late afternoon sun, unaware of his approach because she was listening to Melissa Etheridge on her Walkman's headphones. She looked good, he thought, strawberry blonde hair with a two-day Rocky Mountain fire-engine tan (two hours in the sun at 8,000 feet created a sunburn like a whole day at the beach), small ripe breasts, and a trimmed vector of pubic hair.

He had gathered her up and pulled her along through the timber, where they hid together in a dry spring wash until the man with the pistol gave up and went home. She had giggled while he held her—*this was real adventure,* she'd said—and he had used the opportunity to run his hands tentatively over her naked shoulders and hips and had found out, happily, that she did not object. They made their way back to where she had been sunbathing and while she dressed, they introduced themselves.

She told him she liked the idea of meeting a famous environmental outlaw in the woods while she was naked, and he appreciated that. She said she had seen his picture before, maybe in *Outside Magazine*?, and admired his looks—tall and raw-boned, with round rimless glasses, a short-cropped full beard, and his famous red bandana on his head.

Her story was that she had been camping alone in a dome tent, taking a few days off from her free-wheeling cross-continent trip that had begun with her divorce from an anal retentive investment banker named Nathan in her home town of Pawtucket, Rhode Island. She was bound, eventually, for Seattle.

"I'm falling in love with your mind," he lied.

"Already?" she asked.

He encouraged her to travel with him, and they took her vehicle since the lone crewmember had disabled Stewie's Subaru with three bullets into the engine block. Stewie was astonished by his good fortune. Every time he looked over at her and she smiled back, he was pole-axed with exuberance.

Keeping to dirt roads, they crossed into Montana. The next afternoon, in the backseat of her SUV during a thunderstorm that rocked the car and blew shroud-like sheets of rain through the mountain passes, he asked her to marry him. Given the circumstances and the super-charged atmosphere, she accepted. When the rain stopped, they drove to Ennis, Montana and asked around about who could marry them, fast. Stewie did not want to take the chance of letting her get away. She kept saying she couldn't believe she was doing this. He couldn't believe she was doing this either, and he loved her even more for it.

At the Sportsman Inn in Ennis, Montana, which was bustling with fly fishermen bound for the trout-rich waters of the Madison River, the desk clerk gave them a name and they looked up Judge Ace Cooper (Ret.) in the telephone book.

Judge Cooper was a tired and rotund man who wore a stained white cowboy shirt and an elk horn bolo tie with his shirt collar open. He performed the ceremony in a room adjacent to his living room that was bare except for a single filing cabinet, a desk and three chairs, and two framed photographs—one of the Judge and President George H. W. Bush, who had once been up there fishing, and the other of the Judge on a horse before the Cooper family lost their ranch in the 1980s.

The wedding ceremony had taken eleven minutes, which was just about average for Judge Cooper, although he had once performed it in eight minutes for two Indians.

"Do you, Allan Stewart Woods, take thee Annabeth to be your lawful wedded wife?" Judge Cooper had asked, reading from the marriage application form.

"Anna*bel*," Annabel had corrected in her biting Rhode Island accent.

"I do," Stewie had said. He was beside himself with pure joy.

Stewie twisted the ring off his finger and placed it on hers. It was unique; hand-made gold mounted with sterling silver monkey wrenches. It was also three sizes too large. The Judge studied the ring.

"Monkey wrenches?" the Judge had asked.

"It's symbolic," Stewie had said.

"I'm aware of the symbolism," the Judge said darkly, before finishing the passage.

Annabel and Stewie had beamed at each other. Annabel said that this was, like, the *wildest* vacation ever. They were Mr. and Mrs. Outlaw Couple. He was now *her* famous outlaw, although as yet untamed. She said her father would be scandalized, and her mother would have to wear dark glasses at Newport. Only her Aunt Tildie, the one with the wild streak who had corresponded with, but never met, a Texas serial killer until he died of lethal injection, would understand.

Stewie had to borrow a hundred dollars from her to pay the Judge, and she signed over a traveler's check.

After the couple had left in the SUV with Rhode Island plates, Judge Ace Cooper had gone to his lone filing cabinet and found the file. He pulled a single piece of paper out and read it as he dialed the telephone. While he waited for the right man to come to the telephone, he stared at the framed photo on the wall of himself on the horse at his former ranch. The ranch, north of Yellowstone Park, had been subdivided by a Bozeman real estate company into over thirty 50-acre "ranchettes." Famous Hollywood celebrities, including the one who's early-career photos he had recently seen in *Penthouse*, now lived there. Movies had been filmed there. There was even a crackhouse, but it was rumored that the owner wintered in LA. The only cattle that existed were purely for visual effect, like landscaping that moved and crapped and looked good when the sun threatened to drop below the mountains.

The man he was waiting for came to the telephone.

"It was Stewie Woods, all right," he said. "The man himself. I recognized him right off, and his ID proved it." There was a pause as the man on the other end of the telephone asked Cooper something. "Yeah, I heard him say that to her just before they left. They're headed for the Bighorns in Wyoming. Somewhere near Saddlestring."

Annabel told Stewie that their honeymoon was quite unlike what she had ever imagined a honeymoon to be, and she contrasted it with her first one with Nathan. Nathan was about sailing boats, champagne, and Barbados. Stewie was about spiking trees in stifling heat in a national forest in Wyoming. He had even asked her to carry his pack.

Neither of them had noticed the late-model black Ford pickup that had trailed them up the mountain road and continued on when Stewie pulled over to park.

Deep into the forest, Stewie now removed his shirt and tied the sleeves around his waist. A heavy bag of nails hung from his belt and tinkled while he strode through the undergrowth. There was a sheen of sweat on his bare chest as he straddled a three-foot thick Douglas Fir and drove in spikes. He was obviously well practiced, and he got into a rhythm where he could bury the 6-inch spikes into the soft wood with three heavy blows from his sledgehammer; one tap to set the spike and two blows to bury it beyond the nail head in the bark.

He moved from tree to tree, but didn't spike all of them. He attacked each tree in the same method. The first of the spikes went in at eye level. A quarter-turn around the trunk, he pounded in another a foot lower than the first. He continued pounding in spikes until he had placed them in a spiral on the trunk nearly to the grass.

"Won't it hurt the trees?" Annabel asked as she unloaded his pack and leaned it against a tree.

"Of course not," he said, moving across the pine needle floor to another target. "I wouldn't be doing this if it hurt the trees. You've got a lot to learn about me, Annabel."

"Why do you put so many in?" she asked.

"Good question," he said, burying a spike in three blows. "It used to be we could put in four right at knee level, at the compass points, where the trees are usually cut. But the lumber companies got wise to that and told their loggers to go higher or lower. So now we fill up a four-foot radius."

"And what will happen if they try to cut it down?"

Stewie smiled, resting for a moment. "When a chainsaw blade hits a steel spike, the blade can snap and whip back. Busts the saw-teeth. That can take an eye or a nose right off."

"That's horrible," she said, wincing, wondering what she was getting into.

"I've never been responsible for any injuries," Stewie said quickly, looking hard at her. "The purpose isn't to hurt anyone. The purpose is to save trees. After we're done here, I'll call the local ranger station and tell them what we've done. I won't say exactly where we spiked the trees or how many trees we spiked. It should be enough to keep them out of here for decades, and that's the point."

"Have you ever been caught?" she asked.

"Once," Stewie said, and his face clouded. "A forest ranger caught me by Jackson Hole. He marched me into downtown Jackson on foot during tourist season at gunpoint. Half of the tourists in town cheered and the other half started chanting, 'Hang him high! Hang him high!'. I was sent to the Wyoming State Penitentiary in Rawlins for seven months."

"Now that you mention it, I think I read about that," she mused.

"You probably did. The wire services picked it up. I was interviewed on *Nightline* and *60 Minutes*. *Outside Magazine* put me on the cover. My boyhood friend Hayden Powell wrote the cover story for them, and he coined the word 'eco-terrorist'." This memory made him feel bold. "There were reporters from all over the country at that trial," Stewie said. "Even the *New York Times*. It was the first time most people had ever heard of One Globe, or knew I was the founder of it. Memberships started pouring in from all over the world."

*One Globe*. The ecological action group that used the logo of crossed monkey wrenches, in deference to late author Edward Abbey's *The Monkey Wrench Gang*. One Globe had once dropped a shroud over Mt. Rushmore for the President's speech, she recalled. It had been on the nightly news.

"Stewie," she said happily, "you are the real thing." He could feel her eyes on him as he drove in the spiral of spikes and moved to the next tree.

"When you are done with that tree I want you," she said, her voice husky. "Right here and right now, my sweet, sweaty . . . *husband*."

He turned and smiled. His face glistened and his muscles were swelled from swinging the sledgehammer. She slid her T-shirt over her head and stood waiting for him, her lips parted and her legs tense.

Stewie slung his own pack now and, for the time being, had stopped spiking trees. Fat black thunderheads, pregnant with rain, nosed across the late-afternoon sky. They were hiking at a fast pace toward the peak, holding hands, with the hope of getting there and pitching camp before the rain started. Stewie said they would hike out of the forest tomorrow and he would call the ranger station. Then they would get in the SUV and head southeast, toward the Bridger-Teton Forest.

When they walked into the herd of cattle, Stewie felt a dark cloud of anger envelop him.

"Range maggots!" Stewie said, spitting. "If they're not letting the logging companies in to cut all the trees at taxpayer's expense, they're letting the local ranchers run their cows in here so they can eat all the grass and shit in all the streams."

"Can't we just go around them?" Annabel asked.

"It's not that, Annabel," he said patiently. "Of course we can go around them. It's just the principal of the thing. We have cattle fouling what is left of the natural ecosystem. Cows don't belong in the trees in the Bighorn Mountains. You have so much to learn, darling."

"I know," she said, determined.

"These ranchers out here run their cows on public land—our land—at the expense of not only us but the wildlife. They pay something like four dollars an acre when they should be paying ten times that, even though it would be best if they were completely gone."

"But we need meat, don't we?" she asked. "You're not a vegetarian, are you?"

"Did you forget that cheeseburger I had for lunch in Cameron?" he said. "No, I'm not a vegetarian, although sometimes I wish I had the will to be one."

"I tried it once and it made me lethargic," Annabel confessed.

"All these western cows produce about five percent of the beef we eat in this whole country," Stewie said. "All the rest comes from down South, in Texas, Florida, and Louisiana, where there's plenty of grass and plenty of private land to graze them on."

Stewie picked up a pinecone, threw it accurately through the trees, and struck a black baldy heifer on the snout. The cow bolted, turned, and lumbered away. The rest of the herd, about a dozen, followed it. The small herd moved loudly, clumsily cracking branches and throwing up fist-sized pieces of black earth from their hooves.

"I wish I could chase them right back to the ranch they belong on," Stewie said, watching. "Right up the ass of the rancher who has lease rights for this part of the Bighorns."

One cow had not moved. It stood broadside and looked at them.

"What's wrong with that cow?" Stewie asked.

"Shoo!" Annabel shouted. "Shoo!"

Stewie stifled a smile at his new wife's shooing and slid out of his pack. The temperature had dropped twenty degrees in the last ten minutes and rain was inevitable. The sky had darkened and black coils of clouds enveloped the peak. The sudden low pressure had made the forest quieter, the sounds muffled and the smell of cows stronger.

Stewie Woods walked straight toward the heifer, with Annabel several steps behind.

"Something's wrong with that cow," Stewie said, trying to figure out what about it seemed out of place.

When Stewie was close enough he saw everything at once: the cow trying to run with the others but straining at the end of a tight nylon line; the heifer's wild white eyes; the misshapen profile of something strapped on it's back that was large and square and didn't belong; the thin reed of antenna that quivered from the package on the heifer's back.

"Annabel!" Stewie yelled, turning to reach out to her—but

she had walked around him and was now squarely between him and the cow.

She absorbed the full, frontal blast when the heifer detonated, the explosion shattering the mountain stillness with the subtlety of a sledgehammer bludgeoning bone.

Four miles away, a fire lookout heard the guttural boom and ran to the railing with binoculars. Over a red-rimmed plume of smoke and dirt, he could see a Douglas fir launch like a rocket into the air, where it turned, hung suspended for a moment, then crashed into the forest below.

Shaking, he reached for his radio.

# 2

Eight miles out of Saddlestring, Wyoming, Game Warden Joe
Pickett was watching his wife Marybeth work their new Tobiano
paint horse, Toby, in the round pen when the call came from
the Twelve Sleep County Sheriff's office.

It was early evening, the time of night when the setting sun
ballooned and softened and defined the deep velvet folds and
piercing tree greens of Wolf Mountain. The normally dull pastel
colors of the weathered barn and the red rock canyon behind
the house suddenly looked as if they had been repainted in acryl-
ics. Toby, a big dark bay gelding swirled with brilliant white
that ran up over his haunches like thick spilled paint upside
down, shone deep red in the evening light and looked especially
striking. So did Marybeth, in Joe's opinion, in her worn Wran-
glers, sleeveless cotton shirt, and her blonde hair in a ponytail.
There was no wind, and the only sound was the rhythmic thump-
ing of Toby's hooves in the round pen as Marybeth waved the
whip and encouraged the gelding to shift from a trot into a slow
lope.

The Saddlestring District was considered a "two-horse district" by the Game and Fish Department, meaning that the department would provide feed and tack for two mounts to be
used for patrolling. Toby was their second horse.

Joe stood with his boot on the bottom rail and his arms folded
over the top, his chin nestled between his forearms. He was still
wearing his red cotton Game and Fish uniform shirt with the
pronghorn antelope patch on the sleeve and his sweat-stained
gray Stetson. He could feel the pounding of the earth as Toby
passed in front of him in a circle. He watched Marybeth stay in

position in the center of the pen, shuffling her feet so she stayed on Toby's back flank. She talked to her horse in a soothing voice, urging him to gallop—something he clearly didn't want to do.

Persistent, Marybeth stepped closer to Toby and commanded him to run. Marybeth still had a slight limp from when she had been shot nearly two years before, but she was nimble and quick. Toby pinned his ears back and twitched his tail but finally broke into a full-fledged gallop, raising the dust in the pen, his mane and tail snapping behind him like a flag in a stiff wind. After several rotations, Marybeth called. "Whoa!" and Toby hit the brakes, skidding to a quick stop where he stood breathing hard, his muscles swelled, his back shiny with sweat, smacking and licking his lips as if he was eating peanut butter. Marybeth approached him and patted him down, telling him what a good boy he was, and blowing gently into his nostrils to soothe him.

"He's a stubborn guy—and lazy," she told Joe. "He did *not* want to lope fast. Did you notice how he pinned his ears back and threw his head around?"

Joe said *yup*.

"That's how he was telling me he was mad about it. When he's doing that he's either going to break out of the circle and do whatever he wants to, or stop, or do what I'm asking him to do. In this case he did what I asked and went into the fast lope. He's finally learning that things will go a lot easier on him when he does what I ask him."

"I know it works for me," Joe said and smiled.

Marybeth crinkled her nose at Joe, then turned back to Toby. "See how he licks his lips? That's a sign of obedience. He's conceding that I am the boss. That's a good sign."

Joe fought the urge to theatrically lick his lips when she looked over at him.

"Why did you blow in his nose like that?"

"Horses in the herd do that to each other to show affection. It's another way they bond with each other." Marybeth paused. "I know it sounds hokey, but blowing in his nose is kind of like giving him a hug. A horse hug."

"You seem to know what you're doing."

Joe had been around horses most of his life. He had now taken his buckskin mare Lizzie over most of the mountains in the Twelve Sleep Range of the Bighorns in his District. But what Marybeth was doing with her new horse Toby, what she was getting out of him, was a different kind of thing. Joe was duly impressed.

A shout behind him shook Joe from his thoughts. He turned toward the sound, and saw ten-year-old Sheridan, five-year-old Lucy, and their eight-year-old foster daughter April stream through the back-yard gate and across the field. Sheridan held the cordless phone out in front of her like an Olympic torch, and the other two girls followed.

"Dad, it's for you," Sheridan called. "A man says it's very important."

Joe and Marybeth exchanged looks and Joe took the telephone. It was County Sheriff O. R. "Bud" Barnum.

There had been a big explosion in the Bighorn National Forest, Barnum told Joe. A fire lookout had called it in, and had reported that through his binoculars he could see fat dark forms littered throughout the trees. It looked like a "shitload" of animals were dead, which is why he was calling Joe. Dead game animals were Joe's concern. They assumed at this point that they were game animals, Barnum said, but they might be cows. A couple of local ranchers had grazing leases up there. Barnum asked if Joe could meet him at the Winchester exit off of the interstate in twenty minutes. That way, they could get to the scene before it was completely dark.

Joe handed the telephone back to Sheridan and looked over his shoulder at Marybeth.

"When will you be back?" she asked.

"Late," Joe told her. "There was an explosion in the mountains."

"You mean like a plane crash?"

"He didn't say that. The explosion was a few miles off of the Hazelton Road in the mountains, in elk country. Barnum thinks there may be some game animals down."

She looked at Joe for further explanation. He shrugged to indicate that was all he knew.

"I'll save you some dinner."

Joe met the Sheriff and Deputy McLanahan at the exit to Winchester and followed them through the small town. The three-vehicle fleet—two County GMC Blazers and Joe's dark green Game and Fish pickup—entered and exited the tiny town within minutes. Even though it was an hour and a half away from darkness, the only establishments open were the two bars with identical red neon Coors signs in their windows and a convenience store. Winchester's lone public artwork, located on the front lawn of the branch bank, was an outsized and gruesome metal sculpture of a wounded grizzly bear straining at the end of a thick chain, it's metal leg encased in a massive saw-toothed bear trap. Joe did not find the sculpture lovely but it captured the mood, style, and inbred frontier culture of the area as well as anything else could have.

Deputy McLanahan led the way through the timber in the direction where the explosion had been reported and Joe walked behind him alongside Sheriff Barnum. Joe and McLanahan had acknowledged each other with curt nods and said nothing. Their relationship had been rocky ever since McLanahan had sprayed the outfitter's camp with shotgun blasts two years before and Joe had received a wayward pellet under his eye. He still had a scar to show for it.

Barnum's hangdog face grimaced as he limped beside Joe through the underbrush. He complained about his hip. He complained about the distance from the road to the crime scene. He complained about McLanahan, and said to Joe *sotto voce* that he should have fired the deputy years before and would have if he weren't his nephew. Joe suspected, however, that Barnum also kept McLanahan around because McLanahan's quick-draw reputation had added—however untrue and unlikely—an air of toughness to the Sheriff's Department that didn't hurt at election time.

The sun had dropped below the top of the mountains and instantly turned them into craggy black silhouettes. The light dimmed in the forest, fusing the treetops and branches that were discernable just a moment before into a shadowy muddle. Joe reached back on his belt to make sure he had his flashlight. He let his arm brush his .357 Smith & Wesson revolver to confirm it was there. He didn't want Barnum to notice the movement since Barnum still chided him about the time he lost his gun to a poacher Joe was arresting.

There was an unnatural silence in the woods, with the exception of Barnum's grumbling. The absence of normal sounds— the chattering of squirrels sending a warning up the line, the panicked scrambling of deer, the airy winged drumbeat of flushed Spruce grouse—confirmed that something big had happened here. Something so big it had either cleared the wildlife out of the area or frightened them mute. Joe could feel that they were getting closer before he could see anything to confirm it. Whatever it was, it was just ahead.

McLanahan quickly stopped and there was a sharp intake of breath.

"Holy shit," McLanahan whispered in awe. "*Holy shit.*"

The still-smoking crater was fifteen yards across. It was three feet deep at its center. A half dozen trees had been blown out of the ground and their shallow rootpans were exposed like black outstretched hands. Eight or nine black baldy cattle were dead and still, strewn among the trunks of trees. The earth below the thick turf rim of the crater was dark and wet. Several large white roots, the size of leg bones, were pulled up from the ground by the explosion and now pointed at the sky. Cordite from the explosives, pine from broken branches, and upturned mulch had combined in the air to produce a sickeningly sweet and heavy smell.

Darkness enveloped them as they slowly circled the crater. Pools of light from their flashlights lit up twisted roots and lacy pale yellow undergrowth.

Joe checked the cattle, moving among them away from the crater. Most had visible injuries as a result of fist-sized rocks being blown into them from the explosion. One heifer was impaled on the fallen tip of a dead pine tree. The rest of the herd, apparently unhurt, stood as silent shadows just beyond his flashlight. He could see dark heavy shapes and hear the sound of chewing, and a pair of eyes reflected back blue as a cow raised its head to look at him. They all had the same brand—a "v" on top and a "u" on the bottom divided by a single line. Joe recognized it as the Vee Bar U Ranch. These were Ed Finolla's cows.

McLanahan suddenly grunted in alarm and Joe raised his flashlight to see the Deputy in a wild, self-slapping panic, dancing away from the rim of the crater and ripping his jacket off of himself as quickly as he could. He threw it violently to the ground in a heap and stood staring at it.

"What in the hell is wrong with you?" Barnum asked, annoyed.

"Something landed on my shoulder. Something heavy and wet," McLanahan said, his face contorted. "I thought it was somebody's hand grabbing me. It scared me half to death."

McLanahan had dropped his flashlight, so from across the crater Joe lowered his light onto the jacket and focused his Mag Light into a tight beam. McLanahan bent down into the light and gingerly unfolded the jacket, poised to jump back if whatever had fallen on him was still in his clothing. He threw back a fold and cursed. Joe couldn't see for sure what McLanahan was looking at other than that the object was dark and moist.

"What is it?" Barnum demanded.

"It looks like . . . well . . . it looks like a piece of *meat*." McLanahan looked up at Joe vacantly.

Slowly, Joe raised the beam of his flashlight, sweeping upward over McLanahan and following it up the trunk of a lodgepole pine and into the branches. What Joe saw, he would never forget. . . .